SPECIAL MESSAGE TO READERS

THE ULVERSCROFT FOUNDATION

(registered UK charity number 264873)

was established in 1972 to provide funds for research, diagnosis and treatment of eye diseases. Examples of major projects funded by the Ulverscroft Foundation are:-

- The Children's Eye Unit at Moorfields Eye Hospital, London
- The Ulverscroft Children's Eye Unit at Great Ormond Street Hospital for Sick Children
- Funding research into eye diseases and treatment at the Department of Ophthalmology, University of Leicester
- The Ulverscroft Vision Research Group, Institute of Child Health
- Twin operating theatres at the Western Ophthalmic Hospital, London
- The Chair of Ophthalmology at the Royal Australian College of Ophthalmologists

You can help further the work of the Foundation by making a donation or leaving a legacy. Every contribution is gratefully received. If you would like to help support the Foundation or require further information, please contact:

THE ULVERSCROFT FOUNDATION
The Green, Bradgate Road, Anstey
Leicester LE7 7FU, England
Tel: (0116) 236 4325

website: www.foundation.ulverscroft.com

Jason Hewitt is a novelist, playwright and actor. Born in Oxford, he has a Bachelor of Arts degree in History and English from the University of Winchester and an MA with distinction in Creative Writing from Bath Spa University. After completing his degrees, he spent a number of years working in a bookshop in Oxford before moving into the publishing industry, where he worked primarily as a marketing manager. Jason went on to become a published author, playwright and actor. He is also currently Associate Lecturer for the BA Publishing Media degree at Oxford Brookes University.

You can discover more about the author at jason-hewitt.com

DEVASTATION ROAD

Spring, 1945: A man wakes in a field in a country he does not know. His name is Owen. Injured and confused, he gets to his feet and starts to walk. A war he has only a vague memory of joining is in its dying days, and as he tries to get back to England he becomes caught up in the flood of refugees pouring through Europe. Among them is a teenage boy, Janek, and together they form an unlikely alliance on their way across battle-worn Germany. When they meet a troubled young woman, tempers flare and scars are revealed as Owen gathers up the shattered pieces of his life. Nothing is as he remembers, not even himself — and how can he truly return home when he hardly recalls what home is?

JASON HEWITT

DEVASTATION ROAD

Complete and Unabridged

CHARNWOOD
Leicester

First published in Great Britain in 2015 by
Scribner
an imprint of
Simon & Schuster UK Ltd
London

First Charnwood Edition
published 2017
by arrangement with
Simon & Schuster UK Ltd
London

This book is a work of fiction. Names, characters, places and incidents are either a product of the author's imagination or are used fictitiously. Any resemblance to actual people living or dead, events or locales is entirely coincidental.

A catalogue record for this book is available from the British Library.

ISBN 978–1–4448–3248–8

Published by
F. A. Thorpe (Publishing)
Anstey, Leicestershire

Set by Words & Graphics Ltd.
Anstey, Leicestershire
Printed and bound in Great Britain by
T. J. International Ltd., Padstow, Cornwall

This book is printed on acid-free paper

To my brother

This only is denied to God,
The power to make what has been done undone.

Agathon

He woke to the insistent pip of a bird, its distant trill coming to him through a dream. He felt heavy, lying on his back, as if every organ within him had sunk to its lowest position and now could not be lifted. One hand on his chest, head turned, not a position he usually slept in, and now he could feel an awkward crick pulling in his neck. He lay for a while, mind groggy, the last remnants of sleep still swilling in his head. He was cold but the sun was warm on him. He listened but there was no sound of traffic or distant voices, just the stir of leaves and the pip of the bird. He shifted and a pain shot through his head as something crinkled against his ear.

His eyes opened.

For a moment he was blind but for a sharp light that wouldn't shift, even when he tried to blink it away, and then its brightness slowly receded as a watery sun burnt through. The sky was blue and blurred above him with wisps of cloud hanging, duplicated. His fingers flexed and there it was again, the tickle and lick of grass.

He sat up. The pain pulled.

He was not in a bed. He was in a field.

He was in a field and sitting in the grass.

He looked around, unsure. Everything was smudged and ill-defined: the field tilting away from under him, the blurry line of trees on every side, and nothing between him and them but the shifting grass and occasional blink of a daisy. The pain sharpened, and a wave of nausea washed through him so that he was forced to hold his head between his knees as a sour taste filled his throat.

Head still swimming, he stared down at his hands, scratched and stained with tidelines of dirt. A button was missing from the linen shirt he was wearing — not a shirt he recognized, but nevertheless it hung open at his belly like a lopsided mouth.

He looked about again, carefully twisting right around this time, and thought that for some reason he was in one of the fields behind his parents' house in Hampshire, but he couldn't understand why and nothing looked familiar anyway; there was just the hazy perimeter of trees and the sudden streak of a chaffinch that blurred into two and then one again. He rubbed his eyes. He was still asleep. But the ground felt real and the bird was real, and so was the breeze and the ache in his head. When he brought his fingers to it he could feel a swelling against the back of his scalp, and a pain biting beneath his ribs.

In a field in Hampshire, he told himself. He couldn't think where else. He'd see his father in a minute come huffing through the hedge in his tweeds and brandishing one of his walking sticks, Cedar bounding on ahead. There would be some explanation.

I should be at work, he thought. Mr Camm would be having kittens.

He struggled to his feet and squinted at the

flaring sun. He wavered for a moment, unsure if he could move, then checked his pockets, looking for something — wallet, keys, papers — but there was nothing but grit and some red cotton threads; and the jacket wasn't his anyway. It was a blue-grey serge and tatty. Not at all like something he'd wear. No bag, he thought. Nothing lying about. Nothing fallen from his pockets. He tried to focus on a pair of sparrows as they darted over the grass at the bottom of the slope and disappeared into the trees in a furious bluster of wings. Then, unsure what else to do, he decided to follow after them. It seemed as good a direction as any.

As he took his first uncertain steps he could feel the ache in his head expanding, groping into every corner of his skull and fingering its way down the back of his neck. He felt bruised all over, the waistband of the trousers rubbing at a soreness at his hip, and his bottom lip split and swollen and crusted with dirt. Another wave of nausea flooded through him, and when he stopped and hunched over his knees, a sticky liquid seeped from his nostril and was salty in his mouth.

As he set off again, the grey flannel trousers flapped at his ankles and pinched around his crotch. These couldn't be his trousers. Even the shirt was too tight, the sleeves not even reaching his wrists; and the jacket, though it fitted, was ripped and scuffed at the shoulders.

He cautiously glanced back, hoping something might jog his memory, but there was only a trail of trodden-down grass. It wasn't far to the edge of the field where a rock with a painted face sat half buried among the undergrowth: white rings for eyes and a snout and teeth. It watched him, hunched like a stone golem. Beyond the trees he could hear the rippling of water, so he pushed his way through the branches, the ground steady for the first few feet but then quickly tumbling away, until before he knew it he was crashing through a mesh of twigs and spasms of light, falling out on to a narrow and stony riverbank.

The river was fast-flowing, with rocks protruding here and there. He stood for a moment taking it in: the weeds coasting through it like long lingering thoughts and the bank on the other side rising up over him. He crouched at the edge and cupped water over his face, washing the blood and dirt from his hands and pressing his fingers over his eyes. He took a few deep breaths, feeling the pain pull beneath his rib as he breathed. But when he looked again he was still there, the sun splashing down on him, the river's slop and swill and leap of droplets spattering over the stones. As he watched, strange bits of debris drifted past: branches with sprigs of leaves still attached; clothing — a grey cap, a shawl, a handkerchief; the sodden pages of a newspaper; a single book; another branch; another shawl; a flimsy shoe. He would wake in a minute. Perhaps he *was* awake. If he saw someone he might call out and ask them where he was.

He lifted the side of his shirt and looked at where the pain was, but he could see no mark. He cupped his hands in the river again and drank, and for a time at least the water quelled the empty ache of his stomach. The river drifted away.

* * *

He made his way upstream, picking his way over the narrow streamlets that threaded out from the trees and lost themselves in the flow. He tried to think of the names of tributaries, as if in the finding of a name he might then find himself, but the only thing that came to him was the line of a hymn that looped in his head, something about redeemers and pilgrims.

He stopped and listened. He scanned the trees. Nothing seemed real.

He rubbed at his eyes, trying again to clear his vision, but everything looked watery and barely there at all. The swill of the river slopped in his head; it was hard to keep his balance. *You're being bloody ridiculous. You know where you are*, he thought. *You just need to think*.

As he walked on an empty crate floated into view, bobbing and turning in the water, a magpie strutting around its rim and peering in; and then the smeared shape of a handbag, a half-eaten apple, and a pamphlet, and there, glinting in the shallows, a tin with its label washed off. He stepped gingerly in to retrieve it, and for several minutes he tried to smash it open on a rock, denting and bashing it out of all shape, and then looked for something to pierce it with before, with frustration, he flung it back into the river. If he could have found a voice somewhere within him he would have shouted out.

* * *

He barely noticed it at first, thinking it to be nothing more than an oddly shaped rock wedged up against others on the opposite bank. It was only as he drew parallel and his vision cleared a little that he saw that what he had also assumed was a trapped branch pulling in the water was in fact an arm. A turned face, grey and bloated, was staring at him. His chest tightened. He glanced around. He couldn't see anyone to call out to. He stared closer, not sure what to do. He had never seen a dead body before, but there it was, still floating, the shirt ballooned with air.

He carried on, walking faster, his heart banging. But barely minutes later he came across two more. They were tangled together on his side of the river this time, caught among the overhanging foliage. One might have drowned, he thought, but surely not three.

He searched the trees, seeing nothing in his hazy vision but the blurring of leaves. Cautiously he edged nearer and saw that they were two men, both smartly dressed: one in shirt, trousers and braces, another in a sodden jacket, his arm sprawled across the other as if they had been lovers. As he dared to lean closer, he saw that beneath the water the face of the first was smashed and raw, while the other floated on his back, a line of ribs bursting through his shredded, bird-pecked shirt.

He turned, fearful now that someone was watching him, and tried scrambling up the bank but it had grown too steep. Instead he drew himself beneath the trees, picking up a dead branch and gripping it tightly. Had they been attacked? *Had he been attacked?* He half expected to hear a voice, someone coming after him, or perhaps not even that but one last piercing shot that would return him to sleep.

Edging on, he approached a bend in the river, the surge of water growing into a tumultuous roar. The banks on either side were rising higher and higher, the land veering up to form a steep and rocky gorge. He had seen no more bodies, only a pair of ladies' stockings snagged on a branch, the empty legs weaving in the water like eels trying to swim upstream.

As the river arced around, he ducked under some branches and was brought to an abrupt halt. Some distance further upriver stood the remains of a stone bridge, both sides fallen away to leave nothing but two central arches standing unbuckled and helpless on their piers among the rubble below. The girders of a railway track stuck out like huge twisted hairpins from one end, bending down towards the water. There beneath it lay the broken wreckage of a locomotive, carriages mangled and up-ended, doors thrown open, piston rods bent and wheels torn away, the carcass of an engine, around and over and through all of which the river thundered. He stared at it, his eyes still blurred and blinking. He would open his eyes for real in a minute. His heart might still be pounding but he would find himself in a bed, in a house, in a home he knew, and all of this would be forgotten.

In front of him the crows nosed around the

bits of wood and metal, and then took to the air in a flurry of wings and water, their sudden laughter filling his ears, but still he did not wake.

* * *

He clawed his way over the carriages, clambering on to the side of one that, overturned in the water, now formed a sloping roof, and from there on to another, occasionally losing his grip and slipping, fighting against the water that blasted and buffeted through every crack and hole. Here and there bodies lay caught among the bent iron and broken wood: pale-faced men in drenched suits or women in buttoned coats and flowered dresses; others were soldiers or guards, their uniforms unmistakable within the carnage.

A single door was now a skylight, and peering down through the hole he saw bodies floating among the benches and luggage racks. A teddy bear with one eye missing bobbed against a shut window. He watched it nudging at the glass and then turned away, the sight of it making his stomach flip and clench into a fist.

He rummaged for a while, climbing over the wreckage as if the piled carriages were rocks on a beach. In the pools and crevices he scavenged for food, one eye nervously on the blurred slopes around him as his feet slipped about on the wet metalwork. In among the broken sleepers and mangled rods of iron, smashed glass glinted like broken shards of sunlight and wet rags of clothes haemorrhaged from burst cases before being carried away downstream.

He found the pistol in the holster of a grey-uniformed soldier crushed between two wagons. With his hands shaking, he pulled out the magazine and counted eight bullets, then somehow fumbled it back together and slipped it into his jacket pocket.

As he carefully made his way down to where the engine was he noticed a backpack caught by a branch. Cautiously he lowered himself and waded in. The water was cold and fierce, pulling at his legs. It took some time to unhook the pack but he managed it and clambered back up on to an iron-frame ladder and then the footplate and the top of the engine's cab. On the tilted side of the tender he perched with the backpack on his knees. There were scratches and rips in the canvas where something had tried to tear it open, and on the top a faded number had been scrawled: 4993. He unfastened the buckles and took out a small parcel wrapped in sodden paper. He peeled the shreds of it away until, buried within its soggy folds, he found a hunk of rye bread, now a sodden mush that disintegrated like oatmeal and crumbled into the water. There was nothing else except, in a side pocket, a clutch of tightly bound letters that were soaked through as well, the ink drained away to a wash of watery lines. He tossed them into the river and then hurled the empty bag in after them, watching as the letters, like waterlilies, drifted away downstream.

* * *

After a while the gorge became shallower but the terrain along the river grew too overgrown to navigate, and he was forced up the slope back into the trees. He struggled through the dense woodland and broke through to open land. He wondered whether he should retrace his steps back to the field, double-check whether he had dropped anything or whether he might see something familiar coming at it from a different angle, around which everything would fall back into place. He must have been robbed. *Had he been robbed?* There would be a simple explanation. He was not the sort that panicked. He simply needed to think.

Yesterday, he thought. Surely he had been at work, seated at his draughtsman's bench with Harry beside him. He remembered his section had been working on the new wing structure of what would be the Typhoon. He had been drawing out the stringers that went across the wings' ribs, his logarithmic tables beside him, and his set squares and rulers. Had that only been yesterday? He tried to remember anything else but there was nothing there.

Ahead and behind him, the fields ebbed away over the horizon. He looked in the direction that he had just come from but even the landscape he had walked through only minutes ago now looked unfamiliar.

He put his fingers to the back of his swelling scalp and winced; then he took his head in both hands and let out a desperate sob. He couldn't walk any further. He couldn't think what had happened. He slumped in the grass, so tired and hungry. He didn't even know how long he'd been walking. Perhaps it had been days.

He looked at his clothes. Not his trousers. Not his shoes. He rummaged in the pockets and, feeling something weighty in the jacket, he was surprised — alarmed, even — to pull out a pistol. Was it his? It couldn't be his. He turned it over in his hand. He didn't remember having a pistol, yet something about it was familiar. He emptied out the magazine — eight bullets — then pushed it back with a click and slipped it back into the pocket. Jesus Christ, he thought. He prayed to God he hadn't shot anyone.

He studied the shoes, the laces twice broken and twice knotted, and the stitching straining to keep them together. When he took them off he found that there was nothing written inside. He felt down each trouser leg, and then to his surprise found that something had been sewn into them: something flat and round and hard, and embedded within a tiny pocket that had been cut into the seam. He prised it out with his finger. It was a rusted metal button. He turned it in his palm, confused by it, then smelt the tin and felt its scratches, the raised ridge around its edge and four tiny eyelets. It seemed an odd thing to have, hidden away like a secret. Someone else's button. Someone else's gun.

He pulled himself to his feet and carried on walking. After an hour he passed a half-buried rock in the undergrowth. It had a painted face on it. He could have sworn that it was grinning.

* * *

The house across the meadow was a ramshackle attempt at a wooden-framed building. Curling paint crumbled on the slatted walls and the veranda rails were loose and leaning, while glass was strewn across the boards from a shattered window at the front. Beneath the broken guttering was a barrel, a bucket, a pair of boots and, pushed against the wall, the mound of an overturned rowboat with a hole the size of a foot through it, the wood all gone to rot.

He didn't know how long he had been watching from under the trees. His thoughts kept sliding out from under him; he could barely keep himself conscious. The only constant was the hymn in his head, that same refrain riding in and jerking him awake.

He should approach and see if someone might help him but, other than the strutting chickens in the yard, everything was still. At the side there was an overgrown vegetable patch and he felt the sudden pang of his hunger. The plants looked underdeveloped for this time of year though, the runner beans no more than scrawny infants reaching their arms up the canes. He stayed nervously crouched. It felt too quiet — just the chickens clearing their throats and the occasional surf of dust.

Eventually he ventured out, stalking low across the grass, the pistol in his hand. He gave the house a wide berth, avoiding the shattered plant pot in the yard and the dead plant limping, saggy-limbed, from it. He crept in closer. He wondered if he should call out something. Hello? Is anyone in?

The chickens clucked around his ankles as he edged between them. The strange liquid seeped from his nostrils again — not mucus but something else that stung at his lip until he wiped it away.

On the veranda the front door was ajar. He nudged it just hard enough to open it, waited and listened, and then cautiously stepped in.

To one side of the hall was a room stuffed with oversized dining furniture: an overbearing redwood table that had been polished so intensely that the sunlight pooled on it, and far too many chairs with narrow backs and finely crafted marquetry of two birds entwined in flight and splintered into different shaded pieces. There were paintings that, like the furniture, were too large for the space, and their gilt frames seemed entirely at odds with the wooden walls and stubby nails that they had been hung from. It was as if two worlds had collided, one consuming the other, the contents of a wealthy townhouse now hiding within the dead shell of a farm.

Across the hallway the sitting room had been ransacked and the window smashed. There was a carved bookcase and matching dresser with a foreign newspaper on it, and a chaise longue and padded chairs, one with several penny-sized holes in it that coughed out puffs of stuffing like spittle on to the seat. His shoes crunched on bits of mirrored glass and the discarded books on the floor. When he turned over a broken photograph frame, the picture inside was gone. Sunlight pierced through two holes in the wall and fell on the debris, illuminating dried spatters of blood. He held still and listened, but heard only the soft crinkle of china quietly splintering beneath his feet.

In the kitchen, drawers hung open, gaping, but he could find nothing to eat. He gripped the sideboard with both hands and tried to shake off his faintness. No sink and no running water. He slammed the work surface hard with his hand and cursed. He couldn't even drink.

At the top of the stairs he found three small bedrooms, all untouched and tidy, bar a double room at the back where the bed had a large dried bloodstain spread across its sheets, the rest of the red-soaked bedding pulled out like innards across the boarded floor. He pressed himself against the wall and then stepped over it all to the window. The sun was shining in through a pale film of fingerprints and the dusty flecks of grime. He realized that he had no idea what time it was and his gaze went to his wrist but there was nothing there. He wiped the window clean with his sleeve and looked out, his breath catching in his throat.

Across the meadow was a figure. A boy, shovelling soil. He was tall and lanky, wearing a grey woollen jacket with what looked like patches on either elbow. He stopped and rested on the shovel, and then started again. There was something foreign about him, like the house and its furnishings, so that he was beginning to wonder if he wasn't in England at all.

There were two plots, one already completed, and he watched as the boy shovelled more on to the second and then threw the spade down. The boy glanced around before wiping his nose on the back of his arm and holding it there for a moment, and then taking a few deep breaths. When he had regained his composure, he picked up a couple of whittled branches and, pulling a ball of some sort of line from his pocket, he tied them into a cross, threading the line around the join several times and pulling it tight with a couple of hard yanks before he finally knotted it. He chewed it off and threw the cross down, but before he started work on the second, something made the boy turn, and in that moment before the man at the window bolted, they both caught each other's eye.

* * *

The pain in his head swelled like a storm. He could feel the pressure of it building, and that niggling discomfort beneath his ribs that felt like the ghost of a bullet. He moved his shoulder stiffly in its socket, feeling the grate of cartilage, and touched the tender split in his lip. If he could find something to eat, he told himself, if he could push the hunger and the pain aside, and roll his thoughts back to the beginning and start the day again . . . Nothing about it seemed familiar. He wanted to kick himself, just to feel it and know that he wasn't asleep. He was not the type of man who lost things. And yet here he was, losing his mind.

Yesterday, he thought.

Had he caught a trolleybus? A murky memory

leaked in of having a bag in his hand and being short of change. *Not to worry, sir. 'Sonly thruppence*. He couldn't recall when this was though. It couldn't have been yesterday. He usually cycled to Hawkers and kept his bike, like most of the others, in the back garden of Mr Levin's. If he'd been on a trolleybus he couldn't think where he would have been going. But there it came again: waiting outside the terrace houses, and a figure in the distance; then on the bus, the babble of other passengers and the sense that even then he hadn't quite been there. He couldn't have been, not yesterday. Somewhere else entirely. The memory felt too distant. And where was the bag now? Where was the ticket? Not in the jacket. Or in his pockets. He searched but nothing was there.

Besides, he thought, that day had been so much hotter than this: people fanning themselves with papers and hankies, all the upper windows of the trolleybus wide open, an English town feverish in the summer heat. When now it felt like a different season entirely. The trees were still in bloom.

It was as if part of him had melted away, an indeterminate amount of time and the memories within it faded to black, or evaporated entirely. He groped in his head but all he could think of was the trolleybus. Was there nothing between that moment and this? A break in time stitched together, so that whatever had been in the middle now simply was not there.

* * *

He found himself on his knees, bending over the water, drops falling from his nose. He stared back at his wavering reflection. He had needed to see his face.

He leant further. He could hardly believe it. The eyes had pulled back into their sockets, and what hair there was — cut short, almost to the skull — was receding at the temples where it had not receded before. It was a face that once had been full but now looked lean and wasted, all its youthful plumpness worn away. A gash of blood above his left eye was thick and dried and scabbing. There was bruising on the opposite temple, a cut along his jawline, a split lip and a bruised forearm, as if he had slammed it against something. The pain in the back of his head still pierced through him, along with the sharp ache beneath his ribs — the bullet that wasn't there.

He brought his fingertips to his cheek and around his jaw, feeling the skin and his fragility, the parts where even beneath the skin's lining he felt raw and ravaged.

My God. It was not a face he remembered. There were just the hidden reminders of his old self buried beneath fresh lines, paler skin, a darkening around his eyes . . . He wondered what on earth had happened to him. One didn't step on to a trolleybus and simply disappear.

He wrote his name on the bank with a twig just to know that it was true, scratching the 'O' into the dirt, and then the 'W', the 'E' and the 'N'.

That at least was automatic, something that he could be sure of, the tip of a first thread by which he might pull everything else back.

* * *

He did not sleep. A cold bit into him that he had not expected after the relative warmth of the day. He had lit a fire quite easily, rubbing a stick between two rocks until the kindling had caught; but keeping it lit was a different matter. A dampness had crept through the countryside so that three times he'd got up to relight the fire until eventually he had given up and pulled the jacket tighter around him, his hands pressed into his armpits.

He lay there trying to recall a house, a room, a bed, a warm arm wrapped around him, but in the thickness of the night — in his own private darkness — there was nothing there.

OWEN

Owen woke as cold as if a frost had set within him, and his head felt muddy and confused. He had hoped the new day would bring with it some clarity or an awakening from the dream. Now, maybe an hour later, the strange world lingered.

He was tired too. Most of the long night had been spent trying to thread his thoughts together, quite convinced that in time he would recall something that would explain everything, but the harder he tried, the less he was certain of. He could find no last fixed point.

The memories that did come were old and childish and looped in his head: a dog called Cedar; another name — Suzie Sue; a picture of himself as a child running through fields with his arms outstretched; flying a kite with his father, its red wings spread like a buzzard's, feeling the tug of the string in his hands as if, in his dreams, the kite was trying to wake him.

As he walked he felt so hungry that he could feel his stomach gnawing. The state of his shoes concerned him, and with that the state of his feet. His head hurt and occasionally, if he turned it too sharply, dizziness soaked through him, or a distant tree or gatepost would divide, doubling in his vision. When that happened he would have to stop and steady himself, and wait for the world to eventually find its form.

As his path took him over the brow of a hill,

paralleling a lower road, he became aware of a line of travellers a short distance below him, moving through the sun-drenched mist. There were two four-wheeled carts, each pulled by a bony horse, their wooden wheels creaking and stumbling over the potholed road. In them he could see piles of furniture: wooden tables, thin-limbed chairs interlocked together, and the antlers of a deer hooked over one of the sides. Children sat on stacks of mattresses, cradling pans or wicker baskets, or clutching the corner of a blanket to their nose, or a doll, or a straw donkey, while adults walked alongside, bundles strapped to their backs.

He followed, keeping out of sight, and watching them as they trudged through the smoky sunlight, their horses straining to haul the carts, and the rickety rattle of their furniture bumping around inside.

After a while the road began to edge westerly, taking the procession with it, until it tipped the travellers over a hill and they disappeared into the sunlight.

He had walked long distances before, he thought, for now a recollection was pooling. Not just the muscle memory of walking for hours, but days, and not in the full blush of spring either, but through deep snow with blizzards buffeting through a pine forest and whipping hard against his face. Then, just as quickly, the memory was gone again. He wondered if there was still a war on — a war that felt so distant in his mind and yet he was quite sure had barely begun.

He remembered a radio announcement, and

the next day at his desk, carefully marking out the lines of a plane — a precision laid out for something that, in his mind at least, had not yet been ruined in its reality — he had barely been able to concentrate. A worry had seeped into him that everything was about to change and with it, him too. Everyone would be altered. Lines would be redrawn, populations recalculated, trajectories of bombs and bullets scrutinized. No one would look for beauty in design any more. The womanly curve of a plane's belly would be bastardized, bloated to make room for parachutists and weapons of destruction. *At least we ain't getting called up*, Harry had said. And yet everything had changed.

As he sat on the verge feeling for other cuts and bruises on a body that no longer felt like his own, and in clothes that weren't his either, he found a pocket in the seam of the trousers and was surprised to find a metal button. He turned it over in his palm. It looked familiar yet he couldn't remember whether he had seen the button before.

* * *

He skirted a wheat field — the crop already waist-high, and the soft stalks rustling in the breeze. He had spent the morning wondering just how long he had been gone. He stopped for a moment and watched the wind casting ripples through the shifting leaves. If he tuned his ears he could hear them whispering to him, the reedy *hush* of their voices.

He glanced around and then, seeing that no one was about, he took a step in, slowly venturing further and then feeling the lure of something stronger than he was pulling him in deeper. The tips of wheat licked at his arms as they had done when he'd been a child, that familiar smell of dusty dirt, and the crop swilling and swaying around him. He wanted to run through it. And then, in the memory that swept in on the breeze, sweeping him into it too, his brother was suddenly in front of him, the back of his head bobbing through the crop, the stark whiteness of his shirt against the tan of his arms. *Max*, he shouted. *No, Max, wait!* The two of them running through the wheat, their arms knocking against the stalks and the sun burning so bright that sometimes Max would disappear in its flare; or, without warning, would drop like a dead bird into the crop so that Owen would lose him and panic. He would stand in the middle of the field calling out to him: *Max*, he would shout, *where are you?* Then Max would burst out through the stalks beside him and with a holler knock him down into the dirt. *I was here all the time, stupid*, he would say, laughing, as Owen picked himself up. But not this time.

Not now.

He stood in the middle of the field, anxiously scanning it for that same movement, that rippling path, an unseen disturbance quickly coming for him through the wheat. He stood, waiting — watching and waiting — until another breath of wind blew through the crop, taking his fear and his brother with it.

* * *

The seven soldiers were laid out along the verge like ninepins, each dressed in red green uniforms and missing their shoes and socks. Around them flies patrolled, alighting on stony faces or disappearing inside an open collar, or up the tunnel of a trouser leg and through a bracken of hairs.

Owen edged closer then nudged one of the soldier's ankles with his boot. Even knowing that they were dead, he squatted down and nervously touched one. The soldier's hand was still warm. He stood up again sharply, pulling the pistol from his pocket and looking around, then pacing back up the path several yards and scanning the trees on one side and the fields that rolled out on the other. He thought he could sense eyes watching him but he could see nothing there. Whoever had shot them must still be close; these men were not long dead.

He made his way back, still alert, and crouched down beside them again. The flies had already moved back in, pitter-pattering over the skin.

After some awkward digging around he found a torn map in the breast pocket of one and a small notebook with a blank page at the back. He ripped it out and slipped it into his pocket along with the stub of a pencil; their pistols, bullets and cigarettes, or any chocolate they might have carried, had already been taken.

For some time he sat on the grass trying to piece the sheets of map together but the place names all looked foreign. He didn't know whether they were German or Dutch or something else entirely. He folded the pieces and pocketed them. When he stood back up, he could have sworn that one of the soldiers had turned his head.

⋆ ⋆ ⋆

If there really was a war on and he had no idea where he was, then it was much safer not to be seen. The pain in his head still felt like eyes drilling into him and several times Owen had abruptly stopped, distinctly sure that someone was following him. He kept hold of the pistol and checked his pockets: paper, maps, button, pencil. He had to keep checking that everything was in place.

The morning slowly dissolved, and at times the train wreck and the soldiers laid out like ninepins were gone from his mind entirely, so that it was only when he saw the scrap of paper in his hand that the recollection sprang back and he remembered it was true.

MAX, he had written.

How despairing of him his brother would be.

Lost? Oh, for God's sake.

Snatches of thought like that constantly peeled away, though he tried hard to cling to them: drawing the stringers of a wing at his desk; the red trolleybus following the overhead wires down the hill. He stepped on the back. *Not to worry, sir. 'Sonly thruppence*. The conductor had punched out a ticket anyway. Names, too, blew in and away again. Barnes and Budgie and Peri . . .

You need to make a note of everything. Nothing in his head felt safe.

And then his father was grabbing the strings just in time and swooping the kite back into the blue. *I say*, he said, *that was close*.

It was only as these thoughts dispersed that he realized that he had somehow wandered on to a narrow road and was standing in the middle of it. The sky had opened up into a rich wide blue. Dandelion seeds drifted like parachutists across his path. He stared behind him at the road he must have walked along, at the gentle haze in the distance shimmering above the dirt. Then, for a moment, there in the watery blur, he thought he saw the silhouette of a boy standing maybe half a mile back — a boy, tall and thin and watching him. The silhouette quivered and disappeared.

⋆ ⋆ ⋆

The terrain hardened, the hills forming into jagged edges and the trees into prickly furze. For a while he sat on the verge and could not stop himself crying.

He wondered if there was someone waiting for him. He had no wedding ring or photograph. If he were married would he not feel it? The memory of it might be gone like so much else but there would surely be something deeper within him that could not so easily be cut away. In time, the sense of someone might come, he told himself; it might bring a face, a name. He would not die. He would not give up. He would somehow get himself home.

He took out the map again with fresh determination and searched within its sheets. Somewhere he was lost within it: the most indistinguishable pinprick trapped beneath its contours. He scanned the symbols, the railway lines, the rivers and the strange-looking place names. Harry had once said that the cartographer was to the land what the draughtsman was to aircraft: bringing a plan and order to something that would otherwise feel unnavigable. The map, though, was faded and stained, and staring at it he realized what nonsense this was, even if he tried to think of the contours as no more than arcs and the rivers as no more than cables wiring the land together.

As he moved the sheet away, his eyes were drawn to a name. *Sagan*. It sat at the edge of the sheet. He faltered, stared and then turned his gaze back to the other parts of the map. But his eyes kept being pulled to it as if within him two wires had touched, sparking the slightest flicker of something in his head. He scanned around the name with his finger but nothing looked familiar. Only perhaps the shading of a forest. A symbol printed below looked like the Roman numeral: *III*.

Sagan. He wondered if he had read about the place recently, or heard it on a broadcast. A place so far at the edge of the map as to be almost hanging off it.

In the end he pulled out the scrap of paper and stub of pencil and wrote it down anyway, then found it again on the map and twice circled it. His finger followed the faint railway lines that threaded away from it in either direction but nothing else caught his eye.

* * *

As the evening drew in, the fields and woods gave way to forests that rose up over the steepening hillsides, capturing the swelling darkness within the clutch of their boughs. He found a clearing and rummaged around for kindling, but beneath the trees everything was damp. As he poked about he sensed movement nearby — a figure, he thought, changing shapes between the trees and shifting with the shadows.

He pulled out the pistol. 'Who's there?'

Then, in German: '*Wer ist da?*'

He held still but all he could hear in the darkness was the nervous fidget of birds.

* * *

He did not sleep but lay for hours, shivering and surrounded by the sounds of the forest. He squeezed his hands into his armpits once more and pulled his knees in tight, the ground growing damp beneath him until it soaked through his clothes.

He would not be afraid. But twice he sat bolt upright, swinging the pistol furiously about at the shapes of bats that were sweeping between the trees.

Images, recent and opaque, and untethered to anything else, rose in his mind like air bubbles to the surface and just as quickly burst: sunlight burning through a skin of leaves; water rushing around him. They flashed when he least expected: these leaves so close to his face; or the scuff and scratch of grass being hauled away from under him as if it was the earth, not him, that was sliding. There was no catching them — these sudden openings into what might have been yesterday or the day before or even the year before; it was difficult to tell.

The trolleybus came. He sat by the window. The street melted away.

He jerked awake, aware of the stench of smoke and the fizzle of flames. When he turned on his side he found that a shabby-looking boy was squatting in the undergrowth, staring right at him. Owen scrambled to his feet, dropping the jacket that had been draped over him, and pulled out his pistol, but the boy did not flinch.

In the clearing a fire had been lit and a crude spit constructed with a small animal roasting on it. Moisture from its skinned body dripped and the flames hissed and flared. The smoke was so infused with cooked meat that Owen felt it pulling at his stomach.

The boy didn't look much older than fifteen, and was squatting with his outstretched arms resting on his knees and hands lightly clasped. He had an impish quality: unkempt hair with dried bits of leaf caught in it, and a small snub nose. His eyes were narrow and dark, and he scrutinized Owen, then shifted and cleared his throat. He didn't look in the slightest bit scared, but gauged Owen and the shaking gun with little more than curious suspicion. There was a dried smear of mud across each cheek and another across his forehead. His trousers were dusty at the knees, and he wore a khaki-coloured shirt and black scuffed shoes. The jacket that had been draped over Owen must have been the boy's too; it had darker patches curling at the elbows. A tatty canvas bag lay beside him, with loose pockets and buckles, and something drawn on it in faded red ink.

The boy shuffled and tilted his head, chewing on his lips as if he had something sour in his mouth.

Owen took a step closer. 'What do you want?'

Instantly the boy was on his feet and much taller than he had expected. He unleashed a torrent of words and sounds that Owen couldn't understand. He came closer and Owen backed away. He was still talking, fast.

'I don't know what you're saying.'

'*Hledal jsem vás*,' the boy shouted. '*Dva dny. Dva dny!*'

'For God's sake . . . ' Owen stumbled backwards over the jacket.

The boy gave him a hard shove and then another, and then grabbed at Owen's gun. Owen pulled it away and made for the trees, but before he knew it the boy had twisted him around with surprising force, tipping him over his foot and bringing him to the ground so that he hit it hard with a gasp and was winded. The boy snatched the gun from his hand, unleashing another string of words that Owen didn't understand.

He stood over Owen, pointing the gun.

'All right, all right,' said Owen, submitting. He was on his back and still breathless. 'Look, I don't know who you are or what you want but I don't have anything. I promise.'

He could see then that the boy was shaking. He pressed the heel of his hand to his eye and then, turning away, he threw the pistol down at

Owen's side. He said something but the venom was gone. He took a few deep breaths as he paced away and then, finding some self-control, came back. He looked down at Owen and then nodded, and Owen hauled himself up on to his elbows. The boy signalled at the fire.

'*Máte hlad?*' he said. His anger had almost entirely drained but his frown still puckered. Whatever had happened between them was over. The faintest smile of acceptance flickered across his face.

* * *

They sat cross-legged across the fire from each other, the boy's eyes interrogating Owen as they both hungrily ate. Owen couldn't make him out. Using a small flick knife, the boy had cut the meat from the animal with a swift and practised butchery that was equally impressive and disturbing, before serving the slices in wooden bowls with a watery broth and bits of root vegetable that had been simmering in a pan. Owen didn't know whether to be afraid or thankful. The food was slowly reviving him but doing little to quell his unease.

Did he know the boy? Had he forgotten? He wondered if more days had fallen away into the abyss. Nothing about the boy looked familiar, yet still he stared with an unflinching curiosity. Only occasionally did he get up to serve more broth or carve more meat from what Owen hoped was a rabbit and not a small cat. He poked encouragement into the fire while Owen discreetly felt in his pockets: pistol, paper, button, map. He pulled out the scrap of paper. There were notes he'd written on it in pencil — the words MAX and SAGAN and HARRY and HAWKERS — but nothing about a boy.

The boy lifted the bowl and drank the dregs, his dark eyes like polished wood still fixed on Owen.

Not an imp, he thought, but a bird, in the way he cocked his head or turned it at every sound. He had a nervy alertness, as if he and everything around them was balanced on a wire.

He untied a canister from his belt and, without saying a word, offered it. Owen sniffed it and then took a sip. The water was warm and stale but he took another mouthful and handed it back. The boy took a swig himself and refastened the cap.

'Do I know you?' Owen asked.

The boy said nothing.

'Do you know where I am?'

The boy's nose twitched.

'I'm lost. I don't know where I am. Do you understand? *Wo bin ich?*' he said, trying German instead. 'Yes? Do you speak English? Where am I?' He signalled around at the trees.

The boy said something that might have been a name.

'I mean the country,' said Owen. 'England, yes? Do you understand?' He pulled out the scraps of map but the boy was already talking.

'*Čechy*,' the boy said. '*Sudety . . . Protektorát Čechy a Morava*.' He shrugged, as if you could call it what you liked; it didn't much matter.

'I don't know what you're saying. What are you?' The boy sounded Polish or Russian or something. His words came out buttery but like nothing Owen had heard before.

'*Československo*.'

'Chesko — ?'

'*Československo*,' the boy said.

It sounded like Czechoslovakia, but that was ridiculous.

Owen stared at the scrap of paper, trying to make sense of the notes he'd written and the pieces of map.

'Here.' He held out the paper and pencil. 'Will you write the date?'

'Date?' said the boy, unsure.

'The date. Yes. Today. I need to know what the date is. What's the bloody date?'

'*Je květen*.'

'No,' Owen said, losing his temper. 'The numbers.' He held up his hand splaying his fingers and shook them. 'The numbers, yes? Do you understand?'

The boy took the paper and wrote something. He handed it back.

Owen looked.

3–5

What was that? March? May? That couldn't be right. He felt a heat starting to engulf him.

'The year . . . Now the year. *Jahr*,' he said in German. 'Write the year. Please.'

The boy grinned. He wrote, slow and purposeful this time, as if this were a game that he now knew he was winning. He handed it over.

Owen stared at the numbers.

1945

His stomach tightened. His mind went blank.

'Forty-five?'

'*Čtyřicet pět.*' He nodded.

No, Owen thought. That wasn't right. 1940. 1941, perhaps, but . . . He couldn't have lost . . . what? That was four years. It couldn't be true.

He wasn't sure that his legs could take him, but without thinking he started to walk. He pushed hurriedly away through the trees. He needed to get out, to get away, but the boy was suddenly coming after him.

'*Musíte tady zůstat!*' He grabbed Owen's arm but Owen pushed him off.

'No, let me go!'

He stumbled, crashing through the trees, away from the boy and his mouthful of lies. By the time he came out on to the lane he was breathless. He looked about in every direction at the steep slopes and fields and the endless woods. None of it looked real. It was as if he'd fallen through into another world. He didn't know what to do.

* * *

He didn't know how far he had gone before he sensed something behind him. When he turned around he could see the figure of the boy down the lane. He carried on, picking up his pace, but he could still feel the boy following him, the bag hauled over his shoulder, the water canister bumping at his thigh.

'What do you want?' he shouted. 'Leave me alone!'

He had no idea where he was going. Sagan, he thought, but he didn't know why.

At least we ain't getting called up, Harry had said, but for some reason here he was.

He kept taking out the piece of paper and looking at it, uncomprehending.

3–5–1945

Nothing about it made sense.

When he stopped again and turned the boy had stopped as well, and was standing in the road, staring. Owen carried on, trying to ignore him, but he could feel the boy's stare at the back of his head. He stopped and turned. The boy stopped too. The sunlight was burning around his frame but the distance between them was no different from before. Was he following him on purpose? Did he think this was a bloody game?

Oh, let him, he thought. I don't care.

But he did. He carried on and then glanced back again.

He's like a bloody lost dog.

When eventually he reached a junction he turned right, following the lane through a tunnel of trees. His anger with the boy was starting to dissipate. He was even beginning to feel strangely indebted to him. The boy had fed him, after all. He had watched over Owen while he slept. Again, Owen stopped and turned. The boy was teetering on the cusp of the hillock beneath the dark overhang of trees, the sunlight shining through from behind. This time Owen stood and waited. Oh, let him come if he wanted to, he thought. The boy would slope off to wherever he was going soon enough.

* * *

For over an hour they walked in silence. Owen felt as if he'd been taken hostage, and without a shared language he was completely disarmed. His fingers fumbled in his pockets as he walked for the telltale shape of the button.

'Where are you going anyway?' he asked, but the boy did not reply.

As the morning progressed the air became bracing as they kept climbing to higher ground. The boy lingered behind him but with increasing frequency he walked parallel on the opposite side of the lane and threw Owen cursory glances. Whenever Owen stopped to consider the map, trying to match a point on it with something he'd seen — the pinnacles of a remote chateau or the tops of cone-like mountains blurred by distant rain — the boy would stop too, and empty a stone from his battered shoe, or swipe at something with a stick while he waited. And then Owen would pocket the map and carry on, and the boy would fall into line.

* * *

They followed the edge of a field that had recently been set ablaze, patches of the volcanic earth still black and burning. Behind it the trees seemed to melt, and with every change of wind the burning ash blew across their path so that they had to turn their backs to it and cover their eyes, some of the flecks still orange, pricking their cheeks and the backs of their hands.

They joined a lane that swerved down into a valley, a loosely woven fence separating the road from the farmland. At the bottom of the slope there was an entrance and a grey stone house in a yard with open-fronted wooden outbuildings housing a plough and a wagon. Parked behind the house a couple of small trucks could be seen. Three soldiers in olive drab uniforms were loitering in the yard.

The boy grabbed Owen's arm and pulled them both into a crouch. He then pelted, head stooped, across the grass and ducked behind the fence. He glanced over the top and slumped back down.

'*Honem!*' he hissed, signalling to Owen, who ran over and then squatted down beside the boy, both of them breathless with their knees up and backs to the fence.

'What is it?' Owen said. He turned to take a look.

Through the latticework of branches he could see the house and the uniformed men, bulky rifles in their hands, each held by a strap over a shoulder. One of them sat on an upturned pail, digging around in the dirt with the toe of his boot. The other two stood by the trucks, lounging against the bonnets, and talking the same Slavic language as the boy.

The boy squinted through the thin gap in the fence, glanced over the top and then through the gap again, trying to get a clearer look. Owen held the pistol against his chest. He could hear the boy's agitation in the heaviness of his breath.

Then, from inside the house, there came a commotion. A stout uniformed man with severely cropped silver hair and a square reddened face appeared in the doorway. He was dragging out a woman who was struggling and shouting in his arms.

The boy clenched Owen's arm, his fingertips digging in. The woman clung on to the doorframe and yelled desperately to someone inside — *Aleši! Ondřeji!* — before the soldier shouted something and wrenched her away.

The boy stood but Owen yanked him back down.

'Don't!'

The men at the trucks were opening the doors, one of them flicking a catch on his gun. Another soldier appeared from within the house hauling out two young boys. He gripped each by the upper arm and dragged them as they struggled and fought across the yard. He forced them viciously into one of the trucks, while the woman was digging her heels into the dirt, trying to lower herself to the ground, but the silver-haired man heaved her up as she screamed and shouted, and, with his comrades, pushed her into the second vehicle.

The door slammed as, beside Owen, the boy

tried to stand again, shouting, '*Nacistický sráči!*' but Owen hauled him down harder.

'You'll get yourself shot.'

Then from behind the fence came a ferocious roar of air. Through the gaps between the woven strips of bark they saw flaring jets of flames as two of the men torched the outbuildings, great projections of dragon-fire issuing from flamethrowers, while another stood in the doorway of the farmhouse, a silhouette against the glowing fireball as the hallway was engulfed. The trucks started. Voices shouted. Through a truck window the woman was shrieking as the flames broke through the roof of one of the outbuildings, already crackling at the sky. The downstairs windows of the house splintered as smoke began to issue.

Owen wrapped his arms around the struggling boy.

'*Nacistický sráči*,' he yelled, before they were forced to bury their heads, the heat so intense against the latticed strips of wood that they could hear the dried crackle of bark on the other side of the fence slowly peeling away.

* * *

It was not that he was lost that concerned him most. Nor was it that he had found himself in a war that he remembered so little about, which now seemed to be consuming everything and everyone within it. Nor was it that he had ended up in an obscure country that in the past had been nothing more than a strange name in the news broadcasts, or, even, that somehow he seemed to have wiped several years from his mind. No, what concerned him most was that things he now knew for sure — and knew that he knew — could suddenly be lost again, and then found, and lost once more, as if they had never been there in the first place. Not things from years past, securely embedded, but things learnt yesterday, or an hour ago, or five minutes. He had to work hard just to keep them in his head. Like the train wreck. Or the ransacked house. Or the button. Or even the boy.

Owen was still not sure if he should know him. Or how long they had been together. Or even what his name was — if, indeed, he had asked. All he knew was that he was Czech, and had quite likely fed him.

BOY = CZECH = BREAKFAST

He had found it on the scrap of paper — a formula for remembering.

* * *

He was sitting beside a pool sunk within a sunlit dell, surrounded by boulders and overhanging trees. A small waterfall surged down through a line of rocks littered with broken branches and coursed some eight or nine feet into the pool. Thin-framed dragonflies motored about like silent biplanes, coming in low to scuff the water and swerving the bomb blasts of droplets that splashed from the waterfall. Leaves tumbled around him, spiralling whirligigs drifting down.

He was alone, with no idea of how long he had been there. He thought he might be waiting for someone but he couldn't think who.

At the lip of shore between two rocks, where the soil was sandy and beach-like, there were the fresh remnants of a campfire and a wooden chair that he was sitting on, painted white but flaking. He wondered who had brought it here, clambering with it up and down the steep slopes of the wood. A couple of empty bottles lay about, the labels scraped off, and above him, in a tree, a rusted paraffin lamp had been squeezed into the fork of two branches.

He poked idly at the damp ash in the fire and thought about whether he should build a fresh one. Among the remains were charred bits of paper that looked like documents with photographs attached, each with the same outlined face but the features scraped away.

Every time he heard a sound he turned to see if someone was coming. Somebody would come. He just needed to see who it was.

He took out the piece of paper and scanned his notes: MAX, a date in someone else's writing, an inventory of things in his pocket. HAWKERS, he had written. DRAUGHTSMAN. Next to the word SAGAN he had added the symbol he'd found beneath it on the map: III. He'd found other Roman numerals by other places. He didn't know what they meant.

He kept expecting to see his brother or his father, or hear Cedar's bark as he bounded out through the ferns and tore down the slope to him, snuffling up the scents.

For pity's sake, there you are.

He was not a child now though. He was a man older than his years who would retrace his steps and find his way home, picking up the pieces of him as he went. He would put himself back together. All he needed was to remember.

⋆ ⋆ ⋆

The lad was tall and lanky, wearing a grubby charcoal jacket with a different coloured patch on each elbow, dusty brown trousers and a bag thrown over his shoulder. He stumbled through the sun-soaked leaves with an upturned cap in his hand, a loaf of bread tucked under his arm, and a tin canister that he swung by its handle, the contents sloshing inside. He made his way down the slope, sliding down on his heels to the pool's shore, careful not to spill whatever was collected in the cap.

Was this the same boy? He didn't know. The boy nodded at the white-painted chair as if Owen had constructed it himself while he had been away.

'Good,' he said, praising Owen for his handicraft.

Must be the same boy, Owen thought. He seemed friendly enough.

The boy thrust the cap into Owen's hands. It was full of thin-stemmed mushrooms.

Owen poked at them. 'Are you sure you can eat these?'

The boy put the loaf down on the chair and

unscrewed the lid from the canister to show Owen the milk.

'Where did you get all of this?'

The boy grinned, then pressed the canister against Owen for him to hold. He made his way, stepping light-footed from stone to stone, to the waterfall, where he stood, balanced precariously on a rock, and vigorously washed his hands.

'*To je krása*,' he shouted, still grinning, as he looked up at the pouring sunlight. 'Eh?'

Owen didn't know but nodded.

The boy pointed at the overhanging branches and smiled. 'Good,' he said. 'Yes?'

* * *

The broth was watery and tasted stale, but the mushrooms weren't bad and the bread, although dry, was perfectly palatable if dunked long enough and chewed on for a while. They shared the canister of milk, passing a smile between them at each other's moustaches.

'Owen,' Owen said, leaning forward a little and tapping at his chest. 'English. And you? Your name?'

The boy smiled again and raised the canister as if it were a glass. He took a generous swig, his cheeks full, then put it down between his feet and swallowed.

'Janek,' he said. He stood up and opened his arms to display himself. 'Janek Věnceslav Sokol.' He took a bow and sat down again. 'Janek. Janek — Owen,' he said, motioning to them both and nodding. 'Good. *Dobře*.'

Owen pulled the paper and pencil out of his pocket and finished the equation:

BOY = CZECH = BREAKFAST = YANECK

'Well . . . hello.' He smiled awkwardly, and then tipped his bowl upside down. 'Empty again. Thank you.' Because he now remembered the boy had fed him once before. 'That was very good.'

'Petr,' Janek said. 'I . . . er . . . ' His eyes roved about, seemingly trying to find the word hanging somewhere from a tree. '*To mě naučil Petr*. Teach me.'

'Oh. To cook? I see,' said Owen. 'Yes. Very good.'

'*Petr je můj bratr*. My . . . er . . . ' He paused again, his hand turning as if flipping through a list of words until he found the right one. 'Um . . . *Bruder. Bruder?*'

'Ah, German,' said Owen.

The boy nodded. 'Little.'

'You mean brother.'

'*Ano*. Brother. Petr is . . . er . . . '

'Your brother.'

'Yes, yes. *On je dobrý člověk*. He is good man.'

'Good,' Owen said. 'Well, he's taught you well by the looks of it.'

The boy nodded and faintly smiled, then he rested his elbows on his knees and started to pick at the remnants of bread still held in his hand, breaking it into tiny pieces and then rolling them into balls before he finally ate them.

'There is a war?' Owen asked. '*Ein Krieg?*'

'War?' said the boy. 'Yes.' He laughed.

'What's happened? Who's winning?'

The boy started talking, something about *Nacisti* and *Rusové*, then *Američani*, his hand sweeping in and out — borders changing, tides turning.

'No,' Owen said. 'English, please. In English.'

But the boy didn't have the English. He shook his head and batted the conversation away. It was hopeless.

Owen tried something else, signalling around them as he had done before and getting the map out. He pointed at it. 'Where are we? I need to know. Do you understand?'

He handed the boy the sheets and the boy studied them one by one, discarding the unwanted ones on the ground willy-nilly for Owen to pick up.

'*Jsme tady*,' he said eventually, laying his fingertip at a point. His bitten fingernail circled an area to the top northern edge of the country. '*Jizerské hory. Hory*.' It looked like mountains. His finger tapped a spot.

Owen marked it with the pencil.

Not far north there was a thick line running west to east that might be a border, and towns and villages that he'd not heard of, each with two names: Reichenberg (Liberec), Gablonz (Jablonec), Friedland (Frýdlant) . . .

The boy was watching him closely.

'You want home, yes?'

'Yes,' said Owen. He felt more desperate than ever. His instinct was to head north-west in the vague direction of England, but from what little he could remember of the geography of Europe, he felt quite certain that Germany bordered the west and at least some of the north of Czechoslovakia, which meant that Austria, probably still under the Nazi regime too, must tuck around the south of it. Together, he thought, they would form a clamped mouth around the country, the Czech lands already swallowed midway down the German gullet.

The only other option seemed to be to head back into the heart of the country to Prague — but to do what? — or head out to the east in entirely the wrong direction, and as to what lay there anyway, he wasn't sure. Russia somewhere. Poland somewhere. Countries so alien that even their names — Hungary, Romania, Ukraine — filled him with unease. Poland, he thought. Wasn't that north, and bordering Czechoslovakia? Then he felt quite sure that the Poles had fallen as well.

He felt everything within him sink; whichever way he went it seemed that he was trapped and he'd be caught by someone somewhere. They would think he was a spy or an escaped prisoner. He would have to come up with a story of some sort. No one would believe the truth: that he didn't know *what* he was doing there.

His gaze lifted northerly up the map over the line that might have marked a border, until it reached that familiar name again.

'You don't know this place, do you?' he asked Janek. He pointed at Sagan. It looked to be about thirty-odd miles north. Walking distance. Maybe a day and a half.

Janek shook his head but he ran his fingertip up and down a route anyway, pulling a maybe-yes-maybe-no face, before nodding and handing the map back.

Perhaps he would walk to Sagan, Owen thought. It was close enough and he was damned whichever way he went. Besides, the name had been niggling at his thoughts all day, the uncomfortable sensation that he knew the name already, and whenever he let his eyes drift across the map, the name, for some reason, always pulled him back.

He gathered up the bowls, spoons and pan and took them to the waterfall to wash them out, then refilled the boy's water canister and slopped water over his face. When he came back the boy had taken a watch from his wrist that Owen hadn't noticed before and was scrutinizing it. He held it to the light, the watch glass winking, and turned it in his hand, studying the back as if searching for an inscription. He held it to his ear, tapped the glass and shook it, then tried to prise the back from it.

'*Jsou rozbité*,' he said, shrugging his shoulders and tossing it into the ashes.

'Perhaps I can mend it,' Owen offered.

The boy dismissed this with a wave of a hand as if it was hardly worth the bother.

* * *

When Owen came back from relieving himself in the ferns, the boy was scratching something into one of the boulders with a knife.

'Aha, good,' he said. 'We go.'

As they started to make their way up between the rock formations, the boy caught hold of Owen's arm and stopped him, and then pulled the mushroom cap over Owen's head.

Owen took it off again and handed it back.

'Thank you, but no.' He didn't know where the cap had come from or whose cap it was.

'*Vy jste Angličan*, yes?' said Janek.

'Yes,' said Owen. He'd already told him that.

'*Ano*.' He pulled the cap firmly over Owen's head again and slapped him on the back. 'Now *Čech*. Yes?' He laughed.

* * *

The ground in the wood was rarely flat and either dropped suddenly away beneath them or rose at such a steep angle that it was almost impossible to clamber. The undergrowth was treacherous, thick with dead leaves that hid the thin trailing branches of bushes that pulled tight like tripwires around your ankles or, disturbed by your passing, whipped up from the leaves and bit like vipers at the backs of your calves. Owen found himself grasping at trunks and branches as what seemed like a delicate slope slipped perilously away beneath the leaves, and he grabbed at anything to stop himself sliding, the boy coming down fast as well, swearing all the way. Owen hauled himself up until he stood on the bridge of a sharp incline. He could hear Janek huffing behind him, and then from another slope he dropkicked a pine cone.

'*Gól!*' he shouted, his arms in the air as if he had suddenly scored.

Before long the ground seemed to steady, the tumbling contours of the land finding a gentler rhythm. Owen watched the boy as he wiped spiderwebs from his face and then peeled their sticky trails from the tips of his fingers. He seemed quite at ease out here among the trees.

They reached a wire fence ringing a perimeter. On the other side a fresh green rye field rolled on wide and deep before it reached another line of trees, the apex of a barn poking out from behind them. The field was empty but for the wavering sea of crop and a gnarled, spindly tree that stood stark against the horizon. On every branch, scraps of white material had been tied like ribbons, the sun catching on them as they curled in the breeze.

'Look!' Owen cried. He picked up his pace. He fancied sitting beneath it, resting his eyes, and looking up at the white tokens of material tied as if every one of them was something lost and found; memories now safely tethered, or promises, or vows.

He followed the fence, trying to find a way through, one eye on the glimmering tree, the other aware of the boy stumbling behind him and jabbering on about something that Owen didn't understand. Then he saw a gap where the wire fence had been pulled away.

'This way,' he called. 'Through here.'

He was aware of the boy starting to run behind him as Owen reached the gap and turned to step through, and then he was yanked back as the boy yelled and the pull took Owen off his feet. Suddenly the boy was on top and winding him, one arm pressing Owen's head down, the other held over his own, his sour breath blasting against Owen's neck, and all his elbows and knees digging into him.

'Get off,' Owen shouted.

But Janek wouldn't. Then he slowly lifted his head and looked up, and scrambled to his feet and away.

Owen hauled himself up. He could barely catch his breath.

'*Musíte si dávat pozor!*' the boy exclaimed. He was pointing angrily at a thin grey line pulled taut across the gap, and then something grey and egg-like wedged into the tree. 'Boom!' he shouted. He threw his arms up. 'BOOM!'

Jesus Christ. Owen's hand instinctively went to his throat where the wire stretched between the gap would have caught him, the pull ring from the grenade tugging free. His heart was beating fast. The boy jabbed his finger at him, still furious.

'Yes, I know,' Owen said. 'I'm sorry.'

'*Musíte být moc opatrný!*'

'But I didn't see it.'

The boy signalled around them and then with a pair of fingers he pointed to his eyes — they needed to be alert.

'Two!' he said, jabbing his finger at Owen. 'Yes? Two now. Hmm?'

'Two what?' said Owen.

But the boy did not reply.

* * *

It was the sight of the Red Cross food parcels that did it — scattered along the side of the road, the boy stumbling along the ditch and looking at each in turn before someone else could come along and steal the contents.

He was a deliveryman, not a soldier, and he was not here because once, in another lifetime, he had been a draughtsman or a son or a brother or even somebody's lover.

Delivering packages, that's all, Max had said. *So I don't know why you're making such a bloody fuss about it*.

But what those packages were, Owen could not remember. This was how the day was going, falling into moments of clarity and then confusion, as if in his mind they kept walking through patches of fog. Not Red Cross parcels — that he would have remembered.

Further along the road, the boy hurled one over the hedge, furious that they were all empty.

'*Do prdele!*' he shouted.

* * *

His father had been a doctor dealing with amputees. It was the boy splicing the tops off nettles with a stick that brought a recollection of his father — curling white moustache, large flopping sun hat and white summer jacket, strolling around the garden, a pair of secateurs clasped discreetly behind his back. He would deadhead the roses and, with nimble surgical precision, nip off any broken stems, just as he did the ruined limbs of soldiers. *There*, he would mumble to himself as he stepped back to admire his handiwork. *Oh yes, that's better*.

There was something comforting, familiar even, in logging everything that came back to him.

DELIVERYMAN
BOY = YANECK
FATHER — DOCTOR — AMPUTEES

There was no knowing what might be needed; what might trigger something, that might trigger something else; that finally, and in a roundabout kind of way, might tell him what he was doing here and what he might be walking back to. A home somewhere. A wife somewhere. The cold and empty side of a bed.

* * *

They followed a narrow road up a ridge through thick forest, until it curved around a deep gully high on the hillside and they saw a sentry hut and a number of soldiers, tall wire fencing and a pull-up gate.

They slowed and Janek ushered him quietly down a slope through a cover of trees. When they had crept some distance and had found a vantage point from which they could spy on the crossing, Janek settled himself in the undergrowth, stretching his legs out and leaning back on his elbow among the leaves.

'Now what?' Owen said.

The boy motioned him to sit as well.

'We wait?' said Owen. 'What is this, anyway? Is this the German border?'

The boy didn't answer.

The wind stirred the leaves and after a while there came the patter of rain, which rapidly grew heavier and turned the early evening light from silver to lead grey. Still they waited. They watched the soldiers up at the crossing. In time the rain abated but not before it had dampened them through to the skin.

Owen watched the boy beside him sprawled out on his side, scratching shapes into the earth. The slightest disturbance and his sharp eyes darted.

He couldn't see why Janek had latched on to him. He was beginning to feel like a fugitive; or as if he had two lives running in parallel — the one he remembered and the one here and now — and yet they had no point of connection as far as he could tell.

Perhaps he should give himself up. These men at the border crossing would have food and water, a line of command. He'd tell them that he was a British citizen, that he needed to speak to someone, goddamn it, he needed to get home.

Through the dimming twilight he could barely see them now. Just the murmur of their voices and the reassurance of a laugh. What was to say the boy wasn't leading Owen on a wild goose chase anyway? That Owen could trust the boy when he couldn't even trust himself?

'These men,' he whispered, 'are they German? *Deutsch?*'

The boy shook his head. '*Rusové*.'

'Russian? But I thought . . . Look, what's going on here? Where are we? Isn't this a German border? *Deutschland?*'

'*Ano*,' said the boy, nodding.

'So, where are they? *Wo sind sie? Die Deutschen?*'

The boy threw his stick away and mumbled something.

'Look, I don't think we should be going into Germany, do you?' said Owen. 'That sounds like a ruddy suicide mission.'

Janek stared at him.

'*Deutschland. Nein*,' Owen said. '*Das ist* . . . I don't know — not good.'

'I look for Petr,' Janek said. 'Yes?'

Owen stood up. He'd had enough but the boy pulled him down again.

'*Ani hnout*,' he hissed.

'But I don't know what we're doing here,' Owen said. 'I don't even know why you're still with me. Look, I don't need your help. I'll make my own way. What do you want from me anyway?'

But the boy wasn't listening. His eyes were fixed on the sentry crossing.

Owen pulled at his arm and Janek turned sharply.

'You want home?' Janek demanded.

'Yes. Of course I do.'

'That way then. England. Yes? You. Me. We go.'

* * *

It was almost dark when they heard the carts. Janek pushed him awake and on to his feet, gathering up his bag. '*Rychle. Rychle*,' he whispered urgently, then he set off, Owen stumbling blindly after him through the steep woodland as it arced around towards the patrol.

There seemed to be only a narrow stretch of woodland where it was level enough for them to stand any chance of clambering over the high barbed fence. There, though, a single soldier leant against a post, rifle in one hand, sucking on a cigarette.

They got as close as they dared and squatted in the shadows around a denser clump of trees. Up the sharp incline to their right they could barely see the road above them or the sentry hut through the pines. The silhouetted soldiers drifted like ghosts in the gloom. He could hear them talking more clearly now, the crack of a laugh.

The two carts drew near, wheels creaking and rattling, each pulled by a horse and flanked on either side by men, women and children; some sitting, tired and grizzly, in the carts, clutching pots and pans, others held in parents' arms or walking beside them and gripping a hand. Something about them looked familiar: the rickety piles of furniture, the deer antlers hooked over one side. As the carts pulled up at the crossing, the soldiers gathered around, crowding them. There was a dialogue that soon became heated. The Russian soldiers poked at the adults, nudging them with their guns or giving them a shove against the wagon, laughing, jeering and shouting. One of them called to their comrade down at the fence — *Ey! Georgiy!* — and signalled him. The soldier stubbed his cigarette out on the post and Owen watched as he struggled up the incline through the trees to join the others. By the time he reached the top, two of his colleagues were already in one of the carts and throwing things out to be caught. They would take whatever they fancied. The refugees were helpless to stop them.

'What do we do?' Owen whispered, but the boy wasn't listening, his attention fixed on the road.

There was a cheer as something smashed. The refugees were pleading, trying to pull the Russians away from their possessions, but the soldiers took no notice. They raised their voices and pushed them about from one to another, while more clambered into the carts. One of them held the antlers on top of his head, mooing like a bull, and they laughed. Another had a woman by the wrist. He wanted something from her and wouldn't let go. Owen could hear the children crying. The woman pulled hard and then slapped at the man, and a tussle broke out.

'*Ted!*' said Janek, and with that he was suddenly up and running, going stooped and swift through the undergrowth, across the steeply tilted hillside.

'Fuck.' Owen scrambled after him as fast as he could. High on the roadside he could hear one of the Russians yelling, the scared horses clattering their hooves and the creaking of the cart as the animals tried to push back. He could feel his heart thumping, a sharp stitch in his chest, while Janek was fast on his feet ahead of him through the brambles and ferns that snatched at their legs, all the while Owen aware that if they weren't careful they might step on a mine or he might run through a booby trap, setting off a grenade for real this time.

When they reached the fence it was higher than Owen had imagined, barbed wire prongs lining the top. Janek held it steady so that Owen could go first. He hauled his way up, the wire straining and rattling under the weight as his feet found foot holes and the wire lines bit deep into his hands. As he reached the top, the fence wavering precariously beneath him, he lifted his leg over, steadied himself and then jumped down, Janek's bag and canisters quickly landing in the undergrowth next to him. Janek clambered up and over, and then, with a heavy thump, he was down as well, gathering up his things and they were running; and Owen didn't once look back, but as they slid and scrambled down another slope, disappearing into the dark gully of the forest below, he heard a single sharp shot and a woman started to shriek.

⋆ ⋆ ⋆

His mother had fits. He wondered if that was what had happened, whether it was something hereditary. He remembered her on the kitchen floor, her whole body convulsing as if it was rejecting who she was. Everyone dashing around. Max crying. Cedar had retreated into his basket and was shaking, while in the hallway Agatha, who had only popped in for clematis clippings, was hollering up the stairs for Owen's father to come and be quick. And all the time Owen had stood there in the kitchen doorway, staring. His father came, pushing past, syringe in hand, for this had happened many times before and, of course, in the end everything was fine. His lasting memory was of his mother apologizing over and over again — as was her way after every episode — for the thing she had no recollection of happening, the trauma she had no memory of putting them all through.

* * *

He woke to voices and flashlights. He was lying on his side among rubble on the floor of a large concrete bunker, his back to the wall where there were six square holes along its length and the lights were shining in. The concrete beneath him felt hard and frozen, and his hand was gripping a round piece of metal — a button or a badge. He didn't know how long he'd been there. Nothing looked familiar.

He listened to the voices, three of them: male and hushed and German. He could hear the soft crunch of their feet, and sense the grass and trees around them. The torchlight shone right over him, lying undetected and pressed against the wall, the side of his face on the cold grit floor. Their footsteps came closer until they were right outside, two then three lights shining in, their beams dancing over the back wall and sweeping across the floor and all its moonscape litter.

He quietly lifted his head. There was a boy standing motionless behind the entrance. Owen could just about make out the shape of a flick knife in his hand. He held one finger to his lip to Owen. A *Don't move, don't make a sound*.

Outside, there seemed to be some disagreement — perhaps whether to come in or just leave it. Owen held his breath. He could feel a cramp entering his foot and the sharp bits of concrete beneath him burrowing into his side. The lights swept about the room again, over the rubble and animal droppings, and the rotting carcass of a half-eaten fish, its bones lifting out in a fan. One of the beams passed over an abandoned bag on the floor, a red painted symbol on it, but with its dusty colour among the rubble, the torchlight did not stall. The lights swept out again and he heard the men retreating, their mumbled conversations soon lost within the forest, until eventually they were gone and all he could see was the moonlit whites of the boy's staring eyes.

JANEK

The face fused into clarity and then came the recognition, but the boy's name was lost.

'*Půjdem!*'

He kicked the bottom of Owen's foot and Owen propped himself up.

It took a while before he could place where he was. He had barely slept and had spent most of the night watching the shallow mass of the boy laid out on the floor, listening to his breathing. Outside the new day was just hatching, a dim bluish grey filling the empty frames along the concrete wall.

Janek — the name came back to him — swung his bag over his shoulder.

'*Půjdem!*' he said again, getting impatient. Then he huffed and walked out into the morning, and Owen could hear him traipsing away through the forest before he yelled, '*Proboha, jdeme!*'

Owen struggled up, trying to tread the numbness from his feet, and uncurling his fingers from around the strange button that he had found clasped in his hand when he woke. A large symbol was on the back wall, drawn in charcoal — a flattened 'V', like wings in flight, with another, smaller like an arrowhead, directly underneath, and all framed within a square. He stared at it. Had it been there before? He checked his pockets — pistol, paper, button, map — and stepped out into the dawn.

* * *

They walked all day, skirting hamlets and farmsteads, clinging to the woods. Now that they'd crossed the border, the boy was anxious that they weren't seen.

'*Honem! Honem!*' he called, urging Owen on, the map held at arm's length in front of him, as if even the vague trails he led them down were thinly sketched within its folds.

The going was hard, the ground uneven. Owen could feel his blisters rubbing, and his calves stung, as did his thighs. The invisible pain beneath his ribs bit with every step. As they walked his mind drifted, looking for Max in the wheat fields, either as a boy, the lingering memory still playing out, or as a man striding through the crop towards him, not a delivery but a collection.

Oh, bloody hell, he'd say. *There you are. Mother's going spare*.

He wondered where Max was. He wished for him to suddenly appear on his motorbike or in his Austin 12/14 with the roof down. *Hop in. We're going home*.

He pulled out the piece of paper: SAGAN. He needed to get to Sagan. He had no idea why, but the more he said the name, rolling it around in his head, the more familiar and urgent it had become. He *did* know it. He had *always* known it. It could be no coincidence that it was there in his head and circled on the map, drawing his eye to it again and again as if no other place mattered. When he got to Sagan it would all make sense. Something or someone would be there for him. It was this that was pulling him on.

He looked at the writing. Beneath his sweating fingers the pencil letters were starting to smudge. If he lost the paper or what was written on it there would be nothing for him to cling to but the vagaries in his head; and if his memories went, maybe he would go with them, all the particles of who he was being lifted from him one by one until, with a single puff of wind, he would be blown away like dust across the field.

Then another name fell through his thoughts like a stone — something he had been straining for — and he tried to grab it but was too late.

When are you going to get yourself a girl? Max was always teasing. But there had been someone. Not a Margaret or a Ruth or a Charlotte or a Hetty. They had been Max's. And not Suzie Sue — a name that kept coming to him; a girl so beautiful that they had named her twice.

He watched the misshapen silhouette of the boy up ahead against the midday sun, his long gait and the water canister banging against his hip. Across a far barley field to the right he glimpsed a woman carrying bags and ushering two small children along. The smallest kept stopping to pick things up out of the soil and Owen could hear the mother's distant voice.

'*Matouši! Pojd'!*' She grabbed at the child's wrist and hurriedly began to drag him as the boy started to cry.

* * *

Walking, he sometimes thought it was the back of another that he was seeing in front of him, not Janek. He had stared at the same back for hours on that walk — from where and to where he was still unsure — but the jacket was quite clear now. It had been heavy grey wool that attracted the snow much like the others did — seeping in through the outer material, the clothing and then the skin. He remembered the thickness of the arms, the scuffed right elbow, the man's narrow body lost somewhere within the folds, the way the back of the collar was fraying, the glimpse of threads hanging from beneath the man's tightly wrapped scarf.

The name was gone but he had known it once. There were others in his head — Barnes, Budgie, Peri, Smithy — but none of them seemed to fit. The memory of the back of the man's coat remained quite clear though, even the points in it where the creases came and went, as if it had formed a union with the man within it, so that if clothes had muscle memory you could have taken this man out of them and they would still have walked through the snow without him, those trousers and those shoes, but most of all that jacket. Its arms would swing this way and that; the same creases would come and go.

* * *

They rested in a copse of chopped trees, dozens and dozens each taken down to a stump so that it looked like a crop of seats. A few stumps away Janek puffed on a cigarette, the smell of the smoke bringing back memories of Max. Owen had no idea where the cigarette had come from.

After a few minutes Janek wandered across to the edge of the field and draped himself over the fence, still sucking on the cigarette, while Owen poked around with the watch, the air where Janek had sat infused with the tang of tobacco. He wondered if he could mend it. He had managed to prise the back off. Inside, the springs and wheels stood stationary. He gave each a gentle nudge with the blunt tip of the pencil but nothing wanted to move. He took the watch to pieces and emptied all its cogs and coils and tiny screws into his hand. Now though, scattered out across his palm, none of the parts seemed to bear any correlation to the others. He poked at one or two of them with his fingernail, uncertain even what they were. If he could navigate his way around anything as complex as an instrument panel, he could navigate his way around something as simple as a watch.

Even as a child he had taken things to pieces — clocks, wirelesses, gearboxes and carburettors — and then tried to rebuild them, only better. He liked to see how things worked, the design and construction — even of a living creature. He had dissected a frog once, all on his own. He had pinned it to a slab of wood while it was still alive and then had been disappointed when, the moment he had nervously cut it open, it had promptly died. He had so wanted to watch its tiny pumping heart.

Janek wandered back, pinging his cigarette stub into the grass and then stepping up on to one of the stumps, and then from that on to another and to another, having to jump sometimes, barely crossing the gap. He suddenly appeared on the same stump as Owen, behind him, his toe kicking at Owen's backside. He peered over Owen's shoulder at what he was doing before leaping off on to the next.

Owen turned back to the task in hand. These were the sorts of things he had liked to draw: cogs and wheels, the workings of a watch, every mechanical piece like a biological organ, pumping life into the machine. At his board in the Experimental Drawing Office on Canbury Park Road he had drawn the workings of aeroplanes, knowledgeable of their thermodynamics, and detailing everything to the peak of precision. *We'll be designing bombers before long*, Harry had said, although Owen had no recollection of that.

On warm days like this on the second floor of the old furniture depository he would often open the sash pane beside him, using a spare shoe as a wedge to keep the window open. The smell of the rail tracks on the other side would waft in or the fumes from the Experimental workshop, or sometimes, when the wind was right, the smell of Mr Birch's Fish and Chips.

He had enjoyed the neat orderliness of his craft — the careful angles and finely drawn lines, the precision of his calculations — and also the grace and beauty of his work, as if it were not just a plane he was creating on the clean crispness of the paper, but a bird of human design. He was the creator: its wings envisaged and crafted by him, the almost feminine nose, the taut tail at the back, the mechanics of its aviation, so that sometimes if you glanced up at the sky it was hard to distinguish the organic from the mechanical. That, at least, was his aspiration as he hunched over the drawing board, the window propped open and the high jinks of the factory shop boys drifting in from below.

The sound of a plane over them, its metal skin glinting in the sun, brought him back. He couldn't be here because he was a draughtsman. He felt the boy's eyes on him. There must have been something else.

* * *

By late afternoon the deciduous trees had given way to pine, the forest growing airy and the trunks rising over them, naked and tall. Beneath them the ground was carpeted in spongy moss as if the forest floor had been bubbling, and was covered in needles and a scattering of ferns and gangly saplings. Birds bickered above them and there was a pattering of distant gunfire and then a boom so deep that it throbbed within the ground.

He watched the boy hurriedly tramping on ahead. He had shown Owen on the map how close he thought they were. Up ahead he bent to pick something from the curling branches of a fern and held it up, saying something. It was a grey woollen mitten. And twenty minutes later, by chance, he found its pair.

They cut across two railway tracks and continued through the trees, the boy now walking with his hands in the mittens and snapping at midges as if he had lobster claws. As the dying sun burst through the lofty heads, it threw corridors of light through the forest and turned the trunks metallic: silver, copper and brass. Janek then found a woollen hat in some nettles and hooked it out with a stick. It made Owen think of a man he'd once seen lying face down in the snow.

⋆ ⋆ ⋆

It was this increasing light that was the first sign. The edge of the forest, he had thought, or a clearing, or another railway line. Then, through the pines, he spied a watchtower high on its bandy-legged perch. He dropped down and held still.

'Janek, get down,' he hissed.

The watchtower seemed to be empty but it wasn't that that was making his heart quicken. He edged forward through the trees, his eyes searching for any movement and scanning for guards as they both crept closer. He couldn't believe what he was seeing. This was where three days' journey had taken him; this was the Sagan that had been written and twice circled on a scrap of paper, the pull that he'd felt in the pit of his stomach, the only spot on the map that had caught his eye and kept luring it back. He remembered the *III*. He saw what it meant now. He scrambled closer and lay down.

'*Pane bože* . . . ' Janek said under his breath behind him, who had probably seen nothing like it, but Owen had. Like a key clicking open a lock, the memory suddenly opened, his mind foretelling everything that he saw the split second before he saw it — the shapes of the buildings, the long huts with shallow roofs and high, wired fencing and double set of gates, the second and third sentry posts; sight and memory compounding in a fused moment of connection.

I've been here, he realized. My God. But how could it be so familiar? He felt the undeniable sensation that he had stood on that other side of the wire, that he had stared out through it to where he stood now to see — yes, he thought, glancing behind him — this view, this vista, this very same forest. Yet, staring through the fence and along the stretch of compounds, the rows of single-storey barracks and then up at the lookout post, something *had* changed. He kept expecting to see movement, to hear voices, maybe even shots being fired at them, but wherever he looked there was nothing. Not the sight of a single soul.

They nervously walked the fringes of the camp, eyes alert and ears pricked, but within it the barracks stood like wooden husks. The only movement Owen could see was a loose sheet of paper in the dirt occasionally lifting in the breeze. Two high perimeter fences spanned the length, both with a barbed wire overhang at the top that tipped inwards. Between the fences were tangles of wire, and then, another thirty or so feet in, a taut line of wire fixed a couple of feet above the ground that he wanted to call 'the ditch'. There were empty guard towers at each corner and every hundred yards in between. Some of the windows were still in place, while around one, smashed glass lay among the bandy legs, pressed into the dirt.

The gates had been forced open and they squeezed through the gap. Owen walked with the pistol held ready in his hand, Janek with his knife, both expecting at any moment to be ambushed. As they cautiously crept through the compound there were dozens of familiar-looking barracks, each raised a little off the ground for the ferrets to poke around beneath. He knew the kitchens, the theatre, the bathrooms where there had been metal tubs for sinks and soap that never lathered. And yet how or why or for how long he had been here he was still unsure.

He stopped at an intersection where the ground was compacted hard by footfall, and felt the hot surge of panic burning out from his collar and sweeping across his head. The buildings so oddly familiar now spread as far as the eye could see, all desolate and empty and yet full in his mind with ghosts.

'There's no one here.'

'*Hm, nikdo*,' said Janek, nodding.

The air was filled with the faint smell of kerosene.

* * *

In time, he would describe it as a cloud lifting to reveal a landscape that secretly his mind had always known was there. The longer he stood between the barracks with their blinking windows, his reflection captured for him within every glass, the more he saw and knew: the stumps where trees had been felled to clear more space; the two shallow steps up to each barrack; the one step that was broken and had, he saw now, never been fixed; the double-fronted windows; the shutters at each frame hooked open, one or two of the catches snapped so that they groaned on their hinges. Even the old split barrel was there that they had pelted a ball against. And there was the boy watching him. He could so easily have been one of the others, strangely returned, just like Owen.

* * *

They walked through it like sole survivors, Janek staring in through one window after another, rubbing the dirt off with his sleeve or knocking in the broken teeth of glass with the butt of his knife. One of the huts had been burnt to the ground and was now nothing but charred timber. In another they found a pile of empty food containers, and in another loose faeces that were fresh and looked human.

When they reached Hut 105, the door was open as if it was already summer. The place, like the others, had been turned over: bits of burnt wood, discarded books and an overturned pot of nails that were hard beneath their feet. Janek picked a magazine out from the debris, the pages one by one curling away from his fingers.

Owen had been in the end room. Teddy Williams, the son of an artist, had bunked above him. He lifted the stained and shallow mattress, and then Teddy's too, seeing, as he knew he would, that each bunk was missing a plank. They had taken one out of each to craft wickets and cricket bats from.

It was then, staring at the bunks, that he realized that his head was hurting and it had been for some time, as if he were being cracked and prised open. Names came tumbling in and, with them, faces: Joe Hallam, Guy Fletcher, 'Bugsy', Moe, Mitch Hamble . . .

He unlatched the window and hurriedly pushed it open, leaning out into the empty compound, trying to breathe, his eyes welling. As he felt Janek's hand on his shoulder he was hit by a sudden flash of images. He thought he was going to be sick.

* * *

They found him scuffling around at the back of one of the barracks on the west side of the camp. All the shutters were closed and, with no more than the finest cuts of light breaking in, he was hardly visible, shuffling about in the gloom like a troglodyte among the desks and upturned filing cabinets. He was bent double, gathering scattered papers from the floor with long bony fingers and murmuring to himself as he held them, pinned to his chest as if they were precious to him.

Without straightening he turned to look at them and, as he took a step into the light, they saw that he was a small-framed man in uniform with round-rimmed glasses. He stared, the untidy pile of papers slipping from his grip until a couple of sheets fell carelessly about his feet.

They held still in the doorway and Owen fumbled for his pistol, thinking for the first time that he might not have shot anyone after all and now, of all times, might find himself incapable.

From behind his thick lenses the little man blinked and darted his eyes about the room. What once must have been a smart uniform was now dirty and sodden. The wire spectacles had been bent and reshaped many times. His hair was short with a once neat parting still greased into place and flecked with debris, and his jowls bristled with stubble. *A man gone to the dogs*, Owen's father would have grumbled, who had come across such creatures in his hospital work; tramps and vagabonds and general no-gooders, he had said.

'What do you know about this place?' said Owen.

The man seemed surprised by the question.

'Do you speak English?'

He nodded.

'Who are you?'

'No one,' the man said.

Janek stiffened. The man's English was articulate but his accent was German.

'What are you doing here then?' said Owen.

'What are *you* doing here?' he asked back.

Owen hesitated. 'Looking for someone.'

'Who?'

He paused then motioned with his head to

Janek. 'His brother.'

The man's eyes flicked across and back again.

There was a click as Owen lifted the safety catch on his pistol. 'So what are you doing here?'

'What everyone is,' he said. 'Hiding.'

'What do you mean?'

The man poked the glasses further up his nose with his finger, the other hand still clutching the papers to his chest.

'A reckoning is coming,' he said.

'What do you mean?'

The man didn't answer. Instead he hesitantly bent his knees, lowering himself, his eyes never straying from them, until his outstretched fingers could blindly reach around his ankles for the renegade sheets and gather them up into his pile.

'What are they, anyway?' said Owen.

'They are nothing.'

Janek moved forward and the man hastily retreated further into the shadows, stumbling over the broken bits of furniture in the dark. Then, as Janek went to snatch one of the papers from him, the man abruptly darted, dodging Janek's hand and slamming Owen hard against the wall as he ran past them and out.

'Bloody hell!'

'*Prase nacistický!*' Janek started after him, but the man was already gone, papers fluttering in his wake.

'Don't,' said Owen, calling him back. 'Leave him.'

He pushed himself away from the wall and caught his breath, then picked up the dropped pistol and one of the discarded papers. He pushed open one of the shutters so that the light fell in. It looked like a registration form: boxes completed in neatly printed German and attached on the top left-hand corner was a photograph of a man. He was holding up a card that bore the numbers 5792. Owen scanned the form. There were recognizable English words scattered among the German: place names and family names, an address in Dorset. He stared at the face in the photograph — a man with oiled hair and a cleft in his chin. He was wearing an RAF jacket.

* * *

He leant against a porch rail and looked out at a vegetable patch kicked to smithereens, at the swallows looping over the field beyond, and the distant firs bristling in the breeze. On the post beside him was that same symbol that had appeared in the concrete store — the two 'V's forming wings and a head enclosed in a square. He wondered how it had got there and when he ran his fingertip lightly over the scratches, it felt like it had been freshly cut, the wood still hard and dry.

He turned his attention back to the garden. For a while he watched wind chimes made from cut tins gently spinning on an apple branch, God's last glints of light running down them like melted silver. He tried to cling to the memories that had come to him in the camp. If he could keep playing them in his head, turning them over and over, maybe they would crystallize and then they would be safe.

He wrote down everything he remembered: Joe Hallam, Guy Fletcher, 'Bugsy', Moe, and Teddy Williams — faces that had come back to him and that he could see now in his mind.

HUT 105
RUSSIANS — GERMAN BORDER
BRITISH RAF

He paused and circled it, then added a question mark. He had been quite convinced that Max would be there, that they had been together, but now he couldn't place him there.

He closed his eyes and tried to think, but whatever else he'd remembered of the day had already slipped from his mind.

* * *

In the cellar Janek had discovered a well-stocked food store — the previous incumbents of the house had clearly left in a hurry — and as they ate from the tins, Owen laid the scraps of map out in front of the fire, trying to piece together a route. Granted the boy had navigated them here but the fields and woods were a hard slog. They should find a road and hold their nerve. Keep their head down and make for a town. He was a British citizen, after all. He would hand himself in to the first official and be done with it. The boy — well, he was free to do as he liked.

He scanned the map, hunting out roads, then circled Cottbus several miles to the west. It was a start. He wrote it on the paper. There were railway lines too, leading from Sagan, some heading west, others south. His finger followed them down into Czechoslovakia, pausing at every point where they crossed a river. He had been at one of these spots, he thought — a collapsed bridge. He wondered which of these rivers he had walked along, which railway line out of all these threads was now broken and out of use.

* * *

He remembered a man, Uncle Archie, coming one afternoon in a smart black Bugatti. He had given Owen his driving goggles to wear as they lounged about in the drawing room. The whole summer had been a washout and so, to brighten up an otherwise damp and disappointing day, he had entertained them with tales of his daredevil deeds and near scrapes as a fighter pilot, making the sound effects of the FE2 as it dived, and pumping his arms as if they were guns. *Tat-tat-tat-tat-tat*.

Don't believe a word of it, their mother had said. *Your uncle's a perennial liar. If you're not careful, he'll be telling you next the pope was his co-pilot*.

Wingman, actually, sis, Uncle Archie had said. *Douglas Fairbanks was my co-pilot — as you damn well know*.

Strange how memories were breaking through as if he'd slipped under ice and now there were patches of it starting to melt so he could see snippets of the life he'd once had on the surface. Just when he thought his memory was improving, just when he thought he could retain the events of a day, something always disappeared in turn. Such as where the pistol had come from, or the button or the map or the worn-out shoes he was wearing. It was this circular churn of losing and finding and losing that he found hardest to comprehend. It was as if everything was stored in his head; he just didn't have the light with which to see it all at once.

* * *

It was getting cold and Owen poked at the fire. Janek was sitting on the window seat cleaning the dirt from his fingernails with the tip of his knife. Owen still didn't understand why the boy was with him but he was too nervous now to ask. Janek said that they were *bratři*, which Owen took as 'brothers'.

'You and me?'

'*Ano*. And Petr.'

Ah, yes, Petr.

Then, slipping the blade away and slithering from the seat, Janek brought his bag over and sat on the floor beside Owen in front of the fire. He unbuckled a pocket and pulled out a wallet. It was battered and empty but for a handful of photographs, each folded twice.

He handed Owen a grainy black and white photograph and pointed. The man staring back appeared to be quite a few years older than Janek, and stood proud and handsome in a soldier's uniform. He looked dignified and bear-like, not gangly like his brother, with dark hair, his chest puffed and thumb hooked and heavy in his pocket. He had the same sharp jawline as Janek, the same slender nose and intense deep-set eyes that seemed to stare the cameraman down through the lens.

'Good man,' said Janek. He thumped his chest and Owen wondered whether he had meant 'strong' or 'loyal', or maybe even 'brave'.

'He's a fine-looking chap.'

'Yes.'

'And he is in Germany? *Deutschland?*'

Janek nodded.

'How do you know?'

'They take him.'

'The *Deutschen*?'

He nodded.

'Where?'

The boy shrugged. '*Deutschland*.' He gave Owen a look as if to say, where else? 'I look for Petr. We look. Yes?'

'Well . . . '

'You and me. Two lives. Yes?'

He had no idea what the boy was getting at. 'Yes, of course, but do you understand, I need to get home?'

He passed the photograph back, but Janek seemed to have misunderstood.

'Good. Brothers,' he said.

'No, I didn't mean that,' said Owen, but the boy had already pulled out another photograph and handed it to Owen.

This one was a man and woman sitting

together with straight backs, both of them grey-haired and plump in their Sunday finest.

'*Moje matka. A můj otec*,' he said, pointing. 'Yes?'

'Yes,' said Owen. 'I see.'

In the photograph they were holding each other's hands, the man's focus fixed on the camera, professional and businesslike, unlike his wife who looked awkward and distracted, glancing from the corner of her eye at something that was happening out of shot. Again the same nose, there in the father. His mother had a larger-boned build. Owen nodded and tried to hand the photograph over but Janek shoved it back.

'No. Look. You look.'

'Yes. I've seen. They must be proud.'

'*Podívejte se!*' he said.

Then he snatched the photograph away and pushed it back into the wallet. For some reason Owen had irritated him, and with a slight scowl on his face, Janek fingered through the photographs and then handed Owen another.

A boy and a girl, both five or six years old and dressed in smart summer clothes. The girl was sitting on a doorstep, pulling her dress over her knees, while the boy, grinning toothily, stood in the doorway behind her, savagely brandishing a stick.

'Is that you?' Owen asked with a faint smile.

'Lukáš,' said Janek. He pointed at the girl. 'And Nicol.'

'And where are they now? With your parents?'

The boy said nothing, his eyes starting to

moisten. He carefully tucked the photograph away and then pulled out the last. He sat quite still and stared at it, his hand shaking, and then before Owen had a chance to see, the boy had screwed it up and flung it into the fire. He slapped the wallet shut and firmly set it down.

'Who was that?' Owen asked.

Through the flames, he could just about make out the crumpled face of a girl, older than Janek but younger than Petr. The picture started to curl and wither, the flames slowly taking it.

'Kateřina,' he said.

'Oh?'

'Kateřina is . . . ' He didn't know.

'Your sister?' Owen guessed.

Janek paused, thinking. Then the word came to him.

'Traitor,' he said.

They moved westward, leaving the Silesian forests behind, crossing fields, spinneys and wastelands, and skirting the villages and farmsteads wherever they could, the landscape flattening as they went.

The road they eventually joined was strewn with a ragged trail of people, some heading north as they were, but most passing them in the other direction, hurrying south. The warm air quivered with a shared urgency, mothers steering children along, their hands lightly on their backs; while the few men they passed looked old and weathered, their beady eyes full of suspicion. Occasionally there were even German soldiers, making a weary scramble, some of them so tired it seemed that they could barely hold their rifles.

If the English or the Americans were coming, or even the Russians from the east, it was only a matter of time before they happened upon them, he told Janek.

'And then we will find your brother, and mine too; and they will get us home.'

* * *

In the distance a figure sat on the side of the road, the warm sun so bright that in the gentle heat she shimmered as if she were barely there at all. As the road brought them closer, he watched her offer the passing travellers the bundle she was carrying, presenting it in outstretched arms from the verge, but nobody seemed to want it.

Two men passed, one hauling a trolley piled with sacks and a small dog curled on top like a turd, and after that a lone woman. Once again the figure proffered the bundle. There was a short and clipped conversation, and the girl, for he now saw how young she was, called out to the woman — '*Nein!*' and then '*Bitte!*' — as the woman walked on but, like the others, she would not stop.

The offer and the refusal.

The offer and the refusal.

They saw it running on a constant cycle until, as the road drew them nearer, Owen realized that the bundle contained an infant parcelled in a shawl. The young girl looked tired and thin, in a grubby white dress, a pink cardigan embroidered with fraying flowers, and a headscarf tied tightly over her head.

Without taking his eyes off her, Janek gave Owen's sleeve a tug.

He leant in. '*Nemluvte s ní*,' he said. 'No English. Hm?'

Owen saw how desperate she was, holding out the child to everyone that passed, and her voice tremulous.

'*Bitte, nehmen Sie mein Kind.*'

He tried not to catch her eye, while Janek's hand at his elbow gently urged him on. Then, to his relief, she suddenly cut in front of them, targeting instead a well-dressed woman walking several yards ahead.

'*Bitte, nehmen Sie mein Kind.*'

The woman, who was carrying a leather holdall and had a flowered silk scarf around her neck, tried to ignore her but the girl hurried alongside her.

'*Nehmen Sie doch bitte mein Kind!*'

The woman turned her head away and quickened her pace. The girl seized at her arm.

'*Ich will es nicht*,' the woman said sharply, pulling her arm free, but the girl grabbed at it again.

'*Bitte! Ich kann mich nicht darum kümmern.*'

'*Ich kann es nicht*,' the woman snapped.

The girl tried to force the bundle on her anyway, pressing the crying infant against her and talking fast, imploring her as the woman struggled to push her away, red-faced and flustered now.

Janek shouted, '*Lasst sie los!*' and before Owen could stop him, he was in the middle, giving the girl such a shove that she staggered back against the verge.

'*Sie kann nicht helfen!*' he yelled.

She stopped, her eyes filling as the baby wailed in her arms.

Then they turned and marched on — Janek, Owen, the woman with the holdall — leaving the girl behind.

'*Danke*,' the woman murmured, but she would no more catch Janek's eye than she had the girl's, and after a while they let her pull away, the hard soles of her patent shoes clicking on the road, the leather holdall still in her hand and the silk scarf fluttering out behind her collar.

When Owen glanced back, the road was quiet again. There was only the girl, holding the child to her chest and trying to soothe it, while she looked helplessly around her. She didn't seem to know what to do.

* * *

They walked in silence, an uphill slog, but the girl and her baby played uncomfortably on his mind.

It was another ten minutes before he dared turn again, but the road behind them fell away, as long and straight as a grid-line, and now deserted; just the fields swilling on either side, empty but for the breeze. He stopped, hesitant and suddenly worried.

'Come,' Janek said. He gave Owen a glare and pulled at his arm.

But Owen would not. His eyes were fixed on the spot where the girl had been, a feeling of sickness starting to creep through him. He couldn't see where she could have disappeared to with the child so quickly. Then a terrible thought struck him, and with a growing sense of panic he started to walk back, slowly at first and then faster, his heart bumping up into his throat and thumping in his ears. Like a distant echo he could hear Janek behind him, yelling — '*Ne!*' and '*Ne! Jdeme!*' — but Owen would not stop. As the road took him down the hill, he broke into a run.

* * *

The bundle was in the deep grass on the side of the road, just as he had feared, the infant's small face white within the shawl, its eyes blinking and tiny pink fingers fumbling at the air. He turned and turned and turned again, scanning the corn in every direction for her, and trying to see her in the pockets of trees.

'Hey,' he shouted. 'HEY!'

He waited, and then yelled again, even louder, but the child's mother was gone.

* * *

Janek stalked on ahead, furious and striding hard. He would barely speak to Owen.

'No!' he said. 'No! *To dítě ne!*'

Owen had tried to explain that he couldn't leave it, but Janek kept shouting, a rattling barrage of Czech. She wouldn't come back, if that was what Janek was thinking. But Janek wasn't listening. He paced down the road throwing his hands up in disbelief.

'*Ne dítě, ježišmarjá!*'

Already the infant was crying.

* * *

In the hours that passed he would tell himself that there had been no choice. The truth, though, was that he couldn't rationalize why he had gone back and then picked the child up — it had come from a compulsion within him that he couldn't put his finger on.

The infant now was inconsolable, its pink face

reddening until it was the same colour as the inside of its mouth, and its crying quivered in Owen's chest. He tried to soothe it as best he could, holding it this way and that. He was filled with a growing sense of dread. Dear God, what the hell had he done?

* * *

On a road lined with poplar trees, the panic finally took him and he tried to give the bawling infant to a family in a wagon. He held it up to the elderly mother at the reins but she shooed him off, snapping something at him and spurring the horses on. The man and two daughters, who were hurrying alongside the piled cart and hauling their cases, pushed their way around him.

He stopped the nearest daughter to him, pulling her back. She looked about twenty. Just the right age, he thought. Her face was pale and blotchy, and her greasy hair was sliding out of a clip. She looked at the child grizzling in his arms, its clenched fist waving.

'Please,' he said. If she could just take it . . .

Her eyes were hard.

'*Englisch?*' she said.

'Yes.'

She considered this for a moment. Then, pulling up a force from within her, she spat into his face.

* * *

They sat in the entrance of a field, Owen in the long grass, the baby growing heavy in the crook of his arm. He tried jigging it, turning it, resting it over his shoulder and then holding it again in his arm, but its crying had become incessant and he had no idea how to stop it.

Janek perched on the top bar of the gate, hunched over his knees, and his head tilted with his fingers in his ears.

'I'm sorry,' said Owen, 'but we couldn't have left it. You understand that.'

The boy turned his head away and gazed instead out across the fields.

Owen had never had someone spit at him before, let alone a girl. He still felt the prickle of her saliva on his skin. It felt like shame.

The baby was a boy. No more than a few weeks old, the thinnest wisps of blond hair lifting from the top of his head. The skin of his face looked loose, as if the flesh still needed padding, and there were wrinkles gathering around his neck. His eyes were full of gunk and a thin film of snot was drying into a crust under a nose no bigger than a thumb tip. As they sat, the child's cries tired into a resentful whimper.

'We'll have to do something with him,' Owen said. 'There must be places. Orphanages or something, I don't know. Somebody will have it. Don't you think?'

The boy kicked his heel at the gate bar and arched his shoulders into a shrug.

'He'll need feeding too,' Owen added. 'Can't give him bloody tins of processed meat. We'll need to find him something. And nappies. God!

Milk, clothes . . . Jesus Christ.' The list went on.

The boy remained silent. It was so hard to tell whether he was even listening sometimes. He stared out across the field. Something in the trees where the field dipped had caught his eye — a sudden flash of movement — and he craned to see. For a long time his eyes fixed on a spinney, then he turned to look at Owen.

'No more road,' he said.

'What?'

He swivelled around, jumped off the gate into the field and set off through the furrows.

'Hey! Where are you going?'

But the boy just whistled a call and beckoned him on with a wave.

⋆ ⋆ ⋆

In the small cluttered kitchen of a farmhouse they forced a widow at gunpoint to give them food, while the baby screamed in Owen's arms, and Janek yelled at it and the woman, waving the pistol about, and Owen shouted and the flustered woman cried, '*Nein! Bitte! Nicht schießen!*'

'*Milch*,' Janek shouted. '*Milch*.'

He swung the gun on the baby and Owen, and then on the woman again, who by now was red-faced and sobbing as she bumped around the table, knocking things over, flour dusting the floor and her hands all of a flap.

'And towels,' Owen added.

'*Und Brot!*'

'And soap.'

Janek swung the gun, still yelling.

'Jesus Christ. Will you put that bloody thing down?' He'd fire it if he weren't careful.

The baby screamed and screamed.

* * *

After, as they walked, he held the bottle to the child's mouth and it sucked hungrily on the teat, the bottle old and cracked but good enough until they found something better. His arms were already aching.

Janek strode on ahead, the milk canister he had stolen yesterday swinging at his side, now full again, and another containing hastily slopped-in soup, and a hand towel looped over his belt.

They had left the woman sobbing on the floor. It was the second time she'd been robbed in a week. The camps had been blown open and the inmates were loose. The Poles and Russians were marauding the farmlands, taking everything, she had cried.

But that was not their problem and for now they walked, the adrenalin still pulsing through them, Owen happy that Janek was happy and smiling again. He had slapped Owen on the back as they made their way out to the lane and, for a while, he had walked with his arm draped over Owen's shoulder.

Owen tried to think of something to sing to the child but all he could find in his head was the hymn, those few lines he couldn't shift about pilgrims and redeemers.

They were brothers now, Janek said — brothers looking for brothers. Was that why when

Owen took the lead, he sometimes thought the boy was Max, that it was Max's footfall he could hear behind him? The stone that suddenly scudded past him had been kicked by Max's foot. Max's voice. Max's laugh. *You can't get rid of me that easily*. Another stone skittering past.

In his arms, the baby strained to suck at the last dregs of milk. His face reddened with the effort, and he let out a few grizzly, hungry gasps. Owen lifted him on to his shoulder and tried to comfort him, but in the end the baby started to cry once more.

'*Můža?*' said Janek, offering. He took the infant from Owen and held him out in front of him as if the child was a wet and dripping thing. He manoeuvred him around and then changed his mind, uncertain how to hold him.

'Not like that. Like this,' said Owen, showing him.

'Ah, yes, yes,' said Janek. 'Shh,' he said to the child.

* * *

They rested beneath a willow that overhung a rill, Janek leaning against its trunk, with his knees up and the baby cradled within them. The infant clutched a finger with each hand as Janek softly spoke to him and gently moved his fingers around. The yellow heads of celandine burst up through the thick grass.

Owen lay on his back, studying his notes and trying to make sense of them. COTTBUS, he'd written, and BABY . . . NOT MINE. There were other things written and crossed out, connections made with arrows as if they were electrical circuits mapped out at his drawing board. *We'll be designing bombers soon*, Harry had said.

PILOT, he had written too, although he couldn't work out whether that had been him or one of the other names written beside it. There was no line connecting it; it hung, like a lost thought.

As boys they had always played at fighter planes, running through the fields behind The Ridings with their arms out, or making planes from balsa wood and hurling them from the top of St Catherine's Hill, where they had flown kites.

One summer they had made large paper model gliders, launching them from the guest bedroom. And one day Max had even lit the middle of the model with a match and they had watched in glee and then horror as it had glided down, leaving an impressive trail of smoke, only then for the wind to change and take it straight in through the sitting room window where it had set fire to their mother's rug.

He sat up, disturbed by something in the undergrowth, then turned sharply but whoever was there — a stooped figure, a glimpse of white — quickly pulled away.

⋆ ⋆ ⋆

In the fading afternoon he walked with the infant slumped and sleeping over his shoulder. The longer he held the child, the more it felt like his.

Then a name came and went again, stopping him in his tracks. A woman's name this time. He tried to pull it back but it had fallen right through him.

When the baby woke, to entertain him Janek took him and held him out to one side as if the infant was flying along the road. And again, Max was there in Owen's head, running open-armed through the cornfields, always racing each other. He could see him in the driving goggles Uncle Archie had given them.

Max would never be a pilot — he had always been too rash for that.

He had been with Owen though, in the war — Owen felt quite sure of it. *Two peas in a pod*, Uncle Ernest had said.

He looked back down the lane. He felt a sickening blame for something but he didn't know what.

'Janek,' he called, waving his arms. 'Janek! We have to go back!'

* * *

The barn was old and tumbledown. At the far end, lit by the partial light outside burning through the splits and holes in the wood, six thick pieces of rope were tied from a rafter. Each one hung loose, cut at the same height. Owen tried to pull them down but the knots were too high to reach and there was nothing to stand on. Beneath each one there were dried patches of blood and what looked like piano wire.

The panic that he had left his brother in the

field where he'd woken, or just a trace of him even, had passed. On that lane Janek had hauled him along by the arm. He wouldn't let him go back. *Ne*. *Ne*, he had kept saying, urging him forward and squeezing his shoulder. They would do whatever they needed to do but there would be no going back.

In the barn Owen paced about. With the weight of the child in his arm, a familiar numbness was creeping into him. There was a pinch he remembered digging into his armpits, not as thin as grenade wire or as thick as the ropes, but painful nevertheless. He looked at them still tied to the rafter. He had hung just like that, somewhere.

He put his fingertips to the side of his head, expecting to feel blood.

⋆ ⋆ ⋆

As it got late he walked the child around in the dark. The infant had leaked diarrhoea and vomited all the milk back up and now it screamed with an intensity that was ripping right through him.

'Can you try?' he huffed to Janek but the boy just sat with his back to the wall and his hands over his ears, staring down at the dirt.

'For God's sake,' said Owen. Then he shouted, 'Will you just shut up!'

⋆ ⋆ ⋆

All things were jumbled now. The dark of the night opened him up to them. Blood running down the side of his forehead. A numbness in his armpits. The memory came of a girl's white ankle socks, small feet in sandals, and placed so neatly together next to a child's suitcase.

He stared up at the roof and the patterns the moonshine made through the gaps between the tiles. The lines of it traced around the broken timbers above them like filaments of light.

It was not the fear that he had forgotten her that concerned him most, but that this love he felt had forgotten him — that, after all this time, she could no more remember his face or the sound of his voice than he could hers. And with that they would be lost to each other — both erased from each other's minds.

When sleep did eventually crawl upon him, he dreamt of pulling a house across a frozen sea — he and all the other people, each with a rope tied around their waist and hauling the house across the ice. Seagulls curled noisily around the chimneystack, and on the ice they felt the strain of the weight, their feet sliding and cracks appearing, though the ice did not give way. They pulled and tugged, and the house inched forward. He could feel the cold biting at his hands, while all around them there was nothing but a flat and frozen landscape, and a sky that was giant and blue.

He woke, or dreamt of waking. A shivering body was pressed up against him, warm breath against his neck. In the dark he reached behind and pulled an arm over him. He took the cold hand in his. He held it to his chest.

The morning was miserable. Janek carried the baby, who had the audacity now to sleep. During the night he had fashioned a papoose-like contraption out of a hessian sack. It took the two of them to fasten the child in and Owen wasn't sure how secure it looked, but the child slept happily enough in it, his head resting against Janek's chest and a growing patch of drool spreading across his shirt.

Owen felt tired and twitchy, his eyes and ears playing tricks on him: a hand at a branch, a sudden commotion of birds. *Owen*, a voice called to him, but there wasn't anyone there.

West and north and homeward-bound, they followed the raised ridge of a railway line that ran parallel to their path, the dull sheen of steel above them through the trees acting as a guide. Where the foliage gave way along the top of the ridge, bodies lay about the gully and they had to pick their way through, stepping between the limbs. They were all men with a shared wound at the back of the head. Forty, maybe more, tumbled and sprawled over each other, the rich sunlight around them filled with the frenzy of flies.

* * *

In a cherry orchard littered with petals like snow they found a well and filled their canisters, while an elderly man hoed his vegetable patch nearby, a rifle hanging from his waist, the butt scraping its own furrow neatly through the dirt. They leant against the curve of the well and let the sun shine on their faces. The water was cold and tasted good. The baby wriggled in Owen's arms but was soon made drowsy by the warmth, and Owen wondered if he could leave him there, if the man with his hoe would take the child in for his wife.

Not half an hour after drinking the water, though, they were both being sick. Owen leant with one hand against a fence as he vomited, while a short way down the path Janek did the same. When Owen stood and wiped his mouth, he saw clouds pulling in from the east, a far off smear of rain, and in the distance women and children were bent double, digging with their hands in a field.

* * *

At a junction, an argument ensued. Janek kept pointing down the road, jabbing at the air with his finger while the baby in his arms screamed. He kept saying 'No' and 'This way' and '*Na západ*' — which Owen took to mean 'west' — growing more and more angry and insistent. That was where the camps were. That was where Petr would be.

But Owen thought they were better off turning north.

'Up towards Berlin,' he said. He pulled the map from his pocket to show him, the pieces scattering on the ground so that he had to scrabble around, picking them up before the wind took them. Besides, this road looked wider, he told Janek. They had a better chance of finding help on a major route; they had a child to consider now. He didn't see the point in scrambling through more bloody fields.

But the boy was already walking, taking the baby with him.

'Janek,' he called, but the boy ignored him.

Fine, he thought. Let him go. This would be where they parted then. He'd had enough of Janek anyway. Let the boy see how he got on looking after the child on his own.

He headed off in his own direction, the first drops of rain falling cold and heavy on his face. He would be fine on his own, with only himself to worry about. He had the map after all, and it wouldn't be so hard to find some food.

In the distance shots sounded, their cracks echoing out across the fields.

He stopped and turned, hesitant. The boy was barely visible, almost gone now. With the small bundle held in his arms. Janek didn't seem intent on stopping.

Owen stood for a moment.

Bloody hell.

'Janek!' he called after him.

The rain was getting harder.

* * *

The buildings of the hamlet were nothing but charred and collapsed carcasses: wooden rafters, pillars and posts poking out like blackened bones. The rain had only just dowsed the flames but the fires had been so intense that the heat lifting from them remained hot against their faces. Above, where the wood was still white hot with veins of orange running through it, the air shimmered. Despite the pouring rain, thick smoke lifted, billowing up in sudden whirls that turned and separated; ashen leaves from scorched trees floated about like moths, crumpling and burning in the air.

A woman stood, mutely gathering her three small children to her hips, while soldiers with bulky-looking guns, backpacks and canisters poked around. Two covered trucks were parked nearby. The men took no notice of Janek and Owen as they walked through, strangely lured as if into a dream.

Up ahead there came a calamitous roar as a roof strained and thundered in, and then the crash of another ceiling giving way beneath it. The dust rose up into a mist and then was dampened again by the rain.

Owen clutched the baby hard to him. 'We can't shelter here.'

Janek seemed to agree, then pointed and nodded at the soldiers among the rubble. They were the same men who had been at the burnt-out farmhouse, in the same two trucks.

Owen remembered and it surprised him. How many days ago had that been? Was his memory finally starting to hold firm?

The dust was settling around the house whose roof had fallen in. Half of the front had collapsed in a pile of wooden debris but Janek still entered through the doorway, which had lost its walls on either side and now stood like an empty and blackened picture frame.

Owen pulled the wriggling infant closer as he followed, careful where he placed his feet. The rain fell in streaming rivulets down through the timbers.

'Janek,' he called. 'It's not safe.'

'*Tu pistoli*,' Janek said, beckoning with his fingers.

Owen hadn't meant that but he handed him the gun anyway, and then Janek was pushing through another doorway, Owen stumbling after him.

Here the roof had completely fallen through, and Owen stopped and looked up at the rain firing down like pellets through the broken stanchions. In his arms the baby whimpered.

'I know,' he said, trying to calm him. 'We're going to get you somewhere dry.'

When the voice came from among the carnage, it was breathless and wheezing.

'*Bitte . . . Bitte . . . Helfen Sie mir*.'

Instantly Janek had tucked the pistol into his belt and was climbing over the wood, pulling bits of it aside and hauling planks about as quickly as he could.

The voice came again, desperate.

'Can you see him?' said Owen.

Janek struggled and heaved a timber away, his feet slipping, and pulled aside the blackened door of a wardrobe, then stopped. He stood staring into the wreckage.

'*Bitte*,' came the voice within it, male and deep, but rasping and fighting to catch its breath.

'What is it?' said Owen. He took a couple of steps closer, the rain still streaming down through the broken shell of the building.

He heard the voice again.

'*Janek. Janku, jsi to ty?*'

Then in a slick movement that took Owen by surprise, Janek had drawn the pistol and cocked it at the man half buried under the debris.

It was only when Owen had clambered closer, the baby still held in the papoose, that he saw with a flash of recognition that it was the silver-haired soldier from the burnt-out house across the border. He was wearing the same uniform, and lay trapped beneath a beam, the hunk of timber so heavy across his chest that his breath was short and restricted.

'*Kdo je to?*' he said, his eyes darting across to Owen.

'*On je Angličan*,' said Janek.

'*Angličan?*' the man said with heavy breath. His face was red and the tendons in his thick neck straining. He was clearly in some pain. 'English?' he said to Owen.

'Do you two know each other?'

The man smiled weakly.

Janek pointed the pistol more purposefully.

'Please tell your friend to turn his gun away,' the man said, his accent thick but his English good. 'I am not going to hurt him.'

'He's right,' said Owen. 'Janek, please.'

But Janek did not move.

'Janek,' said the man, gasping for air, the

weight of timber slowly crushing him. '*Prosím, prosím pomoz mi*.'

'For pity's sake,' said Owen. 'We have to help him.' He wanted to pull the boy away, but he couldn't with the baby strapped to his front and teetering on the broken timbers made slippery in the rain.

The man had got his arms beneath the beam and was trying uselessly to lift it. Owen could hear other rafters above them shifting, straining against the unexpected movement.

'Janek, come on!' he shouted. 'It's going to collapse. We need to get this man out.'

'Please,' the man begged. '*Janku, proboha, prosím!*'

He managed to free an arm and reached out a dusty hand.

'*Ne*,' Janek said. '*To je za Bohumíra*.'

The man then raised his hand to protect his face — a *stop, no, wait* — but the blast echoed through the ruins and the man screamed out, his hand suddenly bloody.

'Jesus Christ,' said Owen. 'What the hell do you think you're doing?'

There were voices outside, then shouts.

'For fuck's sake, come on!'

Then the two of them were scrambling through the rubble, the baby held to Owen's chest as they pushed through the charred remains of the doorway and out into the rain. They sprinted across the field, towards a line of trees, a bank and a river. He could hear a lone soldier chasing them and shouting, '*Halt! Halt, oder ich schieße!*'

The trapped man was still shrieking as a shot whistled past, and another, and they heard the clang of a bullet hitting metal.

Owen and Janek ran.

* * *

They let the river take them, the slow current like invisible hands pulling the boat downstream. Around them the rain hissed, hundreds of thousands of droplets spearing the water and splashing up again, every one a heartbeat. There were no oars and they were left to the river's will; only occasionally would one of them lean over the side and paddle a little with a hand to stop the boat from beaching or getting caught up among the overhanging branches. Otherwise they glided, hopelessly adrift.

The boat was flimsy and the water rose up to just beneath the gunwale. Owen held the baby, keeping him as dry as he could within his open jacket. The infant's arms and legs squirmed, and his face screwed up and puckered but no tears came. Owen wore the mushroom cap Janek had given him and the towel requisitioned from the farmer's widow wrapped around his shoulders. The rain stuck his trousers and jacket to him and gradually filled the boat until there was water seeping in through the bottom of his shoes as well.

They did not talk, Owen facing forward, while Janek sat opposite him, his back to the oncoming river, shaking uncontrollably. He would not look at Owen. He stared into the water as it passed beneath them, furiously alive with rain.

They were out of control, Owen thought. This boy was out of control. *Brothers*, Janek had said. But in Owen's mind, whatever bound them together was starting to feel more like a knot tightening around his neck.

* * *

The house was tucked away behind the trees, but even as they stole past in the boat, they had seen that the ruins were empty. They walked around it, warily at first, as the rain pattered down. It had peaked gables and a brown slate roof, and all the windows were without glass, some without even frames. As they came around the side through the thick grass and birch saplings that pressed against the walls, they found stone steps that led up to a missing door, and inside a landslide of rubble where part of the back wall had completely fallen in. Through the paneless windows, branches reached in like stretching arms, and where the roof had collapsed, grass had taken root along the top of the walls as well as nettles that were lined in regimental rows.

There were two rooms downstairs but only one still with a ceiling. The cement rendering was falling away, exhibiting the brickwork beneath that looked pink and sore, as if the rendering had been protecting it like a scab. Against the two window frames, cobwebs hung in drooling rags.

'We ought to make a fire,' said Owen. 'For the child.' He pointed at the grate.

The floor was strewn with concrete dust and crushed bricks, bits of wood and loose nails. By the crumbling stone hearth there were animal bones and a rusty fork, and a man's muddy unlaced shoe.

Janek kicked at a scorched water canister, mumbling something to himself.

'Well, at least it's dry,' offered Owen.

In the adjoining room, where the ceiling was in tatters and there were bars at the window, Janek had found an old bathtub and cleared out the rubble. Now he lay in it beneath the one bit of roof that was still intact, the baby's papoose like a hood pulled deep over his eyes and his bag placed as a lumpy pillow behind his head. His arms and legs dangled like spider legs over the side.

Sitting by the fire, Owen gave the child the last of the milk, though he vomited it up almost immediately and then started to wail. When Owen undid the baby's clothing, the one nappy they had was soiled through. He hesitantly took it off as the baby's little face strained puce, then jerked his head back at the sour stench. He had never seen diarrhoea so yellow. The skin around the baby's bottom and sides was a fiery pink and there was a rash developing across his cheeks that felt like sandpaper.

'No wonder you're making a fuss.' He cleaned him up as best he could. 'I'm sorry, Little Man,' he said. 'I know, I know. I should never have picked you up. But we couldn't leave you, could we, eh? No. And you can kick and scream all you like, Little Man, but I'm going to see you right. I promise. I'm going to see you right.'

* * *

The fire crackled, casting a flickering light across the floor and strange shadows that reached up the brickwork and spread thin-limbed across the ceiling. Clean and warm the baby slept, but his breathing became so light that Owen had to keep checking that he was still alive.

Janek huddled, brooding in the corner. There was no water left, no bread, no tins, just half a packet of biscuits that had got so soggy in the downpour not even Janek would touch them. He poked nonchalantly around with a stick, and then scratched the familiar curling wings of a 'V' into the dirt and then the smaller 'v' beneath it and marked a box around them both.

'What is that?' said Owen. 'You keep drawing it.'

Silent, Janek rubbed it out. He glanced at Owen over his shoulder. Then, with an evident change of mind, he sat himself down again and, pressing the stick hard and flat in the dirt, he swept out a space. With careful precision he drew the two 'V's in the dust.

He pointed at the larger one with his stick. '*To jsou křídla*,' he said. '*Křídla*.' He flapped his arms like wings.

'Ah,' said Owen. He looked more closely. 'Oh. And this one.' He pointed at the smaller 'v' beneath it. 'That must be a head. Yes?'

'*Ano*, yes.'

'Yes,' said Owen, 'I see. It's a bird.'

'*Ano*,' said Janek. He nodded. 'Bird. Yes. How you say . . . ?' He thought hard, his mouth trying to shape words that he couldn't find. He tried coaxing the words out with his hands, and then huffed. 'I not know. Er . . . bird, yes? We say *sokol*. It is *sokol*. Yes?'

Owen nodded. He wasn't sure. It looked like a bird of prey.

Janek then drew the box around it. He put the stick down and motioned with his hands, shaping cubes and squares, then shaking his fists and murmuring words in Czech that Owen didn't understand.

'Box?' Owen guessed. 'Cage? Trap?'

'Cage. Yes, *ano*.' The boy smiled now, pleased with their progress. He pointed at the bird again. '*Československo, ano?* People.' He signalled at the cage.

'You're saying the bird is the people?' Owen said. 'In a cage, yes?'

'Cage. Yes,' said the boy. 'But . . . mm.' He thought about it. 'One day.' He rubbed out the box and fluttered his hand through the air.

'Oh,' said Owen. He nodded. He understood now.

'One day. *Nebudou tady Němci*. No *Deutsch*,' the boy said. 'No *Rusové*. No *bolševici*. No *komunisté. Jenom Češi*. Only Czech. Yes?'

'Yes,' said Owen. 'You'll be free.'

The boy gave Owen a grin.

'And this man today, then?' asked Owen. 'Who was that?'

The boy's smile fell and his face tightened.

'I not understand,' he said. But Owen was certain that he did. He stared at the bird scrawled in the dust.

'He was the same man though, wasn't he?' said Owen. 'The man we saw at the farmhouse. Do you remember? You know who I mean, don't you?'

'He is Nemecek,' said Janek.

'Is that his name?'

'He is traitor,' he said. He gazed into the fire. 'Like Kateřina.'

Then he scuffed out the bird with his hand and walked out of the room.

⋆ ⋆ ⋆

What if she was gone — this wife, this lover, this girlfriend, this missing part? What if she had not forgotten him but had given up on him? How long had she been waiting? He wondered if he had written her letters; if she had written to him, and what she might have said; what private things they might have laughed at, what shared secrets, the codes of lovers trailing back and forth between them in little more than the flow of ink. He wondered at what point she might decide that he was dead; whether, in fact, she had decided already and had put her pen down for the last time, her last words to him already parcelled in an envelope, sealed with a kiss.

He watched Janek dozing, flinching occasionally as if his mind were balanced on the brink of sleep while his body kept trying to yank him back. Plenty old enough for girls himself, Owen thought. He wondered whether the boy had broken hearts like Max had, or perhaps beneath all that Czech bravado he was shy and still unsure of himself — all his mistakes yet to be made.

He shuffled closer to the fire. He sat in nothing but his undergarments while his clothes dried on a makeshift teepee of branches that he'd gathered from outside.

The jacket and the trousers and the shirt still bothered him; he couldn't fathom how he had ended up with them. At least the jacket fit, though both of the shoulders were strangely ripped at the same point, broken cotton threads hanging where something had hastily been removed. There were similar holes and threads around the cuffs. He wondered if there had been an insignia; if it was a pilot's jacket, perhaps.

He slipped the shoes back on and poked at the fire, then unhooked the shirt from the branch and turned the sleeves inside out to dry the other side. He did the same with the trousers, and the jacket. Only then did he see something attached to it — a dead leaf clinging to the lining — but when he shook the jacket out, the leaf was still there.

Not a leaf, he saw as he looked more closely, but a square scrap of grey material the same colour as the lining and lightly tacked to the inside pocket with a fine red thread. He picked at it with the tip of a finger, puzzled. Some of the threads holding it in place were broken and frayed and grubby. The inside of the jacket didn't look ripped; yet the cotton square was stitched there as if it were a patch sewn on and snipped from dead grey skin.

* * *

He sat beneath the window and listened to the rain dripping through the house, holding the baby so that his head touched Owen's chin and he could feel and smell his warmth. The infant was fighting hard to stay awake but the weight of sleep kept pulling him under. Perhaps when Owen fell asleep too this nightmare would fall away and he would wake to find himself somewhere else. In a bed somewhere. A house. A house, he decided, with red geraniums in pots on each of the steps that led down from the door to the small yard and the door in the fence that opened on to the street. He would sit on one of the steps and roll a cigarette, smoking it before he let himself in. A moment with the geraniums and nothing but his thoughts. He would sit and smoke and think and plan, and collect up the fallen petals and hold them, an offering for her, red and curled in the palm of his hand.

* * *

It was still dark when he jerked awake with a strange sensation of being watched. The fire had burnt itself out and the night was thick at the windows. At least twice he had been aware of the baby waking and each time the boy had picked him up and taken him out. Owen had heard crying outside. Now the baby was no more than a curled heap of clothing on the floor, while Janek lay on his side, pressed into the wall, his hands kept warm between his thighs and his leg twitching.

As Owen crossed the room in the darkness, his feet kicked something — a tin — and the baby woke, gave a murmur at first and then started to cry.

'No, shhh, shhh,' he whispered. He scooped the child up, glancing at Janek, and clambered up the rubble mound to look out, jigging the baby up and down. He strained his eyes but he couldn't see anything.

He heard the soft crunch of foliage. A flicker of movement among the trees. Taking the baby with him, he made his way precariously over the debris to the main entrance and stood on the steps. It was cold and he could see the vapours of his breath. He stepped carefully down on to the grass and stopped; he could make out nothing but darkness and shadows. A slight crackle. A quivering breath.

'Who's there?'

With his free hand he groped in his pocket and pulled out the pistol, struggling with it in his hand.

'Who's there?' he said again nervously. Then louder: 'I said, who's there?'

There was silence; and then a figure slowly and cautiously edged out from behind one of the trees.

'*Bitte*,' she said softly. Then, in a familiar accent: 'Please. Don't shoot.'

'Who are you?' he said. 'Jesus Christ. What the hell do you want?'

She took another step forward. It was the girl from the roadside. She wore a long coat but it was the pink cardigan and tightly tied scarf around her head that he recognized in the darkness — and the wildness in her eyes. She gazed at the baby in his arms.

'Take me with you,' she said, her eyes glistening with tears and her voice breathless. 'Please.' She stepped closer. 'You have to take me as well.'

IRENA

'I am Polish,' she said. 'A Jew.'

'Your name?'

'Irena. Irena Borkowski.'

'And where in Poland?'

'Pabianice,' she said. 'Near Łódź. Do you know?'

Owen didn't know any places in Poland. He didn't know why he had asked. He was surprised she'd told him she was Jewish; he rather fancied that given where they were, he would have kept that to himself.

She sat in her long coat, her legs folded to one side, the grubby hem of her white dress showing along with the blotchy scratches on her calves and her filthy patent shoes. The pink cardigan was embroidered with white and orange daisies. She didn't have anything else with her, not even a bag.

Janek had brought kindling in but for some time it was too sodden to do anything other than smoke, and they'd hastily made token attempts at tidying the room: kicking aside the bigger bits of rubble, the dusty shoe and fork, and then shaking out the damp towel and laying it on the floor.

'I am sorry,' she said. 'I do not want to make trouble.'

'Well, that's good to know,' he said, trying to make light of it, 'but a little late, I'd say. I mean, good God, I might have taken your bloody head off.'

She didn't respond.

With the gun, he meant, and outside; although, granted, it was unlikely. However, it wouldn't hurt to let her believe that he was made of tougher grit.

She pulled her legs in a little and murmured to the baby, trying to console him as her eyes scanned the room. The desperate and determined creature that Owen remembered from the road was gone. Instead she sat, small and defeated, all the audaciousness of their last meeting replaced with the nervousness of a wren.

Janek crouched, with his eyes locked on her, while Owen stood with his hands in his pockets then took them out, not wanting her to think that he was anything but proper. He couldn't think what to say or even what to do.

After a while the room began to warm, the wood in the fire finally igniting as outside the skies opened with a rumble and the rain began to fall once more.

'I must feed it,' she said.

'Yes. Of course,' he said with relief. He turned his attention to the wall and the trail of dampness that was bleeding through the mortar. Behind him he was aware of her fumbling with the buttons on her dress and trying to position the baby, who still squirmed and cried. She said something to Janek in German and he took his jacket off and threw it across.

'*Danke*,' she said, but Janek said nothing.

Owen could hear the baby feeding now beneath Janek's jacket, the tiny legs pedalling under the cover, one hand waving in the air and the fingers opening and closing as if it were this exertion of pressure that controlled the flow of milk.

'Better?'

'Yes,' she murmured. 'Thank you. Forgive me. I only wanted . . . '

'What?'

Her eyes lowered. A flash of light.

'No,' she said in the end, changing her mind. 'You would not understand.'

'I might.'

'I had to come. I had to see it.'

'You abandoned him,' Owen said. 'You left him on the side of the road. You left him — '

'I know.'

'On the side of the road.'

'I know.'

'Just lying there — '

'I know! You don't have to tell me,' she said, raising her voice sharply. 'I didn't have a choice.' That he didn't believe. 'I can't look after it.'

'You're his mother, aren't you?'

Silence.

Janek sniffed.

There came another rumble of thunder, then her voice again, quiet and resolute.

'I did not have a choice.'

Owen crunched through the rubble to the window and looked out at the rain, breathing deeply. He could feel the headache, long gone, returning once again. Behind him Janek sat, head tilted, regarding her with that same detached suspicion he had once shown Owen.

'Have you seen anyone?' Owen said. 'Any British troops, I mean?'

She shook her head.

'American?'

'No.'

'You don't know where they might be, then? You've not heard anything?'

She stared at him.

'I'm trying to get home,' he told her. 'I just need — '

'I don't know anything,' she said.

'Right.'

'I have not seen anyone.'

There was a flash and through the window the woods were momentarily lit up, a snapshot of the rain frozen mid-fall.

She was strangely androgynous, he thought, with her scarf tied around her head and whatever hair there was tucked out of sight. It was only the fullness of her lips and softness of her skin that stopped her face from looking like that of a boy.

She kept her head down, reluctant to catch anyone's eye, but Janek gave her no respite — pinning her with his glare. Owen tried to show some English civility and took his attention elsewhere. There was something disturbing about the sound of the baby sucking at her with such animalistic hunger.

She must have seen him take the child. Had she been following them all this way?

'I didn't want to,' she said. 'I tried not to. I kept trying to turn back.'

'But you didn't.'

'I had to know it was all right. That's all,' she said. 'I promise.'

He could feel himself getting angry. His mother had told him too many tales of babies left in bins, bundles, boxes and baskets. During the Great War, she had said, in the days when his father and she had been courting, many young mothers who had lost husbands in the trenches had abandoned infants on the doors of St Mary's, some with notes, some without, some without even a name. She had called them all Little Man, or Little Lady until she could think of something better.

'And what will you do now, then?' Owen said. 'Have you changed your mind? You want him back? Well, take him. Go on. We can't keep him anyway. We can't look after him either.'

She stared at him hard.

The rain dripped through the ceiling into a tin at Janek's feet.

'Take me with you,' she said. 'Please.'

'You're not our responsibility,' he told her. 'Look at us. We can barely look after ourselves.'

'No, you have to take me with you.'

'You don't know where we're going.'

'I don't care,' she said.

* * *

The boat would never have carried three of them, and when they had left the house the following morning, it had slipped its mooring, anyway, and drifted away.

They followed the river by foot. Owen and the girl with her child walked together while Janek strode on some distance ahead, beheading nettles with vicious swipes. Owen wondered if he and Janek were thinking the same thoughts. Another mouth to feed. Another person to concern themselves with. Another inconvenience. Two might have been a partnership but four was a mess.

'Thank you,' she had murmured to Owen. But she hadn't left them much choice.

The river emerged from the trees into flat lands, fields unfurling in both directions to where, in the distance, hills bumped along the horizon. Above them a squadron of planes came over, their growling engines chewing the quietness so that one by one the three of them looked up.

Yakovlev Yak-9. He recognized the clean conventional line of the Russian fighter, even at 30,000 feet. He watched them passing over, their fuselages gleaming in the sun. So free and untethered in all that vast emptiness, their war so much simpler, he thought — clean and precise and distant. Was that what had attracted him? Had the RAF provided a way of taking part without getting his hands dirty or seeing what exactly it was he was doing? Their war was purely mechanical. There was no connection with the enemy pilots they shot down, the destruction they wrought below.

Now though, dropped thousands of feet beneath the planes and cast out in a landscape that was alien but real, the last dregs of the war were all around him. It was the stench of smoke, the grit and sweat, the taste of bile in his mouth; it was the sound of a baby crying or a shot fired through an outstretched hand. And done with such venom, such cold calculation.

The boy strode on ahead, cutting a slim figure in the morning light, and they limped after him.

When Owen glanced back, there were more planes coming, black against the cloud, and further behind them, smaller lines of them like hornets finding their formation.

'Get into the field,' he quickly said, ushering Irena on. He shouted up ahead to the boy, signalling him off the path. 'They're using the river as a flight path,' he called.

'But we are not the enemy,' she said.

'Maybe,' he told her, 'but they don't know that. Are you going to take the risk?'

* * *

He pulled out the map and spread it on the grass while the girl fed the baby. The field had a familiar gentle slope and instinctively he looked around for signs of Max, but there was only Irena sitting on her coat with the infant and further downhill, Janek, his arms resting on his knees. He was picking leaves out of the grass and shredding them. Occasionally he threw the girl a glare but she was absorbed in the baby who was grizzling in her arms.

In the sharp sunlight the dandelions scattered around her burned bright as if their roots were wires connecting them to a power source in the earth that made their yellow heads glow.

At one time he had felt quite confident he knew where they were, but that time was gone and the harder he stared at the map, the less certain he was of not only where they were going but where it was that they had been. Perhaps it didn't matter. Perhaps if he could just pinpoint where they were now, not far from a river . . . But there were lots, and he kept seeing them as threadworms burrowing through the skin of the map.

Now that they had a woman and child, he needed to take responsibility. Perhaps he *had* been in the RAF. It was there on the paper, after all. Next to the word PILOT. If she asked him, he would tell her that, until he remembered anything different. He scrutinized his notes for other clues, but it was becoming a jumble. Words written on it in every direction, many more than he could remember writing: arrows linking them, some circled, others crossed out and then written again.

KINGSTON and HARRY and HAWKER AIRCRAFT.

SAGAN had been circled, and CAMP written. When?

He turned it around and found a number: 4993. And then next to it a name — SUZIE SUE. But that hadn't been her.

He pulled off the jacket. There was the square of grey cotton sewn to the inside pocket. It had niggled him all morning, burning away at his chest. He ran his fingers over the material, longing to pull on the broken threads that tacked it in place. Not that the square of material mattered — the jacket was not his — but it bothered him, as the button bothered him and the pistol that he couldn't remember picking up, and that tender pain at his side where there wasn't even a wound.

He watched Janek haul himself to his feet and come up the slope past Irena, but still she did not look. He slumped heavily next to Owen, resting his elbows on his knees again and his chin on his knuckles, frowning.

'She is bad mother.'

'She is like my mother,' Owen said. Something about the pale oval shape of her face and the milkiness of her skin.

The boy found a twig and poked it into the soil. Before long, Owen thought, there would be a 'V' and then another 'v' and then, more than likely, a box.

At least the baby seemed happier. The rash on his cheeks had gone and he was more inclined to sleep. Irena said nothing to the infant as she fed him, but gently rocked either him or herself — it was hard to tell. She fiddled with the buttons at the front of her dress.

'Where *are* we going?' she said, nodding at the map in his hand.

'I'm not sure. West,' he said. 'Where do you need to go?'

She didn't answer but pulled her blouse closed.

'What have you called him, anyway, the baby?' he asked.

'It does not have a name.'

'You haven't named him?'
'No.'
'Why not?'
'It is not my decision.'
'What do you mean?'
She looked over her shoulder at him and said it again. 'It is not my decision.'

* * *

They cut through a field of rapeseed in a long disconsolate line, the crop waist-high and such a brilliant, dazzling yellow that it was almost too bright to look at. Janek held the child aloft and the yellow pollen peppered their shirts, their jackets and trousers, and left its dust upon the hem of Irena's cardigan.

Owen tried to recall how long he had been walking. Every new field they passed, every wood, brook, stream or road seemed to become more familiar as if he had passed through each one before, and in time he would turn a corner and find himself back in that first field, the river pushing past at the bottom of it, pieces of clothing floating by.

They walked through a copse where there were pheasants rummaging, too quick for Janek to catch, and then a ploughed field that was strewn with a line of bomb blasts blown deep into the soil.

He saw Max's letter in his mind, the sharp spikes of his brother's handwriting scratched across the page. He had been working at the Royal West of England Academy where the

Bristol Aeroplane Company had temporarily relocated their head office. He'd met a girl, and now they had got engaged and he wanted to know when Owen was going up to meet her (Owen had been promising for weeks). Then there was another letter, not long after, and a week after Paris had fallen: four lines, hastily written. This Owen remembered as he glanced up at another plane. He saw the lines so clearly and yet fading as if they might as well have been written in the trail of vapour.

Don't bother. We're coming down.
Can't have the Krauts beating us.
I'm signing up.
You in?

* * *

Janek had deserted them or, rather, had gone off muttering something about food, and he had taken Owen's pistol with him — something Owen now regretted in case the boy actually used it or, worse, didn't come back.

They waited for him under the trees, watching a distant road across the wheat fields where a line of T-34s trundled like armour-plated woodlice, a single proboscis sniffing at the air. He hoped to God Janek hadn't headed that way. He half expected to see a lone figure trying to hold them up and demanding bread with nothing but a pistol and a bent rusty knife; but the tanks moved on, unhindered, and a motorbike buzzed along the road past them like an angry fly.

Irena stood at the fence with an air of agitation, her coat slung over it and the baby sitting at her hip.

'German?' he said.

'Russian. They are everywhere.'

'But aren't they on our side?'

'There are no sides now,' she said. 'All you can do is look after yourself.'

The more Owen considered this war that he had somehow fallen into, the less he realized he knew.

It was the British, Janek had said, who had started it anyway. 'You give Czech land away.'

'What do you mean — gave your land away? When?'

But Janek had dismissed this with the flick of his hand, and Owen wondered whether this was just something that his brother had told him.

'He should come back,' Irena said. 'We must go.'

But the boy did not appear.

Owen took the baby from her and nestled him in his arm. The tiny infant was sedated on milk, his eyes blinking with wonder at the sun, dried crusts of snot clogging his tiny nostrils. Owen wandered up and down the fence with him, scanning the fields for Janek and the road with its slow crawl of trucks and tanks. He rocked the baby a little, soaking up the comfort in his weight and warmth. They couldn't call him nothing. They would have to think of a name.

'What do you do?' he said.

'What do you mean?' She was picking daisies and had them bunched in her clasped hand.

'I mean, do you have a job? And what are you

doing in Germany anyway?'

'I was domestic servant,' she told him.

'Oh?'

'A family in Hoyerswerda.'

'A German family?'

'Yes,' she said. 'Of course.'

'I thought perhaps . . .' He didn't know. 'Your English is very good, that's all. A relief, actually,' he added. 'I can't tell you how exhausting it's been with Janek.'

'Janek?'

'The boy,' he said.

She nodded.

'Yes,' he went on. 'All grunts and hand gestures. A lot of gesticulation.' He laughed. She gave him a thin, polite smile.

'I'm impressed anyway,' he said.

How long must it have been since he'd had a decent conversation? The girl, he had decided, might at least be a mediator between them. He had never been one for chatter — that had always been Max — but, God, he needed it now.

She gave him a coy glance then bent to pick a dandelion. 'I wanted to teach languages,' she told him. 'In university.'

'But you didn't?'

No,' she said. 'The war.'

Oh yes, he thought. That. 'Perhaps you could do it after.'

She didn't seem convinced. She twiddled the flower carelessly in her hand and then, looking at her stained fingertips, discarded it in the grass.

'And you speak German?' he said.

She nodded.

'Excellent. And Czech too? *Český?*' He smiled.
'No.'
'Oh. That's a pity,' he said.
Awkwardly, he reached across and pinched one of the daisies from her bouquet. He tickled the baby's nose with it and held it under his chin, forgetting that it wasn't a buttercup.
'I've been wondering where the father is.'
'He is not here,' she told him.
'I can see that. Is he fighting somewhere?'
She laughed at him. 'No.'
'What about your family then?' he said. 'Your parents?'
'I don't know.'
She was quiet a moment, then, on an impulse, she threw the daisies out into the field, a sudden shower of white and yellow, and draped herself over the fence. 'I don't care anyway.' She kicked at the lowest slat, and then turned to him with a challenging gaze. 'You have children?'
'No,' he said. 'I don't know. I don't think so.'
'You don't know?' She looked surprised. 'Oh. You are good with baby,' she said. 'You have a wife?'
'Yes. Well, I don't know. I think so.'
'You are not so very sure of much.'
'No.'
'Ah,' she said, standing up straight. 'Now I understand. She is leaving you, or she is coming back now, or you don't know. You don't trust her.'
'No, it's not like that.'
'She is one of those women.'
'No, it's not that at all. I don't know. I don't remember.'

'You don't remember.' The way she laughed at him sounded like an accusation.

'No,' he said. 'It's gone. Lots of it's gone. That's all. I fell or hit my head, a bomb blast or something, I don't know. Anyway, it doesn't matter.' He tried to explain, struggling to find the words to express how it was like an empty sea and only now were occasional islands starting to surface, the smallest fragments of land that he might cling to.

'Like this war,' he said. 'I don't know what's happening, what *has* happened, who even is fighting any more. It had barely started, you see, but now this . . . I mean . . . ' He shrugged. 'It might not even be the same one as far as I'm concerned. All of this,' he said, hoisting the baby up on his shoulder and waving his hand across the field at the clogged line of military traffic worming along the road. 'I can hardly believe in it. I don't even know how I got here.'

'You could live through the war like I have and still not believe it,' she said.

'Yes, well, I just want to go home,' he told her.

'And,' she added, 'I do not believe you have lost your memory. You cannot lose memories.'

That's not true, he thought.

'So you are liar, or they are not lost, they are hidden, and you don't want them.'

'Not true,' he said, but she wasn't listening. She was waving at Janek, who was coming up through the field with what looked like a loaf under his arm and, good God, was that a flask of wine?

She smiled. 'I don't think he likes me,' she

said. 'Look. He does not wave.'

'He doesn't know you yet,' Owen said. 'He was the same with me for days.' Or maybe it hadn't been that long. Owen could not be sure.

'You trust him?' she asked, not taking her eyes from the boy as he cut his way up to them through the crop. 'I don't think you should trust him.'

'Why not?'

'You should not trust anyone.'

'Well, that's going to make this rather difficult then, don't you think?'

She turned and gave him a smile. 'Come. We must go.'

* * *

It was Janek, of course, who found the motorcycle and who — commandeering Owen's help — hauled it out of the ditch. He stood with it on the road, holding it upright while he studied it. It was an old BMW R12. Max had been a motorcycle fanatic and had obsessed about such things. This one, though, was battered and covered in dents and prangs, but after Janek had kicked the throttle and it had stalled several times, it eventually belched into life.

He revved the engine and soon he was tearing down the lane, kicking up dust and stones, and then swinging the bike around and pelting back. They stood on the verge and watched, Irena rocking the child.

The boy showed no fear, squeezing the throttle, pushing the bike to go faster as he rode back and forth, head down, back low, the wind shaking his collar and rippling through his trousers. Just like Max, Owen thought, roaring through the country lanes, with him clinging on behind, yelling, *Max, slow down. You're going to have us in the ditch!*

'Waah!' Janek shouted.

He swerved to a halt in front of them. He wanted Irena to get on the back.

'*Nein. Nein,*' she said, laughing, but finally he persuaded her and she pressed the baby into Owen's arms and lifted her dress to hitch her leg over the seat. She wrapped her arms around Janek's waist, looking petrified. He revved the engine and they were off, Irena shrieking all the way, pushing the side of her head into his back and clenching her eyes shut.

It took several runs before she would open them and several more after that before she was laughing and they were both shouting at the thrill of it, the heads of meadow grass bowing as the motorcycle whistled past, and dandelion seeds dancing in the road, whipped up in the backdraught.

Owen followed them along the verge with all the paraphernalia of the baby, the bags and canisters. Just as he was starting to get annoyed, the motorcycle ran out of fuel. He watched as in the distance they freewheeled to a stop, laughing and sticking their legs out like stars. They got off and Janek pushed the bike over to the side of the road and let it clatter down. They waved at Owen and he waved back, setting off to catch them up, but they were already walking on ahead.

* * *

He watched her. He *had* watched her — this other girl who had entered his thoughts and was gone again. There, within that blink of his eye, in the passenger seat of an Austin Eton, or on the back of a disappearing motorcycle, or hurrying down the stairs at a party, and in another blink lost as he stared down from a balcony at the hazy swill of people.

He just wanted to hold her in his mind long enough to see her face.

He watched this girl in the same way: the back of her milky pale calves greasy in the sun, the faint silhouette of her legs through the white fabric of her dress, the curve of her hip, the hump of the infant held in front of her — whom she carried with care but had not cared to name; whom she had given away but could not let go of. She seemed too young to be a mother and yet too bruised now and altered to remain a girl.

Sometimes, as Janek and Irena walked ahead and their outlines blurred in the soft haze and flicker of sunlight and shadow, he could imagine the two of them standing in for him and this woman he so dimly remembered. He wondered if that was the gait of her, the shape of her, her laugh; if what he saw was, in fact, her standing on a distant pavement, gazing at him one last time. But he knew if he ran to her and turned her around she would be gone, just as he was to her, slipping even from himself, bleeding memories and slowly ebbing away.

* * *

The scrap of material lay loose in his hand, a short fringe of frays around each edge and the whole thing no more than two inches square. He turned it over and back again.

'What is that?' Irena asked, her eyes on him as she changed the baby's nappy.

'I don't know,' he told her. 'Nothing.'

Just a plain bit of material and not even cut with any care. It had the same colour as a raincloud, snipped from the sky.

Clouds he knew. Cumulus. Cirrus. Stratus. Altostratus. He had looked down on them and through them, the aircraft barely making more than an indentation as if the clouds were no more than ghosts, so that not even a bullet-shaped plane cutting through the belly of them would distract them from their drift. His first flight as a new recruit in the Air Training Cadet Corps came to him. It was in a small yellow Tiger Moth called Quincy and the updraught had taken her up like an elevator. Seated nervously next to the pilot, he had fallen in love with the sky that day — finding God somewhere in it, and the wonder of the heavens. They had flown low over the Hampshire countryside and then out as far as Bristol and the Severn Estuary. It was early morning and everywhere the fields and countryside were lightly veiled in mist, and at one point steam from a railway locomotive had risen right up through it. He had got his first sense of it that day — the glory of being a pilot.

* * *

The river was fast-flowing as it bumped and splashed over the rocks, scurrying around in whirlpools and leaping the fallen branches. His finger searched up and down the map but he couldn't fathom out where they were.

They struggled along the bank between the trees until first one and then the other direction became unnavigable, the bank so steep and the willows leaning so far over that there was no way around and they had to turn back.

'What now?' said Irena.

Whichever way they looked there was no sign of a shallower calmer stretch and, unable to orient themselves, they didn't know how far they would need to walk until they found a bridge.

'Here is not so deep,' said Janek hopefully. 'I will take baby,' he announced, but Irena wouldn't let him.

'Let me then,' offered Owen.

'I don't need your help,' she said.

They sat on the bank and took off their shoes and socks, Janek and Owen tying the laces and hanging them around their necks. They secured the baby into the papoose to keep him safe, then Owen fastened the milk and water canisters to his belt; their coats and blanket he hooked around his neck as well to keep his hands free.

They edged their way in, Janek first, Irena and the baby in the middle, and Owen bringing up the rear. He could hear the sound of their breath, taut with concentration.

The water was freezing, and the current a lot

stronger than it had looked from the bank. It pulled at his calves as they edged in deeper, using their fingertips to steady themselves against the slippery rocks and their bare feet fumbling in the torrent for each footing. Beneath him he could feel broken branches, the sharp edge of stones, and the sludgy sponge of algae.

'Fish!' Janek exclaimed.

'Where?' Owen felt the unexpected whip of something hard like a snake against his leg. 'An eel!' he said.

It darted away. He saw it tunnelling through the water but then he lost sight of it. He carried on, feeling his way slowly forward, until there was a yelp from Janek and Irena shrieked, and they both splashed in. Their arms flailed as they tried to find their feet again, the water surging around them. Owen scrambled down, slipping in to reach them as they struggled to help each other against the fierce flow.

Irena cried, '*Das Baby!*'

The fall had already taken her several feet downstream and as she tried to stand Owen could see the empty papoose swilling in the water around her neck. He and Janek dived in, struggling against the flow. Irena was feeling around in the water with her hands, dipping her head under to look and then up again as she tried to keep her footing among the rocks. The water crashed and roared around Owen as he surged downriver, desperately searching for a glimpse of the child.

Behind him Janek came up choking.

'I can't see him,' Owen yelled.

'There!' Irena quickly shouted.

Owen turned and saw the infant caught in the relentless tumble of the river, under and up again, turning and turning. Janek flung himself forward to reach him and Owen dived too. He pulled hard strokes, his legs kicking against the rocks and weeds, the canisters banging against his back. In front of him the baby disappeared again, sucked under. Then the child was there and Owen lunged for an arm. He pulled the infant in and held him close as the current washed them against a fallen tree trunk. Then Janek grabbed Owen's shirt to steady him and threw an arm around Owen to keep the three of them upright. They both spluttered and coughed. He was aware of Irena upstream, her hands clutched to her head. He felt Janek's laboured breath against him as the two of them held each other and the child between them. The water splashed hard against their faces. The baby started to howl.

'Thank God,' Owen murmured.

The river churned around them. He clutched the child to his chest.

* * *

They joined a road that grew busier, everyone heading in the same direction it seemed. Many were German soldiers, all exhausted, sometimes walking in small groups but often alone, the abandoned or the deserters, some already holding white handkerchiefs ready to give themselves up. There were families too, dragging tired children with leaden legs or pushing their goods in carts fashioned from crates, or prams, or nothing more than flat pieces of wood attached to rattling wheels and pulled by lengths of rope. Some walked without anything. But all of them were hurrying. Owen could see the anxiety in the tight expression on their faces.

All four of them were still damp and shaken, and slopping in their shoes. There had been little conversation but something in their group had now shifted, like four tiny pieces of a watch mechanism clicking into place. Just a glance sometimes from one to another. A single shared thought.

Janek blamed himself. He had crafted the papoose, after all.

'It wasn't your fault,' Owen told him.

But the boy would not listen. He watched Irena press her cheek to the baby's head.

* * *

Just outside a village the three of them scrambled up on to the verge as four open-topped trucks rattled noisily past. There were hordes of thin-faced men piled in each. They were singing raucously, some sitting, some standing and swirling the French Tricolore. They slapped at the sides of the cart as it rumbled by, banging out a tribal rhythm to accompany an accordion, and in their wake, Owen could hear cheers of '*Liberté*' and '*Vive la France!*'

'What's happened?' he shouted to them. '*Qu'est-il arrivé?*'

'*Votre Hitler est mort*,' one called back. '*La guerre est finie*.' Then the man threw a bottle that shattered on the road at Owen's feet and laughed.

'*Saloperie d'Allemand!*'

★ ★ ★

It was hard to know what to feel — the end of a war that in his mind had barely started. There was not relief or despair. There was simply disbelief, as if he had found out he had been cured of a terminal illness that he had only just learnt he had.

He lay on his back in the long grass staring up at the blue and the soft trail of clouds like smoke from the last guns. Perhaps the sight of a plane would jolt a memory. He stared up at the great expanse, waiting, but nothing came.

He did not know what he had expected from Irena or Janek, but it was not this clenched silence. Their numbness was mirrored everywhere. There was no sigh; no long breath released that had been held for all these years; no joyous hug or sudden embrace that they might later be embarrassed by.

'It's over then,' he had said to Janek, as if perhaps Janek hadn't understood.

'*Ano*,' said the boy. That was all.

He wandered blindly up the road as if Owen had said nothing more than the sun was out or his bag was undone or there might be bread for supper. He kicked along the grass verge, occasionally pulling a stalk of oat grass and flicking it around for a bit before letting it drop from his hand. Irena walked some distance behind, gently jigging the baby, her head nodding in time as if in her thoughts she was quietly agreeing with it.

And so the war had ended — not with a bang but a slow death, a last exhale to nothing.

A mile or so later they passed the remnants of a German battalion scattered along the verge like debris. They sat bent in the grass, or lay flat on their backs, or stood about puffing on cigarettes and staring blankly through the smoke, their sniper rifles lying discarded at their feet. Nobody spoke. Behind them a single soldier stumbled around in the middle of a ploughed field, tripping over the muddy furrows as if drunk and clutching his head in his hands. Even from the road they could hear him moaning and then he pulled a pistol from its holster and, before Owen could register what he was doing, the man had put it to his head and fired.

* * *

They did not speak but walked through the dream. At one point they passed a man sitting in the grass on a milking stool, hunched over and staring at his undone laces as if it were the undoing of these that had been the undoing of his war.

Janek drew a deep breath. He threw them both a look, hands in pockets, saying something and nodding as if something at last had been decided, they could set forth with a longer stride.

'He says everyone will be freed now,' Irena

translated. 'His brother will be free. And we will find him.'

'Yes,' said Owen, smiling at him.

Everyone who was lost would be found. Everything would be mended.

* * *

They sheltered in a hay store that night, in the middle of some woods. Inside it was just large enough for the three of them to lie out, the baby in a bundle between them. One end of the store was entirely open so that they could watch the boughs being blown about, casting shadows across the clearing that were like figures wandering lost in the dark.

After a while, Janek took his rusty knife from his bag and started to scrape away at the side of the shed, etching out the shape of the wings, then a beak. Owen wished he wouldn't; it was starting to annoy him. Like a bloody calling card, as if he were leaving a trail for Czech savages to follow. The scratch and scratch and scratch grated on his nerves.

When he had finished the carving, Janek sat and pulled out photographs to show Irena. Petr, his parents, Lukáš, Nicol. Irena nodded and asked questions that Owen didn't understand. There was no mention of Kateřina.

* * *

They were at a narrow brook near the hay store, lit by the moonlight that fell through the trees and slid over the wet stones like melting wax. Owen dipped the canister in to fill it then watched as Irena slipped her shoes off and stepped into the stream. The moonlight reflecting from it lapped around her calves.

'It's cold,' she said.

'I'm not surprised,' he told her. 'It's late.'

'Are you coming in?'

'No.'

She picked her way over the stones and then, bending down, scooped handfuls of water up over her face. Already, after only a day with her, it felt different. She would be the glue or the wedge between them, he thought; he just didn't know which yet.

'You shouldn't call him 'it',' he said.

'Who?'

'Your child.' Janek had called him '*mala veverka*', but Owen, as his mother would have done, would call him Little Man.

Irena took no notice.

'I could die here,' she suddenly said. Then she threw her arms out wide. 'I am floating in the water,' she shouted. 'I am a little star.'

He smiled and lifted his gaze as he took a sip from the canister.

When he looked again Irena had her back to him and was undoing the knot of her headscarf. He was surprised that her head was completely shaved down to the scalp. She glanced over her shoulder and caught his eye.

Was that almost a smile?

The moonlight dripped from the leaves and washed the curvature of her skull with a soft coral glow, and the water around her ankles was flickering and in pieces.

* * *

He lay beside the fire outside, the patch of material held between finger and thumb. He gently rubbed at it, his forefinger circling the thumb and the fabric, the feeling almost sensual as the material slid around, slowly warming as if, through the skin and knit of fibres, a connection was starting to ignite.

He tried to find her voice tucked away somewhere inside his head, perhaps the sound of her saying his name, as if that might be a way of bringing her back to him. He caught wisps of her: the flurry of her dress, the hem billowing around an ankle as she passed by where he lay, his head in the grass; but she was gone before he could look up and see anything of her but the waft of material, the flash of an ankle, the sun bright upon her pale thin feet.

He rested his head on his outstretched arm and held the square up to the fire. As his hand moved it this way and that, there were tiny pinpricks of light burning through; not accidental or moth-eaten holes but regular ones made by a blunt needle or even perhaps the point of a compass, a loop of them in the top right corner that, as he moved his fingers away, he saw marked the outline of a shape — a circle. No, not a circle. The pinpricks of flickering light shining through formed the outline of a heart.

From the crest of the hill they had seen the road sweep in on a curve and then score a ruled line across the flatlands that swarmed with people as far as the eye could see — a river of them with no end and no beginning, coursing through the fields in an endless trudge of feet and turn of wheel and clump of weary hooves. They walked six or seven thick, and where there was a cart or some other obstruction, they surged around it, moving with a shared momentum. Hundreds. Thousands. And in among them: traps and wagons and carts and barrows, homemade trolleys piled with suitcases, bags, blankets, and children, even battle-beaten soldiers dressed in winter greatcoats, despite the vehement sun.

They called out to Janek as they threaded their way through the throng, Owen almost careering into the back of a bike as a man wheeled it past, and then, turning to avoid it, falling over a child instead who was holding on to her sister's hand, both of them clutching small bags. Someone shouted. Another child was crying. There were books scattered all over the road that people were tripping over, and a motorbike trying to get past. And in among it all, Janek's head would appear in the bobbing crowd or at one side of a cart or another, there for a second and then gone.

'Janek,' Owen shouted. 'Wait!'

Irena had wanted to stay in the fields but Janek had already set off tramping down the hill, taking the baby with him, and now they were caught in it too.

'Janek,' Owen shouted. But the boy would not stop.

When they finally caught up with him he had the baby balanced in one arm and was holding the photograph of his brother in the other hand, flashing it at an elderly couple with a suitcase carried between them, and then a pair of war-torn soldiers, their faces grey with dirt, and then a girl in a mink stole.

'This man,' Janek said, thrusting the photograph into their faces. '*Tady toho muže . . . Neviděli jste? Haben Sie ihn gesehen?* Please. Please, he is Petr Sokol.'

He turned his attention to a younger woman carrying a satchel, with clothes draped over her arm that were still on their hangers. Then another with three children gathered close, herding them like sheep. Then a woman with thin ankles clumping in soldiers' boots. He kept trying, turning in circles, as the crowd on the road peeled around him. He held the photograph in front of them. '*Tady, toho muže. Dieser Mann.*' But none answered. A tired-looking soldier with a dachshund in his arms gave it a cursory glance.

'Leave it, Janek,' Owen said, trying to pull him away.

The boy shoved him off and grabbed a woman's arm as she tried to slip past, holding the picture up to her.

‘*Podívej se na to!*’ he shouted. ‘Look at it!’

The woman pushed him away.

The lucky ones had carts, stacked with belongings and as many people as they could, children spilling out over the sides, holding sticks to the wheels so that they made a steady clicking as the tips hit the turning spokes. Others simply sat, holding something precious to them as the wheels groaned through the dirt. There were prams with children and prams without, piled up with other things. One woman pulled a sledge that kept tipping, everything scattering, cases and books and rusting saucepans, a lid freewheeling towards the ditch. Most, though, had nothing but the clothes they walked in, sometimes not even shoes but rags tied and knotted around their calloused feet.

As they moved westward, Janek seemed intent on trying everyone, the photograph of Petr still clutched in his hand. He disappeared for hours sometimes, pushing through the crowds, and only occasionally coming back with other news that he had unearthed. Irena translated as best she could: the road would take them to the Americans. All of Germany had been taken. The British were further north. There were camps everywhere with people in; hundreds, thousands, no one knew. They had seen terrible things. Some on the road had been liberated. Others were fleeing something. When they got to a town where the Americans were, Janek reported, there would be food, so much food, he said. The Americans were feeding everyone, putting everyone up, and giving them chocolate, cigarettes and clothes. Some were even going to America, he said; they were putting the lucky ones on aeroplanes and flying them to New York. These were the things that some had said. Others said that none of it was true. It was just crazy talk.

'Where are we going then?' said Owen. 'Has anyone said where the road actually goes?'

Janek didn't know. No one did. They all just wanted to get away from the Russians. The war might be over but the Red Army, they had heard, was still coming.

Owen couldn't help but laugh. 'You mean no one knows where the road goes?'

'Leipzig,' Irena said.

'And how do *you* know?'

She hitched the baby further up in her arms. 'I know this road,' she said.

* * *

He was barely conscious of the people around him any more, his mind tumbling deeper and deeper into his own thoughts. Only occasionally did a sight catch his eye: a girl with the head of a small cat poking out through the zip of a bag; a man with an accordion bumping against his waist, so that with every step it made a wheeze, giving sound to his puffing breath. Then, further ahead, he spotted a man with a sawn-off rifle for a leg, the end of the barrel digging into the dirt, the rest of it disappearing up a cut-off trouser leg. As they caught up, the man met Owen's eye and said a few words.

Irena smiled. 'He says, you must not worry. It is not loaded. It is the gun that blew his leg off. Now it is new leg.'

'I can't imagine what my father would make of that,' Owen told her.

'Your father?' She looked confused.

* * *

It came back to him, just as things sometimes did in the night — a memory wrapped within a dream or dream within a memory. He was walking down the corridors of a hospital, his feet clipping the tiles as he tried to keep up with his father.

Our bodies are made up of bits and pieces, his father was saying. *Most of the time everything works just fine. But sometimes something breaks and then it has to be mended. And if it can't be mended, well then, we take it out*.

Like a watch or a wireless or the workings of a motorcar.

Then Owen's father was at an operating table, a throng of nurses around him trying to hold a man down, while Owen's father shouted: *For God's sake, he's not an eel! All I said was hold him*. And then with a bloody arm in his grip, his father started to saw, and despite the strap of leather in the man's mouth, the poor wretch screamed and gagged as the blade crunched through the bone.

Come on, come on then, if you're going to look, his father said. His head appeared for a moment from behind the others and he glared at

Owen, a thin spattering of blood across his mask. *I brought you here to watch*, he said, *not stand back there like a bloody plant pot*.

And then, between the legs of the nurses, the arm dropped into the bucket with a thud, but the fingers hooked over the rim as if the mechanism was still working and it would claw its way back out.

As to what happened next, he was only aware of being lifted from the floor and his father saying: *That's it. You had your chance. I'm not bringing you again*.

Looking around him at the road and surrounding fields, Owen felt as if he were seated instead in a glass box, nothing quite real, as if he weren't there at all.

Perhaps I am not, he thought. Perhaps all of this is nothing but the final deluded imaginings of my dying brain. That is why so much is lost already. Every memory I have ever had will fall into the darkness because, in truth, I am not here at all. I am in a hospital. I am in a field. I am at the side of a bus stop lying on the pavement and quite still, yet within this body I am sliding under. I am sliding away.

* * *

'What's he said about his brother?' he asked, striding to catch up with Irena. 'Do you really think he's in Germany? This Petr is a bit of a mystery, don't you think?'

'He will want something,' she said.

'Petr?'

'Janek. People who give help always want something.'

'I don't think it's like that.'

She laughed. 'Why do you think he is with you? With a war — especially with a war — everything must be paid for. Even help.'

'I don't see why we can't just help each other,' he said. 'We're all looking for someone. You, me, him, us. We'll do it together, I suppose.'

'Yes,' said Irena, appeasing him with a sigh. 'Yes, perhaps it is that.'

'He shot a man in the hand,' said Owen. This was something else that had been plaguing him. 'Another Czech, I think. In the hand. I mean, why would you do that? If you really had a grievance with someone, you'd shoot him dead, surely. I've seen him fire a gun.' From the veranda of a house hitting the silver coils of a wind-chime. 'I don't think he missed his mark.'

'Maybe he wanted this man to remember. Dead men don't remember so much. But alive . . . '

'What do you mean?'

'Every day this man will look at this hand,' she explained, holding her own hand out in front of her, fingers splayed, 'and he will see Janek's face and he will remember why it is ruined, why this boy shot him. Every day he will do this. Every day. Death is too good for some people. Don't you think?'

'I don't know,' said Owen, feeling the softness of his own hand with his thumb, and then that twinge of pain again in his side, the wound that wasn't there.

* * *

It came to him suddenly in a rush, as the memory of his father had not long before. On the road to Leipzig he stopped, the refugees streaming around him. He pressed his hands over his face, his heart beating hard.

Hello soldier. Want a lift?

Yes. If he closed his eyes now he could see her: sitting beside Max in his brother's Austin Eton, just as he had first encountered her, the curls of her short sun-bleached hair caught in a rolled-up headscarf.

That smile. God, that smile.

Hello soldier. Want a lift?

I'm fine, thanks, he'd said, or something like that.

Oh, don't be so silly, she had remarked. *Come on*. She reached out of the car to shake his hand. *Connie, by the way. Your brother's useless*.

Christ, Max had complained, lifting his sunglasses. *Give me a chance*. He introduced them properly.

Well, hello. Then she said: *We can move the bags, can't we, darling?*

Of course, said Max. *Look, for Heaven's sake, O, will you just get in?*

But Owen had been insistent. Better not, he thought.

Can't you just jump in? Max, darling, tell him.

But sometimes, as Owen had learnt at Hawkers, you needed to get a slide rule and draw yourself a firm, hard line.

Suit yourself, said Max. *No dawdling though*.

I know what you're like. He'll be out here bloody hours, and I'm starving. Ma won't want it getting cold.

The tyres skidded. They pulled off with a blast of the horn.

As the Austin Eton picked up speed, his stare fixed firmly on the back of her head. *Turn around*, he thought. *Turn around*.

Then just before the bottle green car vanished around the corner, she had done exactly that.

* * *

The Russians were at Schlieben and then Herzberg, it was said, and then Torgau, all the time getting closer, and then they were right in front of them, a dissolute group of them loitering at the side of the road. Only as they got closer did he see through the crowd that they were taking women at random, one and then another, who screamed and fought as they were pulled from the crowd and across the ditch through the hedge.

The soldiers looked forlorn and weathered, and wore padded cotton jackets that were stained and threadbare, dented helmets with a red star, and ankle boots and puttees — not at all the sight of the unstoppable army that he had believed them to be. Some were swigging from flasks of wine, cheering each other on and laughing, teasing the women as they passed, and fiercely pushing the men from the road if they tried to intervene.

As they drew closer Owen pulled Irena to the other side of him.

'Help me block her,' he said to Janek, tugging him into position. 'And keep hold of the baby,' he told her, thinking that they might be less inclined to take a woman with an infant.

She kept her head down as they passed, as did the other refugees on the road, and their collective pace picked up as the tension thickened. His own beating heart wanted him to sprint, and he could feel Janek beside him stiffening. Don't let him do anything stupid, Owen thought.

Beside him, another girl — Dutch, he thought — was mumbling prayers under her breath.

Up ahead there was a tussle. Shouts. Another woman taken, a large-framed soldier picking her off her feet as she kicked and screamed, his mates on the side bent double and laughing, one of them with a stolen Nazi jacket draped over his shoulders, all medals and badges.

Beyond the hedge, Owen caught a glimpse of someone breaking free. The figure made a run for it across the field and a gun went off, the sound like a slap against his ear.

His hand went instinctively to Irena's elbow.

'Come on,' he said under his breath. 'Hurry, and whatever you do, don't look.'

* * *

They walked as long into the night as they could, putting as much distance as was possible between them and the Russian army, until in a field they eventually gathered, hundreds peeling away from the road to settle for the night. They weren't likely to be bombed any more, but in larger numbers they could withstand the attacks of robbers or lone renegades still determined to take a few down with them to hell.

The night pulled in, the darkness lifting out of the ground and seeping up to fill the sky. Before long the field was a dark sea of burning lights, flames flickering everywhere from freshly lit fires.

Janek wandered, showing people the photograph of Petr and trying to scavenge food or cigarettes from them. Owen's eyes followed his silhouette as he drifted from group to group.

They kept the fire burning, poking at it occasionally with a shared stick, and the baby whimpered softly. For a while, though, they did not talk. Around them people were getting raucous: some drunk, others high on nothing more than their freedom. Bottles were passed around and there was shouting and singing and a man playing a banjo made from a saucepan. The air was thick with ashy smog.

He lay half propped against Janek's bag and coat, while Irena jigged the baby who would not settle. On the back of a grubby German medical form that had blown across the field, he found himself sketching. He filled the paper with the crude mechanics of the bodies around him, sitting at fires or standing about or dancing in front of the flames. For the first time in days — weeks, maybe — he felt oddly at ease, as if there was comfort in doing something that he had always done, another muscle memory slotting into place with every soft and hard stroke of the pencil on paper.

Why do you never put any flesh on them? This was Connie, lying out in another field, on a different day entirely.

That was how he liked them though. It wasn't the flesh or clothes that interested him, or what it was that made them human. It was the muscles inside, the joints, pulleys and pistons; the shapes of an anatomy, how they fitted together and then came to life like the puzzle of a watch or a dissected frog or a plane. He liked that they never looked finished, the cross guidelines left through them that helped give them their dimensions. Like the anatomical sketches of da Vinci or Michelangelo's cartoons that he had seen in the National Gallery in London one summer.

She came back, in that moment. That first family lunch.

The whole afternoon, he remembered, had been unbearable: his father holding court from one end of the table and Max grinning from ear to ear at the other. Owen had purposefully positioned himself where he wouldn't have to look at her, but he couldn't help himself. Every time he'd caught her eye through the silver arms of his mother's prized candelabra, he felt the collar of his starched shirt tighten around his throat.

Across the fire, Irena was holding her hand out.

'I said, you English with your little sketches . . . Can I see?'

He muttered that they weren't much of anything, but she insisted. 'I knew you would draw me. If it is me you have to let me see. Come on.'

He reluctantly handed her the piece of paper, and for a while she stared at it.

'At the top,' he said, pointing.

Her gaze shifted and he watched her expression finally settle into a frown.

'They have no faces,' she said.

'No.'

'Why you not give them faces? Hm.' She handed the paper back.

'I can't really draw faces,' he explained. 'And I'm not interested in them anyway. It's the body really — '

'It is just shapes then,' she said. 'Without a face, what are we? A box. We can't see out. You can't see in. How do you see into someone's ghost?'

'You mean soul,' he said.

'I know what I mean.'

'Anyway, they're just sketches,' he said, wishing now that he'd never started.

'Well, you need to put faces on them.'

Irena sat down and poked again at the fire. The infant was getting fractious and she tried to feed him, but the child was upset and wriggling, simultaneously sucking and crying, so tired and hungry that the poor thing didn't know what to do with himself.

She swapped arms and tried the other breast, and the baby was silent for a moment but then started up again, his toothless mouth wet and furious and his hands in fists, batting at the air.

'We need a proper meal,' he said. 'None of us

can function like this. We need to push on tomorrow. We surely can't be far from Leipzig now.'

'I wish it was not here,' she said.

'The baby? Come on, you don't mean that.'

'I do. When I find its father I'm going to give it to him. I'm going to say, 'Here. Here it is. Is this what you wanted?''

'You have no idea where he is then?'

She held him in her stare, the light from the flames burning orange across her face.

'I don't know,' she said. 'I told you. They took him to a camp. I don't know where.'

'But you are going to find him, for the sake of the child?'

'It is not for the child,' she said. 'It is for me. I did not want it. He forced it on me. It is his child, I tell you. His child, not mine.'

* * *

It was an hour before Janek reappeared, swinging two bottles that he'd procured from somewhere and singing. He stumbled about the fire for a while, looking for his feet, and then offered them the wine, both bottles already opened, half slugged and colouring his cheeks. He swayed for a moment more and then slumped down with an '*oeuf*'.

'Good,' she said, 'you are staying.' Then she laid the child in the grass in front of him and swiped a bottle from his flailing hand. 'The Englishman and I are going to find the biggest fire, aren't we?' she said to Owen, hauling him up by the arm. 'And we are going to drink this, all of this, and dance, and I don't care.'

'*Und was ist mit mir?*' said Janek, slurring. He lolled on to his side.

'You are in charge of baby,' she said, and taking Owen by the arm, she led him out into the middle of the field where they did exactly as she had said.

Owen was awkward at first, everything she'd told him hanging heavy in his mind, but she seemed intent on forgetting. Every time he tried to speak she shushed him with a finger and thrust the bottle into his hand, making him drink before she grabbed it back to take another swig from it herself. She was drunk in no time at all and before long, he too felt strangely careless and happy. They sang and swung each other around, her arms pulling herself into him so that they staggered, laughing and tripping, with a hundred fires burning behind them. He could smell the cherry wine on her breath; the smoke and sweat on her skin. And every word she had said was forgotten, lost within a warm fog.

* * *

That night, as the fires blinked out one by one, he lost sight of her again. He travelled back and forth in his mind, trying to find her in the folds of things remembered, this woman whom he had loved who was now gone. He checked his pockets looking for letters, but there was no note of her on the scrap of paper, no mark on the map where she might have stood. With the light too dim, he couldn't even find the holes in the slip of material, even though his fingers searched and he held it every way he could. He could see no pinpricks of light through it. They had healed in the darkness and were no longer there.

In his dream the house was still there, the frozen sea spreading out around it, endless and empty. The people were gone, as were the ropes by which they'd been pulling it. There was just him standing outside, the ice fast claiming it: the sound of crackling as he watched it creeping up through the lines of mortar and spreading across the bricks, covering and consuming them one by one beneath its frosty skin. Ice trails fingered around the doorframe and up to the windows, and with it came the glassy crinkling sound like a slowly cast spell.

He stepped through the doorway where the frozen sea was the floor, the ice still softly travelling up the walls, the steps and the open entrances to each room like a fast-spreading frost. Where he touched the banisters, the ice crunched like lichen. It ran in clumps along the bottom of the skirting boards like snow-white moss. With every patch and piece the ice consumed, it took the constituent of whatever it touched, draining the colour from it, so that all that was left was an ice replica of what had once been — a step, a chair, a table, everything white and frozen. In each room he found the furniture in disarray, unsettled from their normal positions as the house and all its contents had been hauled across the ice, and now bunched up against the furthest wall.

He stopped. On a mantelpiece, turned to a slab of ice, a frozen candlestick with a frozen candle was now starting to drip, a single ice bead of wax sliding down the stick. Another drip splashed down from beneath the mantelpiece, and when he turned around he saw on one of the ice chairs that there was already a gap in the stretcher where the ice had turned to liquid and melted away. Everything he saw now was dripping, holes appearing in the ceiling, splashing from the light fittings and running down the walls. The house that so quickly turned to ice was just as quickly melting, so that before long he realized there would be nothing left of it, just a frozen sea on which it pooled, endless and empty again.

* * *

His name was Anatol Dubanowski and he was *Polský*, Janek said, dragging Irena and Owen over to where he sat in the grass. In his endless search to find someone who knew something of his brother, Janek had instead unearthed a man who had been in the camp at Sagan. He spoke little English, Janek said, but if they had someone who could translate, he would speak to them.

He was an odd fellow, worn thin like they all were, some of the shine lost from his eyes and the skin loose around his jaw beneath greying stubble. He had a sharp nose and spectacles that he kept pushing up with the back of his hand. He was perhaps in his early forties, Owen thought, although in these strange days it was hard to tell.

Janek introduced them and the man struggled to his feet and shook their hands, then flung himself down on the grass again and set about rolling some dried leaves into a makeshift smoke. With him was a lad he introduced as Henryk, who had a cabbage ear and a hand that constantly shook, the other holding it down as if it had a mind of its own.

They exchanged awkward niceties. The man began chattering in Polish to Irena, who had been reluctant to join them at first but politely answered his questions while trying to skirt his roving eye. A blotchy heat rash, Owen noticed, was slowly spreading up her neck. Janek took the baby and sat him on his knee, while Henryk sprawled long-limbed in the grass and held out a finger for the infant to squeeze.

The man, Anatol, didn't recognize Owen. He continued to speak in Polish, Irena translating back and forth. There had been hundreds, thousands maybe, at the camp, he said. He couldn't be expected to remember everyone. Besides, there were many compounds.

'And when were you there?' asked Owen.

Irena translated and the man answered.

'*Do samego końca . . .*'

'To the end,' she said. 'January. That is when they move. To other camps.'

'What were you?' Owen asked. 'A pilot?'

'*Tak*,' said the man, nodding. '*Kapitan*.'

Owen felt a rush of relief. 'Were you all pilots?' he said.

Irena asked. The man shrugged. The camp was run by the Luftwaffe, he told her. He was a pilot, so yes, there were pilots. But there were other prisoners too. If Owen wanted names and numbers, he should speak to the Germans. Get a list. Although, as far as he knew, everything had been destroyed.

Owen asked instead if he knew of a man called Max, or another, Petr Sokol. A Czech. But the man shook his head. He'd already told them — there were thousands.

'And ask him where they went, as well,' said Owen. 'I need to know the route.'

But Anatol didn't know. All he knew was that they'd rested for two days in a brick factory in Muskau because of the snow, and then they'd moved to Graustein and Spremberg. The whole march, he said, had taken them eight days.

'And then what?' said Owen, but Anatol was still talking.

'Everyone went in different directions,' Irena told Owen. 'Some to Nuremberg — the Americans, he thinks. He is not sure. Each compound went to a different camp further west.'

'And where did you end up?'

Luckenwalde, he told them. Twenty miles or so south-west of Berlin.

'And the British?'

'*Nie wiem.*'

'He does not know,' said Irena.

After that there didn't seem to be much left to say, and the man was on his feet and brushing himself down. They had to get going.

'But what happened to you?' said Owen. 'In the end. When did they let you free?'

She asked him and Anatol told them: he had been liberated by the Russians. That was over a fortnight ago. He had been walking ever since.

'And where are you heading now?' said Owen. 'Surely you should be going east?'

But the man had no intention of returning to Poland. His gaze turned vague as he spoke, glancing behind them over the fields and pushing his spectacles up his nose.

'He says there is nothing left for him there,' Irena translated when he eventually spoke. 'He says he had some family in Switzerland. He is hoping they are there and alive.'

'And your friend?' Owen motioned at Henryk.

The man shrugged. The boy had no one else, he told them. Perhaps he was going with Anatol.

He finally made excuses to leave that Irena didn't bother translating, even though the man's eyes were fixed hard on her. The rash creeping up the side of her neck had almost reached her ear.

Owen shook their hands and thanked them.

'*Powodzenia*,' the man said.

'What was that?'

'Good luck,' said Irena.

'And you.'

Then Anatol went to kiss Irena goodbye, but as he took her arm he pulled her close enough to whisper something, a question perhaps, into her ear. She tugged her hand free and glared at him.

'Is everything all right?' said Owen.

'Ah. *Tak, tak*,' said the man, nodding and

flashing a subservient smile at them all with a mouthful of wonky teeth. Then, beckoning Henryk to follow and raising his hand in a wave, he stepped off the verge and they had soon disappeared into the crowd of bobbing heads.

'Are you sure you're all right?' asked Owen, as Irena took the baby from Janek and gathered him up in her arms.

'Irena?'

She turned.

'What's wrong?'

She hoisted the infant on to her shoulder with so little care that he started to cry. 'I don't have to like all Poles,' she said, 'just because I *am* a Pole.'

'No — '

But she was already out in the road and walking, taking the baby with her.

* * *

How little he knew about her; how little he knew about them both. In time, he supposed, the three of them would disperse just as accidentally as they had come together; Irena disappearing into the haze on the road just as she had appeared, Janek gone when Owen awoke, leaving nothing behind of him but the warm dust of a fire.

She had no brothers or sisters, she told him. Her parents had wanted more. They had wanted a son, she said, but that was not to be.

'And where are they now? You said they were gone.'

'They took my father first,' she said. 'And then

my mother. And then the house. They left me in the street. I don't know where my father is. In a prison somewhere. A camp. I should not allow myself to think that he is dead, but I do.'

They were leaning against a fence, while in the far distance he could see more fields, only these were battle-scarred, the charred remains of spindly trees sticking out like broken wires.

He looked at Irena. 'And your mother?'

She shrugged. 'If one is alive it will be my mother,' she said. 'She speak many languages. She is useful. She is, er . . . ' She struggled for a moment to find the English. 'At a girl school,' she said finally.

'Headmistress?'

'Maybe.' She didn't much care. 'Our house was like her school.' She clenched her fist tight and shook it.

Owen nodded. 'An iron grip. You sound like you don't much like her.'

'What can I say? My mother is a bully. My father is a liar. Thank God for the war,' she said. 'Or I would not know.'

'But you still love them?' he asked.

'You do not have to respect someone to love them,' she told him. 'And you do not have to understand them.' She paused, then asked, 'What is worse, do you think? A road full with people like this, or an empty one?'

'I don't know,' he said. 'Do you hate the Germans?' It was, perhaps, a foolish question, and for a long time she did not answer.

'Some people, they mistook the devil for God,' she said eventually. 'In my opinion it is an easy mistake to make. But, then, I am not like other Poles.'

'What do you mean?' Owen asked.

But she only shrugged and rested her head on her folded arms, leaning into the fence and looking the other way.

'Does your family know about the baby?'

She lifted her head and glanced back at the child. Janek was showing him something he had spotted in the hedge and holding him under his arm as if he was going to toss the baby in after it.

'My mother.'

'And . . . ?'

'Not the truth,' she said.

'Why not? You were raped, weren't you?'

'I don't like that word.' She stood up straight.

'So, what will you tell her about the child, if you find him, this father, and he takes it, which I very much doubt he will?'

'I will tell her that the baby is dead,' she said, matter-of-factly.

'Will you go home, then, when this man is found?'

'No. I told you, they took it. I have no home.'

'So what will you do?'

She took a deep breath. 'What will any of us do?' she said. 'Start a new life somewhere. Pretend none of this happened and that I am happy. What do people do?'

'Find their families, perhaps, like Janek is trying to do, like I am.'

'Janek.' She smirked as if the boy was a joke. 'His brother is dead,' she said. 'You know that. They always are.'

'What do you mean?'

'He is Czech. He is — how you say? — troublemaker. Dangerous. If what he says is true.'

'What's that?'

'They will have no choice. It is like the Jews and the Germans. They will always be as they are.'

'Like what?'

She laughed. 'You can stop a war but you cannot change people's opinions. They will always hate what they hate. Like mushrooms,' she said. 'Or, I don't know, moths. Surround me with them or get rid of every last one, it makes no difference. I will still hate them. That is the Germans and Jews. So, the war is over. What difference does it make? It does not change anything.'

'You can't really believe that.'

'Why would it?' she said.

* * *

She was not like any of the other girls Max had dated. That perhaps had been the problem. A sleeves-rolled-up type of girl, Max had said. *A man's got to change with the times. We need girls like her now. There's a war on. I need someone practical. Someone who gets things done and doesn't sit around all day filing her nails.*

And that's what the others did? Owen had asked.

No, I'm just saying. Margaret and Ruth and

that lot, well, they're all good crack, but take them out of the dance hall and pop them in some overalls and they wouldn't know a spanner from a bloody Spitfire.

Connie was on the patio admiring their mother's geraniums.

Oi, said Max, taking the Woodbine from his mouth and giving Owen's arm a slap. *Dear God, are you listening? I said, what do you think?*

Of what?

Of Connie, you plank.

Oh, I don't know, Max. And he didn't.

I mean, I know she's a bit avant-garde but I think I might like that in a wife. Keep me on my toes.

She's nice, he had eventually offered.

Nice? Bloody hell. Is that it?

The best thing to do, Owen told himself, was to politely avoid her, but that was not easy and not once had he truly wanted that. Max wanted him to get to know her better. *She's just your type*.

A week or two later he and Max had started their training. At Hawkers Mr Camm had been none too pleased, but Owen had needed his personal approval. The design department was moving to Claremont House near Esher anyway. Kingston, they said, wasn't safe.

You're more use to the war effort behind a drawing board. You know that, don't you? Mr Camm had grumbled, but he filled in the form anyway. *Just make sure you come back*.

For a while they were both at No. 11 Recruit Centre at RAF Skegness, and then the

Operational Training Unit at RAF North Luffenham. Connie had got a job at Smiths Industries in Putney, where she made KLG sparking plugs for Hurricanes and Spitfires. He imagined that she looked quite the part in her overalls.

Max was renting the second floor of a house on Caversham Rise and it made sense, he said, for her to save money and move in there while they were both in training — an arrangement that their mother wholeheartedly disapproved of.

It's just a silly infatuation, Owen tried telling himself. She would say it once herself. And what could he do anyway? He would push his feelings down every single time he saw her, even though it hurt.

* * *

In an abandoned munitions factory on the outskirts of a nameless town, they tried to find some space to sleep. In the office areas, hallways and dining room, every inch of floor was taken, huddled groups of people filling the air with their whispers, their coughs and snuffles; while on the main factory floor, which was cavernous, empty and cold, hardier groups clustered around the abandoned machines that were now still and silent like the iron bones of dinosaurs.

They picked their way through, up stairs and along hallways beneath tall arched windows that threw broken squares of moonlight across the grey walls. In the end they crammed into a corner beside the entrance of an office. Irena tried to get the baby to sleep but he was too upset and wouldn't even feed, and soon there were others crying too — disembodied voices sobbing in the dark.

Owen lay there, hungry and exhausted, his eyes growing heavy. He could feel the beat of his heart pumping in his ears. *Don't come back without each other*, his mother had said.

He closed his eyes and slid under.

He was walking. Still walking. Sometimes Janek and Irena were with him, countless faceless people around them and a darkness pushing from behind. Sometimes he walked home along the lane through the Hampshire fields, and he could see his mother in the door of The Ridings except that it wasn't getting any closer. And sometimes he walked through snow, and the image then came to him so vividly: the long trail of weather-beaten men pushing through the forest. The guards drove them on hard. The Russians, they said, were coming. They trudged on with heavy feet, the blizzard blowing and tearing at them, the snow six inches deep, and so cold he could feel his own breath freezing and clogging in his chest. His boots crunched through the snow. There were books dropped, half buried, a hat, a mitten, a glove. And in the dream or the memory that woke him, a figure then came staggering out through the blizzard towards him. He was in a coat thick with snow, and Owen felt the judder in him as he fell, this figure that might have been him.

* * *

Apart from the odd oil lamp wedged within the carpet of bodies and giving a soft glow, the factory was dark and it was hard to tell one face from another, all pale, wide-eyed and staring hard at him. Those who slept clutched their belongings to them, their eyes blinking open as he slipped by. He made his way down a corridor, peering into offices where families had set up home in the shadows, then up some stairs and along another hallway. Occasionally he could hear a clang from somewhere in the bowels of the factory, echoing through the walls like a subterranean death knell. He half hoped it was still a dream.

The boy was in an abandoned turbine room with two others. All three had found crowbars and were shouting and laughing as they brought them crashing against the side of the machine. A detonating *boom*.

'*Za Československo*,' Janek yelled. '*Za svobodu! Za Petra!*'

'*Petr!*' the boys shouted.

'*Za Petrovu armádu!*'

Janek struck again, his voice a battle cry.

Owen shouted: 'Hey! Stop!'

The two other boys scarpered, crowbars clattering to the floor, but Janek took no notice. He struck the machine again, harder, with another bell-like clang that reverberated through them.

'What the hell are you doing? Janek, stop it.'

Janek swung the crowbar again; it hit with a *boom*. 'Petr,' he shouted. '*Za svobodu!* Freedom!'

'Don't be ridiculous!'

Owen tried to wrench the crowbar away but Janek viciously swung it at him, almost taking him off his feet.

'Just put it down. You're going to hurt someone. My God, what's wrong with you? What's this going to achieve?'

But Janek took no notice. He smashed at the machine again and then hurled the crowbar as hard as he could deep into its gullet. He glared at Owen; his eyes were filled with rage.

'Our time.' He jabbed Owen in the chest. 'And you help us.'

'Me?' The boy was crazy. Owen couldn't help but laugh, but that only angered Janek more.

'You owe.'

'What?'

'Two lives,' he said, poking him again. 'Remember?' Then he turned on his heels.

'Janek!' he shouted after him. 'Hey! Wait!'

What did he owe? Two lives, for what? He stood for a minute, his heart kicking and his hand to his chest, still feeling the prod of the boy's finger. He gathered the two crowbars up off the floor, and there it was, scratched on to the side of the machine in chalk. A bird within a box.

* * *

When he woke, Janek and Irena were gone. There was just the baby asleep in a nest of clothes. He sat up, panicked. All around was a sea of sleeping bodies, each one a ripple in the darkness, broken only by those who, like him, could not sleep and sat hunched like rocks, the soft sea-murmurs of breath whispering around them.

The fear that they were truly gone intensified and he stood up, staring.

* * *

He heard them before he saw them, the sound of their breath gasping in and out. He pressed his back against the installation, knowing they were somewhere behind. He bent down and glimpsed through the gaps in the iron framework, catching sight of them through the bars and rods. Her legs were around his waist, dress lifted, hand up his shirt, pressed against the wall. She pulled him into her and he pushed and pushed. In the empty hull of the factory floor, he could hear the quiet echo of her crying.

* * *

In the night, in his dreams, she came to him and curled her arm around him; her smell, her skin, the warm draught of her breath. They fitted quite snugly, wrapped together, the light pooling over her skin like liquid silver in the night. He could draw the curves of her then, if he wanted, her indentations and fragile lines; he could design her on the page as if she was his, and only his, and every inch of her perfect body was of his own making.

On this sea of sleep he felt quite safe, her arms around him through the night, gently keeping him afloat. In the morning, though, she slipped once more from his mind entirely — she drifted casually away.

Sometimes he was painfully conscious, his mind turning over and over the same things as if he were sifting through soil in search of ancient remains. Other times he fell through whole hours without realizing, his feet moving but his thoughts gone, as if somewhere within him part of him had faded away. Each day he tried to rebuild her. Each day something was lost. He walked the lane. Max pulled up. He was on the trolleybus, the heat through the window pulsing right through him. He could never remember what had happened to his bag. Frail tunes came to him, not the hymn but the first tendrils of another memory: the Stowe House Hotel. If only he had been able to draw her face he might remember it more clearly. Sometimes he felt the pain in his side like a bullet and wondered if it was only his soul walking, if he had left his body in a field somewhere, the sun trying to warm his cold, hardening flesh.

Leipzig. Just get to Leipzig. The Americans that everyone said were there would then somehow get him home.

Janek had searched for rags along the verges and hedgerows, and then fashioned a makeshift flag — unfurled wings and a 'v' for a head painted on it in tar. The boys from the factory were gone but there were other recruits beside him now, each with a stick held like a rapier and with a collective swagger in their step.

* * *

For a while he and Irena rode in the back of a cart 'liberated' by an enterprising group of Dutch who had taken pity on her with a crying infant. At Irena's insistence, Owen had squashed in with them among the cases and bedding, the Dutch family perched and propped around them. The cart rattled over the potholes and they could see Janek running boyishly some distance behind them, the red, white and blue flag bright in the sunlight.

Owen held the baby. He sometimes enjoyed the weight of the boy in his arms and his soft, comforting warmth, but there was no doubt he was a worry.

Irena was leaning out over the side of the cart gazing at the rubble-strewn and bomb-blasted road as it disappeared below. They were all miserable and hungry, and the Dutch family had no food.

'Perhaps we could write,' she said. 'When all of this is over.'

He shifted uncomfortably in his seat. 'Yes, if you like,' he said, knowing that neither of them really meant it.

'I've never been to England,' she said. 'You will have to write to me about it.'

'I can tell you now if you like.'

'No,' she said. 'I want it in a letter. It will be something to look forward to.'

Still leaning, she held the end of a twig against the wheel of the cart, just as they had seen the children doing, and it clacked against every turning spoke and rattled through his chest. Then she turned, sitting up a little, and rested her hand on his arm.

'I do know it's impossible, you know. You think I am ridiculous,' she said, 'looking for the father. You think I won't find him, and . . . ' She stalled. 'You are right. I know that. I lied. I'm sorry.' He thought she was going to cry. 'It's hopeless, isn't it?'

'I did think something was rather odd,' he said. 'You weren't looking in the way Janek looks for his brother.'

'Yes, well, Janek is obsessed.'

'Or has more hope.'

'Or has more hope,' she conceded. 'Yes. Perhaps.'

He saw then just how lost she was, how it was desperation that had driven her to them in the first place, to abandon the child as she had.

'Last night . . . ' he began. 'With Janek. You were . . . ' He didn't want to say it. 'Did he . . . ' He took a breath and tried again. 'I mean . . . '

'He did not force me,' she said, looking down once more at the road. 'If that is what you mean.'

'But you were crying,' he said. 'I saw you.'

'You don't know what you saw.' She turned on him. Her voice had changed. 'You don't understand.'

'What do you mean?'

'You know nothing about what has happened here. So how can you ask such things?'

'I'm just worried about you. That's all.'
'It's not your place.'
'I can't help it. And Janek. Both of you.'
'He thinks they will start a revolution,' she said, turning her attention back to the road. 'Did you know that?'
'You sound like you don't care.'
'A new *Tschechoslowakei*,' she said. 'Independence.'
'Independence from what? The war's over.'
She took no notice. 'It is all he says. You are very lucky your German is so bad. I think his brother is in the resilience.'
'The resistance,' he said, correcting her. It would make sense. If Janek's antics were anything to go by, there was plenty of fire in the family. Maybe Petr had been caught and that was why Janek thought he was in Germany.
Beside him, Irena pulled something out from under her — a small oak box — that had been causing some discomfort.
'Sometimes I am like his mother,' she said, checking behind her that no one was looking. 'And he is like a child. Czechs are all the same. Weak.' She undid the clasp and opened the lid. 'Oh.' She smiled, seeing it was a sewing box.
'You've had a child,' he said. 'You've had to grow up.'
She glanced at him, her fingers already in among the sewing bits and bobs.
'We have all had to grow up,' she retorted. 'The war has made us all old now. Everyone but him.'
She rummaged around, unsettling thimbles

and bobbins of thread, before pulling something out. Then she closed the lid and squeezed the box back under her. She unwrapped a snatch of velvet, in which a line of glinting needles had been secured and a tangle of thread.

'I will fix your jacket,' she announced. 'Look, the shoulders are split.'

They laid Little Man in a snug nest of blankets beside them, and for a while they sat in silence as she quietly sewed the tears together and fixed a button, and Owen dozed, the rhythmical bump of the cart lulling him finally to sleep.

When he woke, she was gone and the baby too, and it took him a minute to spot her walking in the road with Janek, the infant in Janek's arms, bundled in his trailing flag, and the three boys he'd recruited lagging behind them like disconsolate courtiers.

The mended jacket lay neatly folded on Owen's lap.

* * *

He rifled frantically through the kitchen cupboards looking for food, while all around dozens of bony hands did the same, grabbing and snatching and breaking things.

Someone yanked a drawer of utensils out and there was a crash of cutlery falling to the floor. Owen threw open a bread bin — empty — and tossed it aside. There was shouting, scuffles and fights breaking out. If he went upstairs might he find clothes? Clothes for Little Man and something for his throbbing head. He looked around, trying to find Janek among all the people — not just boys and men but women and girls too. What they couldn't take they would break. Through the window a girl of no more than twelve was throwing ceramic plant pots through a smashed greenhouse. The sound of shattering seemed to go on and on and on.

Medicine, he thought. Something for Little Man. He pushed his way past those still swarming in, stumbling over the smashed glass and crockery that avalanched beneath his feet.

'Janek!' he yelled. 'Janek!'

He fought his way up the stairs, hordes of people pushing past him with clothes and towels and blankets and shoes. In the bedroom, hands were pulling sheets from beds and curtains from poles, their rings scattering across the landing like exploding stars. There was a smash as something went through the window. He could hear a man shouting in German louder than anyone else.

He spotted a medicine chest on a dressing table, pillboxes thrown about the floor. He scrabbled around on his knees but he couldn't read the labels, and anyway, he didn't know what he was looking for. Something for the baby or was it something for his head?

Downstairs he could hear a cheer and the sounds of a struggle. There were boisterous voices coming from the yard. He grabbed the nearest pill bottle and, pocketing it, scrambled out. The hall below was already emptying of people just as quickly as it had filled.

When he got into the yard a crowd had gathered in a large circle, yelling and taunting. The group swelled as more joined. Owen strained to see, catching glimpses of the figure moving in the middle, waving a piece of wood over the heads of the spectators, who still clutched their spoils.

He elbowed through until, with some force, he managed to squeeze his way to the front. The sight that met him he would never forget; not in the weeks and months and years that followed, when everything else about those times had blurred around the edges. The old man tied to the chair, which had been kicked over so that he was flat on his back, his feet dangling. Janek, pacing feverishly around the circle, the crowd goading him, cheering him on. The piece of wood that looked like a baluster gripped so tight in his hand. The farmer begged in German while Janek prowled around him, wringing the baluster in his hands and squeezing it tighter. His face was red, an aggrieved anger that must have been pent up in him like a dark storm starting to unleash itself. The crowd fed it and stoked it with their hundred voices: '*Zrób to!*' '*Doe het!*' '*Faites-le!*'

'*Nein. Nein!*' the man pleaded.

Then, horrified and frozen as he stood within the circle, Owen watched as Janek approached the man tipped in the dirt. He held the baluster against the man's head as the crowd bayed louder, clenched fists thumping and arms jabbing. Then Janek swung the baluster back, testing the strike, and the excitement of the crowd rose to a melee, before he took aim and swung the wood back again, and Owen yelled: 'Janek! No!'

* * *

They crouched at a shallow river, washing their clothes and bodies. They had left Irena nursing the child at the roadside. Janek was in nothing but his makeshift flag wrapped around him like a towel. Owen wore only his shoes, to protect his feet from the sharp stones, and his grubby underpants. In the past he would have been embarrassed, squatting almost naked and slopping freezing water up into his crotch as he rubbed the shirt that was not his between his knuckles. But not now. His trousers and socks were drip-drying from a stick dug into the soil. Up and down the river, beneath the trees, others were doing the same: thin white figures glinting in the sun, voices subdued, just an occasional splash and giggle bubbling over the rocks.

The incident at the farmhouse hung between them in the air, invisible but heavy. The boy swilled his clothes carelessly about in the water with a finger. His head had that familiar tilt; his eyes rested on Owen with a stern stare.

Part of Owen hankered back for that time when there had just been the two of them and the days had been simpler — without the confusion of Irena and the baby, the road and all its people infecting them with a collective mind that wasn't really theirs.

Owen wrung the shirt out.

'I know you're angry — ' he began.

'*Jste pořád zraněný*,' Janek said, interrupting him and pointing at Owen's bruised ribs.

'Listen, Janek, I know you're angry, but this . . . this one-man retaliation unit . . . It has to stop. Do you understand?'

Of course the boy didn't, but Owen carried on anyway.

'Look, I don't know what you're thinking but if you're angry — you know, *angry*,' he said, trying to make the boy comprehend. 'If you're angry because you think they killed your people, that man did not. He's an ordinary farmer.'

'*Já jsem ho nezabil*,' said Janek. 'Not kill.'

'No. Only because I stopped you.' The boy was exasperating. 'Listen, I'm telling you — '

'*Ne*.' The boy abruptly stood up, the water dripping from him. He threw his sopping shirt down. 'No. You listen. Two lives,' he said. 'You give me.'

As Owen stood up as well, the boy gave him a hard shove and Owen stumbled backwards through the water.

'*To vy. To je vaše vina*,' the boy shouted, and then more words that Owen didn't understand. '*Hledal jsem vás*' and '*Dva dny. Dva dny!*'

'For God's sake,' said Owen. 'What the hell are you doing?'

'I save you,' said Janek. He slammed his fist at his own chest. '*Já!*' Then he jabbed at the air but whatever he wanted to say, he couldn't find the words.

'I don't believe you,' said Owen. 'I don't know what you're saying.'

The boy was glaring at him again. Saved him from what? Pulled him up into the field? It didn't make sense.

Then the boy stepped forward and Owen recoiled, scared that the boy was going to give him another shove that would send him back into the water. But when he spoke, his voice was firm and quiet, an anger still in him that he was trying to contain.

'You help Petr,' he said. 'Yes? We find *Angličany*. English, yes? And you help Petr.'

'But I don't understand. I don't understand what you're saying, Janek. Prove it,' Owen said. 'Prove that you saved me.'

The boy picked his clothes up from around his feet, the water streaming from them, and wrung them out with a few hard twists. He gave Owen a final glare and then slopped out of the river and on to the bank. He grabbed his bag and Owen's clothes, came back with them and shoved the clothes against Owen's chest with another furious burst of Czech before he splashed out again, the flag still wrapped around him, and his pale white back disappeared through the trees.

Owen stood in the river, shaking and clutching his damp clothes to his chest.

'Janek!' he called, but the boy was gone.

Above him the outlines of thinly drawn leaves were ablaze with the evening light.

* * *

The boy slept with his head on Irena's thigh, a soft air issuing out from between his lips. Her fingers stroked lines of comfort into his hair, the tips trailing his face, around his closed eyes, his cheek, his jaw. Little Man lay beside him wrapped in the papoose.

When Irena closed her eyes too, Owen carefully reached across and very delicately dragged the boy's bag out from beneath his arm. He softly unfastened the buckles one by one, opening it and feeling around inside the bag that the boy always kept so close to him, never allowing it out of his sight. He didn't know what he hoped to find; he just knew that he needed to look. Perhaps Janek had taken something that was a clue to who Owen was.

His fingers found the shapes familiar — a pot, a pan, wooden bowls, sodden socks, the bristles of a brush — all of it tangled among what felt like clothes and a hand towel. Then something hard. The tough cover of a book. He inched it out but there was not enough light to read by. He fumbled in the side pockets and felt the sharp prick of gramophone needles wrapped in a handkerchief, and then tucked beneath them a matchbox, the shuffle of matches inside. He darted his eyes over at Irena and Janek, who were both still and sleeping.

The breeze blew out the first struck match. The second was lit just long enough to see the book was written in Czech. With the third he flicked hastily through it, finding at the back several loose pages. He lit another match. Not pages but newspaper clippings. The first was old — 1918 — and had a photograph of thirty-odd men standing in a well-ordered group as if they were part of a political assembly. The next included a map, most of it faded, but he could see that border areas had been shaded and labelled *Sudety*. On the corner of the page a date was visible: *30. září 1938*. As the match burnt out he laid more articles flat on his knee in the dark, and then struck another match to sift through them. Time and again he came across similar-looking photographs in the creased clippings. There were rallies, demonstrations, brawls, a crowd of men clashing with a group of soldiers outside the main doors of an office building and then, in another, what looked like factory gates. Caught within the crush was a dark-haired man waving a baton, his mouth open mid-shout. It was Petr. And there again, in the next photograph and the next, sometimes with his name — Petr Sokol. He lit another match and scanned the text. There were other names: Josef Myska . . . Filip Jankovic . . . A whole article about a boy, Antonín Nemecek, who seemed to be only fifteen. Other words caught his eye, some similar to English so that he could guess their meaning: '*sabotáž*' and '*demonstrace*' and '*politický*'. In the scrum of a demonstration, Petr's face in the thick of it, there was a smaller man fighting alongside him, his fist raised and clenched. He had an armband around his jacket, and as Owen held the clipping closer, keeping the match alight, he noticed that the band had Janek's symbol on it — a flying bird within a box. He riffled through the other clippings, lighting match after match and finding the same man, the same armband, Janek's symbol again and again. Only with the last match did he sense something, and in that brief and final quiver of light, he looked across and saw that Irena's eyes were on him.

* * *

Behind closed eyes that night, fragments of the day came back to him, and an afternoon too. An August weekend back at The Ridings.

Oh, you sketch. Max, you never said.

They were sitting on deckchairs on their parents' lawn, Max and Owen with their sleeves rolled up, sweating in their linen trousers, while Connie languished in a lilac summer dress.

Come on then, she said. *Do me.*

Max had heaved himself up in the chair, saying, *You won't like it.*

I might.

Well, only if you don't mind looking like the inner workings of a Tornado.

Oh, Maxwell, she had said. *Don't be such a child.*

Actually, I'm really not very good, Owen said. He had only brought his sketchbook out so as to distract himself from her, but he'd barely put pencil to paper. Cedar wouldn't sit still.

Why don't I draw you, then? She held her hand out for the pad. *Come on, hand it over.*

Oh, hello. Brace yourselves . . .

For goodness' sake, Max. She turned on him. *You've not even seen it yet.*

She rested the pad on her knees and, repositioning herself, she thoughtfully stared at

Owen with the end of the pencil pressed against her lip and one eye squinting at him as if, in the sunlight, he kept slipping out of focus. Then, holding the pad secretively to her, she made a few flourishing pencil marks in no more than a matter of seconds and proudly handed the pad back.

Max swiped it from Owen's hand and together they looked at it. Max snorted. As stick men went, she'd given Owen an obscenely large head.

And why's one arm half the length of the other? remarked Max. *Good God, has Father been at it?*

They had all laughed at that.

Now don't tell me, she said, leaning into Owen with a playful smile, *that you're not very good. Compared to that I'm sure you're a bloody Rembrandt or, I don't know, what's his name. The one with the* Venus de Milo.

She had been thinking of *The Birth of Venus* so he told her, Venus de Milo*'s a statue*.

Well, you know what I mean.

Besides, he added, *I'm really not very good at faces*.

That's true, grumbled Max.

Well, maybe you've not had the right subject.

And in that moment, on that hot afternoon, he wondered if she had purposefully caught his eye then, or perhaps nothing had happened at all but the rush of heat to his face and the need to turn away.

He lived in constant fear of himself; that at any moment something regrettable might burst from his mouth when he saw her or he might not be able to stop himself from reaching across to touch her hand. At the Falkirks' dinner party that October, he'd had to take himself out of the room entirely and stand in the hallway for a moment, trying to wipe incorrigible thoughts from his head. She had seen what had been going on behind his eyes. Only later did he know that she was starting to feel it too.

Max, of course, was so blind to her that he saw nothing else.

I wish you'd talk to her more. For Heaven's sake, O, she'll think you're bloody mute.

But Owen didn't trust himself, and Max remained oblivious of the Herculean efforts he was making not to let anything show.

Surely then he had tried to stay away, and surely she had too. Yet every time he thought of her, it was of a stolen glance between the arms of a candelabra or the slight curl of a smile seen in the wing mirror of Max's Austin. Then, one evening on the way home from a dance, with a chap called Barnaby sitting up front with his brother and the beams from the car cutting through the night, he had let his leg relax against hers. Even though they had both stared out of opposite windows, deaf to Max and Barnaby's chatter, he could feel her thoughts reaching for him, and the return of pressure against his leg.

The hall was packed, the heat unbearable, the air filled with clamouring voices and the stench of grubby bodies and stale sweat. Around them was a sea of heads in caps and head-scarves. Everywhere Owen looked there were scared eyes and children crying. No one seemed to know what was happening or what it was they were supposed to be doing or why they were even there.

Some miles outside Leipzig a refugee collection point had been established and they had been herded on to a narrow slip road as lines of US military personnel directed them through. Now, along with hundreds of others, they were jostled into the receiving centre that had been hastily improvised from military barracks. All the hope and relief Owen had felt at seeing the American soldiers had sunk to the pit of his stomach. When he finally struggled through the hordes to the rows of desks at the end, dragging Irena and Janek with him, they found that the desks had been abandoned and any system with it. Instead, the uniformed personnel were scattered among the crowd, trying to direct individuals one way or another, or herd groups of people towards transport. One soldier was firing questions at those around him and then pushing them towards different corners.

'We are going to be split,' said Irena.

'We're not.'

But against the walls around the hall, various flags had been hung. Owen caught Janek's eye. For all yesterday's bravado, the boy now looked petrified.

'It's all right,' he told him. 'We won't be split. Do you understand? They're not going to split us.' All the antagonism from the day before was paling into insignificance. 'Come on. This way,' he said. 'We need to get some help.'

He took Irena's wrist and pulled her back into the crowd.

'Don't lose us,' he told Janek.

The boy nodded. Through the crush of people, Owen could feel his fingers around Jarek's arm.

The noise increased at the back of the hall where there were two sliding doors, and around them the crowd started to surge and swell. There was a hissing outside.

'*Podívejte se!*' shouted Janek.

He pointed over Owen's shoulder. Through a window the funnel of a steam engine could be seen pulling past. Others had seen it too. There was a slowing scream of wheels and inside the hall a collective intake of breath, and then a combined swell, everyone straining to look and then starting to push, eager to get nearer the doors. They pressed hard against each other, arms and elbows and shoulders trying to squeeze their way through.

'Get back!' a soldier bellowed. 'Stop pushing.'

'I can't breathe,' Irena gasped.

'Just stay close.'

The crowd inched forward, taking them with it.

Janek's fingers slipped and then grabbed on again. Someone's cigarette breath was against Owen's neck and a girl's head was pressed into his shoulder, a suitcase digging at his side.

The people at the door bottlenecked.

'Get back! Come on, get back!'

This is how he'd lost Connie. In the crush of a party, the swell of a crowd. All the noise — the laughter and music and shouts of excitement — pressing at his head so that he had wanted to shout out: Where are you?

'Let me through.' He pushed. 'I said, let me through!'

The soldier was forcing his way through the crowd and Owen grabbed at his sleeve.

'I'm English,' he said. 'Please. You've got to help us.'

The man turned his head but barely took Owen in.

'I said I'm English. Do you know where I go? Please.'

The man looked at him, young and vaguely dazed, just how Owen had imagined an American farm boy, except that now this boy was herding refugees.

There was a flutter of confusion. 'I don't know,' he said. And then: 'You want Hitchin. Ginger hair. Yeah, over there.' He pointed.

Owen looked.

'Got him?'

Owen looked again.

The man who caught his eye was not ginger.

He was thickset with a square head, short silvery hair and in an altogether different uniform. A man who, in the moment as he slipped through the crowd, twenty or thirty feet away, Owen thought he recognized. Then the man was gone.

'Where?' Owen said, glancing back. But the farm boy was gone as well.

* * *

'Listen,' he said for the second time, trying to make himself clearer. 'I'm a pilot, for God's sake. British RAF.'

'With no papers.'

'No papers, no. Look, I just want to get home.'

The man called Hitchin glanced up from behind his desk. 'With no disrespect, sir, so do the other God knows how many thousand here. As I said, you're going to have to wait.'

'But I'm English.'

This didn't seem to interest Hitchin in the slightest. The war must have washed all sorts of people up at this man's feet, each with a story, when all he wanted was to have as many of them sorted, processed and moved off his patch as quickly as possible.

'You must have British contacts here,' said Owen, 'or ways one could get in touch with someone?'

'I'm sorry, son, but I've got two thousand people here to deal with right now, not just you.'

'Yes, I understand that.'

'But I don't think you do.'

Irena and Janek lingered nervously nearby.

'I tell you what,' said Owen, 'who's your commander? Where do I go for information, for help? I just need to make contact with the British government.'

'You said.'

'Yes, but you're not listening. That's all I'm asking for. Isn't there someone I can speak to? There must be someone in charge.'

The man raised an eyebrow.

'What about in Leipzig?' Owen said. 'Someone must have a line of communication with the British forces.'

'Look,' said the man, finally losing his temper. 'The last thing MG HQ's got time for right now is sorting out the woes of some goddamn rookie pilot like you. I said we'd get to you in good time, sir, but I've got two thousand people here already to deal with and more coming every minute.'

'I just need pointing in the right direction, that's all,' said Owen firmly.

'No, what you need is to fill in the goddamned form, like I said,' he told him, pushing it back across the desk one more time and prodding it with his finger.

'But I can't. I've already explained this.' He waved his hand at the various boxes. 'Half of this information you need, I don't have. I don't know.' He tried another tack. 'Look, can't you at least get someone to look at the child?'

'They're with you?' Hitchin said, at last surprised by something.

'We've been on the road for God knows how many days. We're hungry, do you understand?

Starving. The child needs some attention.'

'We don't have any medical facilities here,' said the man. He turned his attention to Irena. 'What are you anyway? Polish?'

Irena nodded.

'Okay, well, we need you to get yourself over there,' he said, pointing at a disparate group gathering in one of the corners. 'We'll get you packed off somewhere soon.'

'No,' said Owen. 'She's coming with me.'

'No, hero,' said Hitchin. 'She's not going with you. She's going to stand over there with all the others and she's going to do exactly what she's told, without a fuss or a song and a dance, and she's gonna take the kid with her. Is that understood? I don't know who the hell you think you are, soldier, throwing your weight around, but you're not the goddamn cavalry. Okay?'

At that point a man appeared at Hitchin's shoulder. He was thin and nervous-looking, with red splotches of eczema dabbed like thumbprints down his neck.

'Sir?'

'For Christ's sake, what now?'

'Sorry to interrupt, sir.' The man bent down to speak into his ear. 'It's about the train,' he said. 'Bit of a mix-up, I'm afraid. They've sent the wrong boxcars. We can't use them, sir.'

Hitchin took a deep breath and then sharply stood up, bucking the table and shoving it out hard.

'Parsons!' he yelled with a voice one only had in the army. 'Get yourself over here. Jesus Christ. We're gonna have a goddamn riot.'

He started pacing over towards the man and Owen made a last desperate grab for his arm.

'Sir!'

'Oh, for the love of God. Do what the hell you like! Turner!' he yelled. A man with a bandage around his head sprang from his seat. 'Will you just get them out of my goddamn hair?'

'I missed it,' the man called Turner said, as he ushered Owen and Irena out, Janek hurrying after them. 'Where'd he say you guys need to get?'

'MG HQ,' said Owen, whatever that was.

'Ah hell,' muttered Turner. 'Hitchin's orders, right?'

'Right,' said Owen.

* * *

The open-topped jeep took them through the suburbs, Turner at the wheel, and his partner, Anderson, struggling to control a map, which flapped in the wind as he tried to navigate them through the blown-out streets and rubble. In the back, Owen, Janek and Irena were scrunched in so tight that every time they hit a hole, Owen felt the boy's hipbone crunch against his own. Irena tried to protect Little Man from the dust and dirt as it blew up into their faces.

The east of Leipzig looked relatively intact but for the occasional building blown out and the bullet holes pelted like peepholes into the walls. Here and there people were sweeping rubble from the paths. They drove through clouds of scent that wafted from blossoming gardens.

Along the electrical wires, birds chattered in long lines.

The further in they drove, though, the worse it became. Owen's stomach sank as he gazed up in bewilderment at the remains of the buildings leering over the jeep. Some had been flattened to no more than mounds of brick and stone. The bombings had happened quite some time before, but even so, every now and then Turner had to swerve to avoid a scattering of bricks. Some of the buildings were burnt-out shells, blackened and charred around the empty windows; others had parts blown away entirely, leaving nothing but random walls and lonely chimney breasts, the bones of a house with a mountainous avalanche of rubble flooding through, taking walls down with it and flinging them like shingle out across the street. From up above, ash and dust drifted down. It covered the road in thick silt, and the tyres kicked it up around them so that it fell on their hands and Owen's trousers and got caught in Janek's hair.

Bulldozers were shovelling up broken brick and debris into huge heaps.

'We're trying to clear the main through-roads first,' Turner yelled back to them. 'I tell you, though, no sooner have you cleared one bit than a block falls down some place else and the goddamn road gets blocked again. I swear, this thing's gonna take weeks.'

Their route did appear rather circuitous. Turner seemed an erratic driver and was constantly swerving to miss a blasted hole in the road, or a canister that had blown across it, or a splay of bricks where a wall had come down. Twice they found their route blocked, and Anderson scanned the map for a way around while Turner threw the jeep into reverse and backed speedily up the road or made a sharp three-point turn, reversing over rubble, wood and broken glass.

The high buildings that were still upright cast cold shadows across the street. Owen looked up at the blown-out windows, the iron balconies, and the white sheets or pillowcases hanging from them in submission. Janek tipped his head back too, his eyes wide with disbelief. Irena kept her own gaze locked on the road, coughing as the smoke billowed into their faces. Occasionally dusty children could be seen scuttling like beetles over the brick slags, covered in the same dirt that blew in scurvy waves across the road. Old men sat in doorways; with their motionless grey pallor they looked like ancient gargoyles guarding the entrance to a troglodyte world.

* * *

The new US Military Government headquarters was on Leibnizstraße, off what once must have been a busy intersection. Most of the line of houses was still intact: tall, narrow windows lined up along each floor in a style that was almost Georgian, and smaller basement windows that peeped warily like half-closed eyes over the top of the pavement.

Turner pulled up outside. A couple of soldiers with steel helmets were forming a loose guard outside the double doors. From open windows at the top of the adjacent building, the crackly sound of a big band could be heard, and further down the street voices from a wireless.

'Here you go,' said Anderson. He opened his door and got out, nodding at one of the soldiers standing outside, then helped Irena out with the baby, Owen and Janek following.

As Turner and Anderson drove off Owen stood on the pavement and looked up at the countless windows.

The two US privates on the entrance wouldn't let them in. Owen had to admit, they must have looked like an unlikely troop of vagabonds. He went through the speech he'd rehearsed in his head. No, he didn't have any papers, but he was a pilot, British government business, and he had not come all this way to be left on the doorstep.

The two soldiers standing between him and the entrance looked at his clothes.

'Do you honestly believe I would have got halfway across Germany in a British uniform?' he said.

They saw his point but still weren't going to allow Irena and Janek in.

'No refugees, sir,' one of them said. 'Strictly military personnel.'

'At least let the girl through.'

'We're not supposed to let any refugees in,' the man said.

'Especially her lot,' added the other.

'And whose lot is that exactly?' said Owen.

Before the man had a chance to answer there was a voice across the street.

'These two not playing ball?'

The woman was in uniform: light brown pocketed jacket with a red felt title badge stitched to one shoulder, a black glove folded over the top of one pocket, a cream blouse, and army green skirt and cap. She had a document case full of papers under her arm. She pulled at the other glove still on her hand as she walked briskly towards them, her heels crunching on the gravel in the road.

'English?' she said, the accent cheery American.

'Yes,' said Owen.

The only American woman he'd taken much notice of before was Loretta Young. He'd been to see her three times in *The Unguarded Hour* when it had played at the Regal Cinema on Richmond Road. This woman had the same dark curls held in place with a clip.

'Well, that's great. C'mon, Teddy,' she said to one of the men. 'Don't be such a spoiler and let the good man in.'

'It's these two that are the problem, miss,' he said. 'Rules, 'n' all.'

'Oh, rules, snooze,' she said. She took a look at Little Man crying in Irena's arms. 'Wowsers, you've got some lungs. Yours?' she asked Irena. Her smile widened and Irena nodded. 'Sweet.'

Then her eyes scanned Janek up and down. 'As for you . . . Let me guess. *Čech?*'

Owen had no idea how she had been able to tell. The boy grinned.

'I knew it. Damn.' She clicked her fingers. 'This girl's been here too long. You're coming in then, Mister Airman?' She took Owen's arm and glanced at the others, Irena jigging the baby and Janek shouldering his bag. 'Don't worry,' she said to them, 'I'll send him out when we're done.'

* * *

The smartly dressed American lady deposited him in a reception where there was a desk, a secretary and a row of hard-backed seats that gave it the rather uncomfortable air of a well-to-do doctor's surgery. At one side of the room was a set of high double doors. Walnut, Owen thought, or oak, with vines and flamboyantly feathered birds carved into the panels. The woman went to introduce him to the receptionist but she was on the telephone and then they were both distracted by a booming voice coming down the stairs.

'Well, my Lord, would you believe it — '

'Oh my God!' the woman squealed. 'Charlie!'

'Where in devil's name have you been hiding?'

And that was rather the end of it. The pristinely dressed Charlie swept her out of the room, all excitable chatter, and the woman made a vague gesture to Owen to indicate that she was all but a helpless damsel in the company of this man, telling him that the receptionist — Owen hadn't caught her name — would help for sure, and really the colonel was a softy, all bark and no bite. They disappeared, laughing, up the stairs, and Owen took one look at the receptionist, who was giving someone on the telephone an earful, and snuck instead into the toilets to quietly gather himself.

The room was small and a little shabby, and beside the cubicle and a porcelain sink that needed a scrub there wasn't much else to it. The window was open and outside he could hear a commotion — Janek's voice and Little Man's cries and, further down the street, still the distant strains of swing. He leant over the sink and stared into the mirror, trying to pull his thoughts together and compose his story. It was a stroke of luck that had brought them here, but now, faced with an opportunity, he didn't quite know how to handle it.

Each day he seemed to look older and thinner. Once-plump parts of his face were now sinking in, his collarbones like railings, and the skin around his eyes had turned dark. He pressed at his ribs. That bloody ache was still there.

As he filled his cupped hands with water from the trickling tap and held them for a moment to his face, he heard someone crash in behind him, breathless, before the door banged shut and a bolt was hastily pulled across. He turned around.

'Bloody hell. What are you doing?'

She leant back against the door, her hand firmly clutching the handle as she tried to catch her breath.

'I had to see you,' she said.

She wiped at her face as her eyes darted around the room.

'And where's the baby?'

'With Janek.' She went quickly to the window and peered through it, then turned back. 'You do not understand,' she said. 'They were not going to let me in.'

'Well, I know that. What's the matter?'

'I have to tell you,' she blurted. 'Before you see this colonel.'

'What do you mean?'

Her eyes widened. 'You have to help me. You have to make them help me.'

'Yes, I know.' Of course. She meant the baby.

'No, you don't!' She seemed to leap at him.

He raised his hands, trying to pacify her. He had never seen Irena like this, her eyes so wild, stepping anxiously about as if she wanted to pace but there wasn't the room. She pressed her lips together, trying to control herself, and wiped her eyes with the heels of her hand. She took a deep breath.

'The man,' she said, her eyes filling. 'The man that raped me. He was American. An American soldier.'

Owen stared at her.

'Are you sure?'

She nodded.

'Jesus Christ.' He tried to think. 'But . . . My God, Irena, why didn't you tell me?'

'I don't know,' she said. 'I was scared.'

All this time he had known that she was keeping something from him. But did she honestly think that an American here in Leipzig might help them track this man down? She looked so small now in that dirty white dress and the ragged pink cardigan.

'Where did it happen?'

She shook her head. 'I don't know,' she said.

And then: 'In Aachen. It was in Aachen. I tried to stop him. I promise. I didn't want it. You have to tell them. Please.' She drew closer to him, her tears gathering wet around her chin, so that instinctively he backed away, unsure of how to handle her. 'I need them to help me,' she begged. 'Not much, just some money or . . . I don't know, maybe they can give me somewhere to live so I can look after it. I could look after it; I could do that if they helped me. Or, I don't know, fly us away from here — America, I don't care, but they have to help me. They raped me. This man. In Aachen. This American. You have to tell them. Please. It was an American soldier.'

* * *

Colonel Hall would not be seen. The smartly uniformed woman at the reception desk, her arms resting on a leather inlay and fingers rolling a blunt pencil in her hand, was quite firm about that. She reeled off a list of reasons, each one digging her heels in deeper, but Owen was only half listening. He could feel the walls folding in on him. Every sharp tick of the pendulum wall clock chipped a bit of him away.

He had left Irena in the gent's toilet and she had still not reappeared. If she didn't slip out soon she would be found and hauled over the coals — and him with her probably.

'I'll wait,' he said.

'I'm afraid you won't,' said the receptionist. 'I'm going to have to ask you to leave.'

'But I'm British RAF,' he complained.

'And your papers?'

'I don't have any,' he said.

'Proof of identification?'

'I told you!' He could hear his voice rising. 'Isn't my word good enough?'

'Not these days, no,' she said.

'Well, it will bloody well have to be.'

She put the pencil down hard and eyed him over the rim of her glasses with an expression that said: *Well, without any papers, what am I to do?*

Just then the double doors opened and two uniformed men came through. The reception filled with voices.

'Miss Meier here'll sort you out,' the larger of the two said, motioning at the receptionist.

That must be the colonel, Owen thought. He had broad enough shoulders, an eagle badge sewn on each.

'It's a damn mess, though,' he said. 'You'd think these people would be begging for jobs, but no. No, I reckon they're just about used to getting everything done for them.'

'Well, we're gonna have to teach 'em somethin' 'bout that, sir,' said the other. He was young and puppyish, more gung-ho than was necessary.

The colonel smiled thinly, a hand at the man's elbow that clearly signalled: *Off you go*.

'Yes, well . . . I'll be seeing you, Bill. And, don't forget, I'll be needing those cables . . .'

They shook hands again and said goodbye. As the colonel disappeared back into his office, Owen leapt towards the door.

'Excuse me! Colonel Hall?'

The receptionist bolted from her seat. 'Hey! Sir!'

But Owen had already pushed against the closing door and into the room.

'Sir, I said no!'

The colonel had barely got midway across his office.

'So sorry, sir,' Owen and the receptionist both said. She was teetering in the doorway.

'I do apologize,' said Owen. 'Flight sergeant. British RAF.' He saluted.

'I don't care what the hell you are, barging in here like a couple of bloody musketeers.'

'I did try to stop him, sir.'

'I don't rightly care,' snapped the colonel.

'I just need five minutes of your time, sir,' said Owen.

'I don't have five minutes,' said the colonel. 'And who the hell are you anyway? You got an appointment?'

'No, sir, he certainly does not,' said the receptionist tartly.

'No,' admitted Owen, 'and I wouldn't ask, only . . . ' Only now he couldn't think and the colonel was staring. 'Please,' he said. 'You have to see me. I wouldn't ask if I wasn't desperate.'

He could feel his insides melting. He was shaking, everything that was keeping him upright seeming to fall away.

The colonel stared at him, drawing in his pale lips. 'Goddamn it, all right. Five minutes. And that's your lot. Understand?' He looked Owen up and down and moved back to his chair. 'You look like some godforsaken farm boy,' he said, sitting back down heavily. 'British RAF?'

'Yes, sir. Sorry about making an entrance like that, sir.'

'Yeah, well . . . And don't think about sitting down,' he said. He stared at Owen as he stirred a cup of tea on his desk.

Owen heard the door close. He glanced around the room, at the paintings dotted around the walls, mostly pastoral scenes he noted, and the spot above the colonel's desk where a single picture had been removed and there was a rectangle of panelling that was slightly darker than the rest.

'Well?' said the colonel, tapping the spoon against the rim with finality. 'Go on then.'

The room felt unbearably hot, even with the sash window open. Owen drew himself up to his full height. With relief he could hear Irena's voice in the street outside.

'I'd like to report a missing person, sir,' he said, trying at last to catch his breath.

It wasn't what he had planned to say first but it came out of his mouth anyway.

The colonel put the spoon down. 'Oh yeah?' he said. 'And who the hell might that be?'

* * *

The telling of the story was not as simple as it should have been. It had no beginning and even the middle was a tangle.

He had been in a camp, he eventually said, some days' walk east from Leipzig.

'But what happened before that or how I got there, sir, I don't know.'

His memory, he told the colonel — bits of it were gone, broken away, and he was only now starting to reclaim it.

'And then I woke up in a field,' he said, 'and I was in Czechoslovakia, and that's where I met Janek, sir. And Irena, well, she came later. She's the one with the baby.'

'The baby?'

'Yes, sir.' He wasn't explaining himself at all well. He'd come back to the baby later. The problem was that it was all so muddled. 'I wish I could remember what had happened, but I can't. I don't even know where I'm going. I just need to get home.'

'And where's that?' said the colonel.

'Well, I worked in Kingston, sir. I know that. I was a draughtsman at Hawkers.'

'The planes?'

'That's right, sir. Designing Hurricanes and whatnot, and then . . . then . . . ' Well, that's when it started to blur.

'But I thought you said you were a pilot,' said the colonel.

'Yes. I am, sir.'

'But you don't remember?'

'No, sir. Not exactly. I get flashes of flying. I can see it in my head. I can see the cockpit, the instrument panel. I know all the systems. I could draw you any sort of gauge you like, sir: engine oil pressure, oil temperature, coolant temperature, fuel tank, you name it. I know how to read them all.'

'That doesn't make you a pilot.'

'I'm telling you, sir, I flew Avro Lancasters. Mark three. Great big birds,' he said, wanting to shout it out. 'With Max.'

'Max?'

'My brother.'

'And he's there in your head as well, is he?'

Owen lost his temper. 'Look, I'm telling you, I flew. We flew together — Max and I — and I lost him. I bloody lost him.'

He took a gasp of breath. The man across the desk leant back in his chair, the wooden legs slowly creaking. Owen didn't even know what he was doing there any more.

'Okay, so backtrack,' said the colonel. 'Let's go back to this camp of yours.' He jotted something down on a pad beside his elbow. 'Now let me see, was that before you flew or after?'

'After.'

'Only I'm getting confused.'

'It was after, sir. I flew — we flew — and then I was in the camp. And then I woke up and I was in this field. And I don't know what happened.'

'Right. And where exactly was this field?'

'I don't know.'

'And the camp?'

'I don't know. I don't remember. Look, a place called . . . ' He rubbed his head and tried to think. There *had* been names but now he couldn't think of them. Places and people. 'I've been there,' he said. 'I went. I went with Janek. We saw it.'

'But it had a name? This camp?'

'Yes,' he said. 'It would have had a name, but

no, I don't know.' He was getting confused, his head clogged with so much that he couldn't think straight. 'Look, perhaps I wrote it down,' he said, suddenly remembering. 'I've been writing everything down that comes to me, trying to piece it together. And I've got it here. See? I've been writing it down. I'll show you.'

He would lay it out on the desk for the colonel and it would all come back to him: all the names and numbers and circles and arrows, the blueprint for remembering.

He put his hand in his pocket for it and then the other pocket, but there was only a worn-down pencil, the broken watch and bits of grit and thread. Even the square of material was gone. He checked the jacket pocket and then the trouser pockets again, and the jacket for a second time.

'It's a square piece of paper,' he said, still searching. 'It's folded, and I have it. It's here somewhere. Everything's written on it. I promise. I've got it. I've got it. It's just . . . ' He checked the trouser pockets again, digging around in them. He could feel the panic filling him. 'I had it just here,' he said, 'just now. It was here, I'm telling you.'

He checked the breast of the jacket where something else had once been, then fumbled around within the shirt, thinking he might have slipped it inside for some reason, or perhaps it had fallen out where the button was missing; not the button he had but a smaller one, a different one. He looked on the floor for it. No, it was the letter he needed. No, not the letters. He'd thrown the letters away. It was a piece of paper.

A fucking piece of paper with everything he knew on it and now —

'All right, now calm yourself, son.'

'No!' he shouted. 'You don't understand. I was lost. I've lost everything. I've walked for, I don't know, ten *fucking* days, and all I want,' he said, slamming his hand down on the desk, 'is some *fucking* help!' He stood back, aghast.

'I think you need to sit down, soldier,' said the colonel calmly.

Owen sank into the chair, then leant forward for a moment and held his head in his hands, sobbing. He couldn't stop himself. His fingers fumbled in the jacket, but there was nothing there, not even the square of material.

The colonel rubbed at the back of his neck. 'All right,' he said. 'I'll get you home. If that's what you want.'

Owen looked up.

'We got planes going back and forth to England all the time these days. Half of our boys are probably still over there. After that you're on your own, course, but gets you out of this hellhole and back in the fold.'

The relief flooded through him. 'Thank you,' he said, his voice barely a whisper.

'Yeah, well . . . I've got enough to worry about here sorting out these cocksuckers without the likes of you.' The colonel smiled as if perhaps he didn't mean that, then wiped the back of his finger under his nostrils and took a deep breath. 'I hope that's all, mind.'

Owen hesitated. 'Yes,' he said, despite himself. 'Thank you.'

Any moment to say anything about Irena had already passed.

The colonel picked up the telephone. 'I'll speak to Miss Meier. Be here tomorrow morning. And no more favours. Although I guess you'll be wanting somewhere to sack down?'

'Yes,' he said. 'Thank you.'

'Oh, and think yourself lucky,' the colonel said. 'By my watch you've just had double your time.'

Owen nodded and stood up. The man held the telephone receiver to his ear, waiting for Owen to leave.

'Sorry, sir,' said Owen as he got to the door, hoping that something else might be salvaged, 'but the boy I'm with, he's looking for someone. His brother.'

The colonel stared.

'If you were to make a suggestion as to where to start looking for someone . . . ?'

'What is he?' said the colonel.

'Czech.'

The colonel put the phone down, giving up on the call.

'Listen, we've spent the last God knows how long trying to sweep these refugees up. Believe me, it ain't easy. And my problem's getting this city up and running again: safeguarding a supply of food, clearing out the rubble . . . We've an infrastructure that's blown to hell — water, electricity, tramlines, you name it. Accommodating these people is just one of a hundred problems. Then we got Heinie living here up in arms cos they reckon we're gonna hand them over to the goddamn Ruskies.'

'And are you?' said Owen.

'All these displaced persons, we're trying to clear them out, sending them to camps while we work out a way to get them home.' He took a deep breath. 'Listen, pilot — you want my advice? You can't think about these people no more. They're not your concern.'

'You've not heard of a Czech called Petr Sokol?'

'Nope.'

'He's some sort of Czech hero, I think.'

'If you mean a resistance fighter, they're ten to a dozen these days. I swear to God, you own a house in Prague you probably can't cross your kitchen to take a damn piss without tripping over a revolutionary propping up your table. Heroes are cheap tender these days. They're easier to find than bread. And I know what I'd rather have. Now, go on, beat it,' he said. 'Or I'm gonna forget to make this call.'

He picked up the receiver and dialled a single number. Owen could hear the phone ringing out in reception.

'All right, Miss Meier, send her in,' the colonel said. 'And while I got you on the line . . . '

Owen was already opening the door. The woman he had met out in the street was standing in reception with her back to him. She turned as he came through with a raised eyebrow and the slight twist of a smile.

'Oh, it's you holding things up,' she said.

'Sorry,' Owen blustered. 'Government business.'

She laughed. 'I doubt that. Oh, and by the way, your baby's crying.'

'It's not mine.'

'Well, that's not what she said.'

Owen smiled awkwardly. 'It's a marriage of convenience,' he joked, but she was already through the door.

'It seems, Flight Sergeant,' said the woman at the reception desk, emphasizing each syllable with a degree of petulance, 'that I'm lumbered not only with organizing a car but also finding you accommodation.'

'Well, if that's not too much trouble,' he said.

The woman sighed. It clearly was. 'For one, I presume.'

'Three, actually. And an infant.'

The woman raised her eyes to the ceiling and sighed again.

'Be here at seven o'clock sharp tomorrow morning then, sir,' she said. 'I really don't want to have to deal with you again.'

* * *

The building was a former hotel in a narrow street not far from the blown-out remains of Katharinenstraße. All the habitable rooms were housing military personnel now, bar the remaining part of the attic where they were to be accommodated. Half of the roof had fallen away, along with the building beside it. Rumour had it, their driver told Owen, that every brick and board of the house had tumbled down but for a mantelpiece on which a fish bowl had been found, still intact, and with a single goldfish still swimming in it.

As they were led in through the door and up the narrow stairs, a woman and a trail of three children squeezed past, being hurriedly ushered down by a yelling soldier, each of them dragging a suitcase, the sleeve of a knitted mauve jumper trailing out of one.

A US corporal poked his head over the banisters. 'Flight Sergeant?' he called down to Owen. 'All yours now!'

The attic was filled with hotel paraphernalia: broken desk chairs; a pile of mirrors; old wooden coat hangers that had been broken into firewood; a washing line strung up across the room, hung with several dusty tea towels. Two sets of screens divided the attic in three. One had a tin bath in it; the other two each had a shallow single mattress. The colonel's receptionist, despite her haughtiness, had acquired them a Moses basket and sent it on ahead. There were holes in the roof where falling shrapnel had come through, one piece with such force that it had smashed a hole in the floor as big as a footprint. When they crouched down they could spy an American GI through it, asleep on a bed, the fingertips of one hand tucked into the waistband of his trousers, and a half-drunk bottle of red wine that had tipped and leaked like blood into his boot.

'It will be good if it does not rain,' said Irena.

'No. One, two,' said Janek, ostentatiously counting the mattresses. '*Ne, ne*. No good.'

'Yes,' said Owen. 'Someone's going to have to share, I'm afraid. Share. Yes?' He held two fingers up, pressed together. 'We can argue about that later.'

When he glanced down into the street, the woman and children they had passed on the stairs were still standing out on the pavement surrounded by their cases and bags.

'You did not tell him, did you?' said Irena.

She put the sleeping baby into the basket and watched as the infant stirred, and then looked at Owen, waiting for an answer. He felt the shame burning in him.

'I thought you were going to help me. I thought you cared.'

'I'm sorry,' he said. 'I didn't see what good it would do.'

Her eyes filled. 'Yes, well . . . ' She turned away. 'Now we will not know.'

* * *

He picked his way through the labyrinths of rubble where paths had been cleared. A group of dishevelled women were trying to right a tram that was burnt out and laid across the street like a barricade. It was grey, as everything else was, and looking old and dusty. When he passed the half-shattered window front of a looted tobacconist, he caught himself in the glass looking old and dusty too.

It seemed almost impossible that England might be how he had left it. Were these the sights in London as well, he wondered — his neat and tidy draughtsman's desk now covered in bits of rubble, and the window that he had always propped open with a shoe now broken, shards of glass across his drawing board and shattered beneath his seat? Was the house in Hampshire as ruined as these were, or that small rented flat with the geraniums on the steps outside, each pot cracked and broken, the plants flung and hanging down like boneless limbs between the slatted steps? Or perhaps they had survived. Perhaps, as miraculously as the goldfish bowl, they were still there and stark in their colour, while around them everything else had been blasted to grey.

He sat for a moment in a square where only a single lamp-post was left standing and watched as a couple of women in fur coats poked around among the bricks, picking things out to put into a battered pram.

He closed his eyes. His thoughts scattered. He kept thinking of the Stowe House Hotel, and then of a child in white ankle socks and smart red sandals, a child he couldn't place. The New Year's Eve party came back to him: the crush in the banqueting hall spilling out into the hotel foyer and then further out into the cold, where some of the guests from the bomber squadron and their partners stood around laughing and insulated by a concoction of alcohol and festive cheer.

The hall, he remembered, had been unbearably hot, the windows all steamed up and the paper chains crushed and damp against them like lines of languid thoughts. There had been a sea of heads and rumbling voices, and through it all the heavy blasting of the band, while reverb from the microphones occasionally cut across the room, slicing conversations in two.

He had felt perilously drunk and uncomfortable in his service dress, his sweat having soaked right through his shirt. In the spirit of the evening, most of them still had their masks on. The Venetian-themed ball had been the station commander's idea. *So you'd better keep the damn thing on*, Max joked, *if you want a chance of getting out on a sortie any time soon*.

She was there. From behind the anonymity of the mask he had found it almost impossible not to look at her, although now, sitting in the rubble and in an altogether different life, he couldn't picture her at all other than the black velvet of her dress and how it had drawn his attention to the paleness of her skin. Barnes and Budgie were close by, shouting over the din about the rum punch that nobody was touching because some fool, Barnes announced, had spilt milk in it. Owen couldn't help but look at the nape of Connie's neck, thinking then, as he thought now, of kissing it, or the thin ridge of her collarbone that led his eyes down into her dress. Perhaps he would have every bit of her that Max hadn't touched: a spot on her neck, a handful of freckles, an earlobe that he might gently press between his lips.

With one hand at his thigh beside her, Owen hadn't been able to stop a finger lifting to touch, all too briefly, the back of her wrist, before hooking it around her own finger. And she had not pulled it away. The smile had been no more than a hint but he had caught it nevertheless.

* * *

He would leave them and this time tomorrow he would be in a car or on a plane or maybe even back in England, being questioned by the War Office in a smart room in Westminster. In London, at least, there would be people who knew him: there would be records and addresses and names and photographs. His life might even be presented back to him, a string of hard and solid facts that he could thread back together like beads on a necklace.

He had searched through his belongings again but the paper and all that was on it was gone, lost on the road somewhere or fallen from his pocket in the chaos of the receiving centre and trodden underfoot.

He had found the square of material though, sewn into the inside breast of the jacket once more, and the heart rethreaded with neat red stitches. When he put the jacket on again, he could feel it beating against his as if it were alive.

A wave of anger and shame washed through him as he crossed another rubble-strewn street. Why hadn't he told the colonel about Irena? He felt as if he'd betrayed her with his silence, his weak-willed hesitation. *You should not trust anyone*, she had said to him, and he had proven her damn right.

It wasn't that he didn't trust her, he decided, or pity her, or care. It was just that . . . Well, she was so silent sometimes, clamming up over questions she didn't like, and when she did speak it was with such brusqueness that it often took him by surprise. He didn't know how to deal with her or with the way she looked at him, as if she wanted something from him that she could not, dare not, say.

Of course he felt sorry for her, protective over her now in a way that he had not felt earlier. He wanted to ask her what exactly had happened with this American, but he knew that he wouldn't. He thought instead of his mother caring for babies abandoned after the last war. They hadn't all been fathered by dead men, she had told them. Many more had been conceived in a similar manner to this one, he now realized; although, of course, his mother had always been too refined to say exactly what that was.

He needed to somehow ensure that Little Man would be all right. Yet tomorrow Owen would be gone and it would be out of his hands. When he got back to the hotel he would apologize. And tomorrow morning at the military government quarters he would damn well say what he should have said, what Irena had told him to say: that the US army owed her.

He found himself on a street called Klostergasse, and then, passing the entrance to a blown-out shopping arcade, the coloured tiles on the ceiling cracked and dusty, he caught a glimpse of a child running past at the other end, not dissimilar to a child that he had seen before in his mind. White socks. Smart sandals. A child that kept coming back to him, sitting on a bench opposite him in a room that was small and crammed with people. She held a bear with a missing eye and the sunlight, in his mind's eye, was flickering far too fast across her face.

A lorry's engine popped and she was gone from his thoughts. He was at a junction but although he stopped, unsure, he had no choice but to turn left on to Nicholaistraße, the other roads being blocked. Every bombed street looked the same so that it was hard to tell one from another, and it wasn't long before he realized he was lost. He sat on a fallen slab of concrete while he tried to get his bearings. On the street in front of him a satchel was crushed into the dust. On the other side, two sparrows were drinking rainwater from the remnants of a broken plate. All the days that were stacked behind him, and all the things that had been said and had happened, were starting to feel like strange dreams. None more so than the day before. All the things Janek had said still circled in his mind.

He stood up and dusted the dirt from his trousers. From several buildings down, where a blast had taken half a house away, a flurry of wind lifted sheets of newspaper from the arm of a chair that teetered on the cliff of a living room and carried them over the edge. He watched as they blew across the road, and for a while, until they dropped, it was as if they had come to life and were flying like wide-winged birds.

* * *

When he got back to the hotel, a water mains had burst and the ground floor was three inches under water. He slopped through the hallway as people swept it out in waves on to the street, where it swilled around in the dust and tailed away trying to find a drain. When he reached the attic the door was ajar and he could hear them: the rhythmic pants and the fidget of floorboards.

Against his better judgement, he allowed his gaze to fix on the gap in the door. They were on the floorboards beside the bare mattress, Janek gripping on to it with one hand while he pushed into her, his small buttocks clenching and his dirty toes on the floor, the veins worming in his neck. Irena had him clamped between her knees, her unshaven armpits black and bristling. She made soft gasps, her hands sprawled at his back where his bony spine ran like a mountain ridge. Then she turned her head. She had seen him. Tears rolled down her cheeks but she did not take her eyes from Owen.

* * *

They shared the bath water, one after the other so that by the time Owen got in, it was no more than a few inches deep and dirty, but he washed himself in it anyway, picking off the curling hairs of someone else that attached themselves to his skin.

Irena appeared from around the screen, clothed again but her hair still sopping.

'I found a clean cloth,' she said. 'You can have it.'

'This water is filthy.'

'I had to wash him out of me.' She walked over to the side of the tub and stood there looking at him as he covered himself with his hand.

'Can I have some privacy?' he said. 'And the cloth then.'

She still had it in her hand.

'Do you like watching people fuck?'

'I don't know what you're talking about.'

Her stare was making him self-conscious, sitting in no more than a dirty puddle with only a hand defending his dignity.

'Look, can I just have five minutes to myself, please?'

'You did not answer the question.'

'I don't know,' he said. 'Do you like people watching?'

'Sit up.'

She scooted him forward in the tub and then, hoisting up her skirt, she stepped into the bath behind him.

'What are you doing?'

She perched on the rim of the bath with him sitting between her knees and leant over his shoulder to soak the cloth.

'Lean back,' she said. 'Don't you want to be clean?'

'I want some time on my own,' he told her.

'I don't believe you,' she said.

She took the cloth from the water and began to clean his back. And he didn't stop her. He let her toes nestle under his buttocks. He let her take the cloth over his shoulders, rub at his neck, covering him with all their dirty water. He let her; and he said nothing. He let her run the cloth down one arm and then the next, lifting the hand that covered himself and then the other that had taken its place; and he felt her breath against the side of his neck, the press of her body against him; and when she reached over him once again, she dropped the cloth and it was only her hand that took water down his chest. She leant over him, her fingers sliding down his stomach, down, down . . .

'Don't,' he said.

'What?'

'Don't.'

She sat back up.

'Do you wish I was your lover?' she said.

'Don't play games,' he told her.

'I'm not.'

'You'll get your fingers burnt.'

'We are all burnt,' she said. 'We are past saving. All of us.'

She put a hand on his shoulder and squeezed it.

'I said don't. Please.'

'Do you really not remember what she looks like?'

He said nothing.

Then she said, quite matter-of-factly, 'Perhaps she looks like me.'

He stood up abruptly and stepped out, the water draining from him, grabbed a blanket for a towel and wrapped it hastily around him.

'I'm sorry,' she said. 'I didn't mean that.'

But it was too late. It was said.

* * *

Pushing through the crowd of party revellers, he searched for Connie. Max was missing too. He forced his way out into the hallway and then into the bar, but she wasn't there and nor were they in the library. How was it that he had got so drunk? He could feel his senses disengaging, masked faces becoming a blur.

He stumbled up the wide staircase, tripping over the lip of a step and gathering himself again, before he pushed against a flow of people all cascading down.

Max! he called. *Are you up there?*

Then, *Connie! Connie!* he yelled.

Along the landing he found guest rooms and tried a few at random, but they were all locked. A group of revellers in uniforms and evening gowns were coming down the corridor, arms lolling over each other, giggling. He held himself against the wall as they passed, then called out again, louder, the hubbub of the party below ringing in his ears.

Was that when she had appeared, coming from a doorway or out through an arch? She looked like a fox, her eyes and nose covered beneath the black snout of the mask. She stood midway down the corridor, where one of the light bulbs was blinking, her back to the wall and her eyes fixed on him. He went to her.

Are you all right?

I don't know you, she said to him. It had almost been a whisper.

He laughed. *Of course you do. It's* — He went to lift his mask but she said: *No. Don't*.

She rested her hand on his jacket and through the eyeholes of her disguise she looked at him, her lips opening wider and her fingertips curling and closing around his lapel. He knew then that he should pull away. He was aware of the rise and fall of her chest, the quiver of her breath.

Then, with a glance down the corridor, he had kissed her, soft at first and then harder, her hands at the back of his head and around his shoulder, pulling him into her, kissing him hard. Behind those masks, they might later have said, they could have been anyone. They could have been nothing but strangers, caught in a moment's mistake. But they weren't, and he kissed that earlobe, that neck, that collarbone. Then he pushed her forcefully against the wall. He would take those lips, that breast.

⋆ ⋆ ⋆

He woke to the sound of crying. Then he realized that it was not the baby. It was Janek, sitting on the floor with his back to the attic wall and his arms wrapped tight around his knees. In the darkness of the night, he was sobbing like a child.

Owen sat up, the figure across the room like a mound of deeper blackness gathered against the wall, and the other side of the mattress where the boy had been sleeping now cold to the touch. Janek's crying came in quivering blasts of breath and, as the clouds above them thinned, the moonlight seeping in through the small window and the holes in the ceiling gave a silvery sheen to his face. Owen saw the tears seeping down his cheek like oil.

He crossed the room and sat down beside him, their shoulders almost touching. He didn't know what to say or do, other than to lightly rest his hand on the boy's knee so that the boy could be sure he was there. The foliage of darkness drew in around them again as the clouds pulled back over. He could vaguely make out the silhouette of Irena sprawled across her own mattress as if she had been washed up on a raft, carried in on the tide of her breath.

How far they had come, he thought, his hand still resting on Janek's knee as the boy sniffed and quietly gasped through his tears. And yet, how little he knew of them both. He had no idea how many days he and Janek had travelled, this boy who had appeared out of nowhere and had insisted on being with him as if there was something deeper that had threaded them together; something passing between them even now, in the shared warmth of hand to knee.

And in that hour that they sat, and maybe with that touch, like sand it quietly sifted in and he slowly remembered. Everything, he realized, that the boy had said was true. This boy beside him had pulled him from the river, and now his hand, his thin fingers, the now familiar arm of his jacket were there in Owen's memory, where maybe they had always been — two hands that had dragged him out by the armpits, struggling with his sodden weight and the cold rush of water pummelling so hard around them.

He had dragged him out and Owen remembered being hauled up a bank through the trees, the grass pulling away from under him, and the struggle to keep himself conscious, a sunset across his eyes like watery blood eventually fading to black. He had woken again, but only for a moment, to hear the boy's struggles and shouts of frustration. He had felt an almost debilitating cold spreading through him, and the ebb and flow of consciousness slipping; and as it did — before the darkness closed over him completely — he was vaguely aware of two shots and then another, and in the darkness the boy had run.

He felt the press of a shoulder, his hand still there on a knee. Janek had stopped crying but for some time neither of them moved. They listened to the sounds of Irena and the baby sleeping, while outside across the graveyard of a city, the night was strangely silent and darker than it had ever been.

MARTHA

The plane came and went without him, and he wondered what the hell he had done.

At dawn he had slipped with purpose from the attic and down the narrow stairs, leaving them asleep. No note, no goodbye; he would simply disappear. But at the entrance to the thick-bricked building on the corner of Leibnizstraße, he hesitated and dropped into a crouch, his back to the wall. The early morning sun washed light down the street, casting the receptionist's shadow as she walked around the front of the building looking for him, her footfall echoing as she complained to the driver who was meant to take him to the airfield. *Seven o'clock. I was quite clear. And now here we are, quarter past.*

He closed his eyes and tried to decide. This wasn't about Irena and Janek, he told himself; this was about him. There was the car. Just bloody well go. But in his mind he couldn't get past them: the boy sobbing in the dark, a boy he had come so far with and to whom he realized now he owed so much; or the weight of his guilt about Irena; or even the feeling of Little Man's hand around his finger. To leave them now felt like another betrayal, even as he kept telling himself not to be an idiot, to step out with whatever mouthful of apologies he could think of and get into the car.

Two lives. You owe me.

Well, didn't he owe them both? He needed to protect them. He was a British pilot, for God's sake. Where was his sense of duty?

Get into that car and drive away and he would never know what happened to them. Could he live with that? Could he be so selfish as to abandon them, and make the same mistake again — just as a voice kept telling him that somehow he had done with Max?

He waited for that instinctive lurch to kick him into action at the last moment, to propel him out from behind the corner with a raised hand and a cheery *sorry I'm late*, but the kick did not come.

The receptionist said something to the driver. The car door slammed. He heard the engine starting, still wondering why the hell he wasn't moving, but he didn't, and the car drove off.

⋆ ⋆ ⋆

They had to leave the attic room and so there seemed no option but to walk. The road was busy with refugees and took them west towards the city of Halle. They had not walked much more than three miles, the suburbs of Leipzig giving way to fields, when the jeep pulled up.

The woman in the driver seat called to them: 'Hey! I remember you four. You guys wanna lift?'

It was the American woman. His Loretta Young. And now here she was in an open-topped jeep. She peeled the sunglasses from her eyes and looked them up and down.

'Jeez, you guys are like the goddamn League of Nations.'

Irena pulled the headscarf tighter over the back of her head and considered the woman with suspicion. Little Man was still bawling, his tiny purple face screwed up in anger and his tight fists flailing.

'Is this little woodchip all right?' she asked.

'I don't know,' said Owen. 'He's been like this all morning. He won't keep anything down,' he added.

The child had certainly worsened. When you held him in your arms you could feel the heat burning from him, and earlier he had leaked a foul-smelling diarrhoea all over Janek's arm.

'You'd better hop in,' she said. 'He doesn't look at all right. Where you troops off to, anyway?'

'Not sure,' said Owen. 'We're trying to locate a few people. The colonel mentioned some camps.'

'*Ano*. Petr Sokol,' Janek said. He took his wallet from his pocket and pulled out the photograph.

The woman's glance was cursory. 'Nice.'

'His brother,' explained Owen.

'*Můj bratr*.'

'Yes, and . . . ' Owen looked at Irena. He realized that for all this time he'd thought they had been looking for the baby's father and now it turned out that he was an American GI.

'So you're going where exactly?' said the woman.

'North,' he said.

'That specific, huh?' She had a point. 'Good job I stopped then. I'm on my way to a place near Celle,' she said, 'if that helps, and you've got the guts for it. It's not exactly home from home but there's a hospital and some medical support for the little one, and then perhaps from there — ' she nodded at Irena and Janek — 'we can maybe see about getting you guys home.'

Other people in the road were beginning to show interest in them and had stopped to look or were sidling closer, eyeing the jeep's empty seats that could take them anywhere and the boxes piled in the back that might be food or medicine.

'Well, are you coming or not?' she said. 'If it's not you, it'll be someone else.'

They clambered in, Owen in the front, the others piling in the back between the boxes, a shovel and an Olivetti typewriter squeezed in on its side. Then the woman parped the horn to clear the road and they pulled out, Janek giving an exclamation of delight as her foot pressed hard to the pedal and the jeep accelerated.

'So, how did it go with my uncle?' she yelled, over the sound of the engine and whistling air as they picked up speed.

He didn't know what she was talking about.

'The colonel,' she said.

'Colonel Hall's your uncle? I didn't know.'

She laughed. 'Why would you? I didn't tell you. And he sure as hell won't. Don't worry — it's only through marriage. Although for how long, God knows. That will be down to Roger, my husband.' She glanced at him, both hands at the wheel as they hit a bump and the jeep lurched. In the back Janek whooped. 'Some of us have been fighting a war on all fronts,' she said, 'if you know what I mean.'

'Oh,' he said. 'I'm sorry.'

'Ah, heck, don't be. I'm not. Anyway, I don't think you rightly answered the question.'

'Oh, well . . . He was rather nice.'

'You mean an idiot, right?' she said.

'No. He did organize a car and a flight home, actually.'

'Both of which you've turned down by the looks of things,' she said. 'You're not going to be very popular. New loyalties?' She motioned with her head to the back of the jeep where the infant mewled against the wind.

'Yes. Something like that,' he said.

'You must be a soft touch.'

* * *

Her name was Martha, a welfare officer with UNRRA — the United Nations Relief and Rehabilitation Agency, she explained.

'Don't worry,' she said. 'No one out here's heard of us. We're new. It's some international set-up, sent out to feed the starving, fix the broken, rehouse the homeless and all that.'

'God,' he said.

'Oh, don't be too impressed,' she said. 'Between you and me, we're making a goddamn mess of it.'

He introduced himself and Irena, who leant forward and said, 'You are a good lady. Thank you.'

'Well, we get your kid fixed, that's good enough for me. Besides, I rarely do a trip out here without someone cadging a lift. You wouldn't believe how hard it is to get gasoline in this place.'

Janek insisted on introducing himself with theatrical gusto, standing up in the back of the jeep and throwing his arms open. 'Janek Vĕnceslav Sokol,' he announced, the wind ruffling furiously at his sleeves. 'I love you, America!'

'That's great,' said Martha, 'but could I ask you to sit down?'

Before long, Janek had the photograph of his brother out again and was leaning through the gap to show it her. 'You know? Petr Sokol.'

'I don't think so.'

'He asks everyone,' said Owen, not meaning it to sound so much like an apology.

'Oh, they're all the same,' she said. 'It's understandable. Half of Europe's been tipped out across the map. No one knows where the hell anyone is. If you're a Polish Jew, you could be anywhere from Westerbork to goddamn Janowska. And that's assuming you're alive.'

'You find Petr?' said Janek, still holding out the photograph.

She laughed. 'I'm sorry but at the moment getting any information is practically impossible. We've got no systems in place yet and besides, there're too many DPs out there. I might as well be trying to hold Lake Michigan in my hand.' She leant back over her shoulder as the jeep slowed, held up by a truck. 'I'll try to find your brother. I'll ask. But I can't make no promises. You understand? *To . . . nebýt . . . možný*. Too many.'

'No,' he said. '*To je možné!* We speak to Czech. Czech people know Petr. Czech people need Petr.'

'He's some sort of resistance fighter, I think,' Owen explained.

'Well, that's one thing we sure as hell don't need,' Martha told him. 'Another rookie revolutionary.'

She swerved to avoid a speeding Russian truck that was veering from side to side. Two Red Army soldiers were leaning out of the window, clasping bottles and yelling. She slammed on the brake to let the truck pass and swore at them. '*Przeklęte dupki!*'

'Russian as well?' he said. 'Goodness.'

'Polish, actually,' she said, 'but I think they got the point.' Then she threw a smile over her shoulder at Irena but Irena did not catch her eye.

* * *

They travelled west, following the River Helme for some way before finally turning north through the town of Nordhausen where, Martha said, only a month ago the British RAF had destroyed three quarters of the town, killing a thousand prisoners.

'Oh, it's okay. Our guys are there now,' she said as they drove through. 'It'll go to the Russians soon though, like Leipzig. They used to build rockets there. V-2s. That's what made it a target.'

The town was devastated. It was becoming a familiar picture. They passed through in silence,

Janek's arm lolling over the side while Irena held the crying infant tight to her chest. They kept having to wipe the dust from their faces.

'A few weeks ago we found a camp,' Martha said, 'just outside of here. It was supplying the workers for the factories. There were five thousand bodies.'

'Five thousand?' said Owen.

Martha sniffed. 'You think that's shocking. That's nothing,' she said.

After a while she pulled over so that Irena could try feeding the baby, who was still bawling, and Martha could fill the petrol tank from a canister she had in the back. She seemed surprisingly capable.

Irena sat in the grass trying to feed Little Man but he was writhing and screaming in her arms and wouldn't take to the breast.

'When we get to the camp I'll ask Dr Haynes to take a look at him,' Martha said to Owen. 'A kid cries for that long and you know something ain't right.' She replaced the petrol cap and screwed the top on the canister. 'What's the story anyway?'

'What do you mean?'

'With the little guy. There's always a story. I take it the baby's not his,' she said, giving a nod at Janek.

'A bit of a sore subject, actually,' he said. 'It's something I should have raised with your uncle.'

'Oh?' She fastened the hook back under the bonnet.

'She says she was raped.'

The bonnet dropped with a clang.

'One of ours?'
'Why do you say that?'
'You wouldn't be 'raising it with my uncle' if it wasn't.'
'That's the point. I didn't and I should have. She specifically asked me and I didn't say a bloody word.'
'Why not? Not buying it?'
'No, it's not that. It's just . . . ' But now he didn't know.
'Where'd it happen, anyway?'
'Aachen, she says.'
Martha leant against the side of the jeep and blew out a puff of air. 'That's quite some haul.'
'Yes, well, I don't know the full story . . . '
'If it was one of our boys, though, I doubt he's going to make himself known, and if he does, well, with so much else going on, the military here have got pretty good at turning their heads.'
'I was rather hoping we could help her.'
'Is that guilt talking?'
'Maybe,' he said. 'I just think she's had a rough deal.'
'Well, if she's a Pole come out of a camp, I'd say you're putting that pretty mildly.'
'Will you talk to her then?' he asked. 'I don't think she wants to be entirely honest with me.'
Martha called something across to Irena in Polish and the girl nodded. Martha gave the bonnet a slap.
'Looks like you boys are all in the back then.'

* * *

They joined the Berlin-Hanover autobahn heading west. Owen had never seen a road like it. Wide and sleek with four lanes, the trees on either side cut right back to allow the road in all its glory to pass through unhindered. It was flat but curved gently through the countryside, the road elegant but in tatters. The concrete was torn up in places by the weight of vehicles that it could not hold and it was littered with holes caused from bomb blasts that created bottlenecks in the traffic where the trucks and cars and lorries ferrying military personnel in and out of Berlin slowed to weave a precarious route around and through the rubble.

From the rear seat he watched Martha and Irena up front, snatches of German and Polish whipped back by the wind. As the road grew clearer Martha accelerated, the sound of the road and the engine and a rattling draught combined into a storm that blew hard across his ears. He stared over the side of the jeep. Beside him, Janek had wrapped the baby within the jacket he was wearing, protecting him from the wind.

Five thousand corpses. It was barely conceivable. *We're just deliverymen*, Max had said. Or perhaps that had been him.

If he let them, the passing fields fused into a blur. He could detach himself from the world that way. The juddering under him felt familiar. The roar of engine noise and pounding of wind. He could hear it shrieking against the windscreen. He could feel how the plane had strained and quaked, the air thundering so hard against it. He could hear voices, people shouting. Owen's eyes closed.

* * *

He was on a train, the fur of hedges whistling past. He kept checking the documents in his hand: names and addresses and a photograph. There had been others that he'd thrown away, or burnt near a woodland pool sitting on a chair, scratching his face from all of them except these still in his hand, sitting on the train with a canvas bag by his side, a number scrawled on it: 4993.

When they empty the camp, we'll need to be ready, someone had said. *Government says we need to stay in line, but if you make a run for it, don't get caught*.

Now he was on a train; how long later, he didn't know, only that through the windows the snow had gone and for some unknown reason he was heading east. The carriage was busy and around him the other passengers seemed agitated. A girl in stark white ankle socks sat opposite him, a suitcase beside her, a bear with one eye sitting in her lap. The train's wheels ground on the tracks and clattered in his chest. The sun blinked and flared through the window, flickering too fast across her face.

The little girl leant to one side and peered along the gangway. They had not spoken all journey but they had been playing a game of shadows. When she leant one way, he leant out the same; when she lifted a finger, he did too. It was like a conversation. Now, when she leant, he did as well, only this time she shook her head and he glanced behind him. Two SS officers were making their way through the crowded aisle and checking papers. He held the documents a little tighter. Where his palm was perspiring it was lifting the ink from the paper and smudging it. His heart quickened. The train jolted. Those standing grabbed at something to steady themselves, then the train tilted again as the track curved.

He carefully peeled his hand away. The ink stains were now there on his fingers. The documents were so clearly a forgery. The little girl had noticed too. Then she looked up at the officers approaching. The train rattled and lurched.

* * *

They left the autobahn, heading north. Janek sat in the front now, holding his hand out to feel the rush of air blowing between his fingers.

They passed through a town called Celle where they crossed a river. Along the streets there were hundreds of old timber-framed houses with the now familiar white sheets still hanging from the windows. The town, Martha said, had saved itself by surrendering. Then they were out in the fields again. The road led them across a heath and through dense and fragrant woods where whole patches had been burnt down-to flush out snipers, Martha revealed. Then they passed through a field, enclosed by trees, where lines of labourers were digging, turning over the soil, and there were boards with skull and crossbones.

They drove alongside some fencing, criss-crossing like the bars of a cage behind the branches of the hedge. Through the blinks of light, mesh of wire and leaves, he kept thinking he could see thin figures and pale lumpy mounds. They had to cover their noses to the stench of burning and the billowing clouds of smoke that blew out across the road. In the distance he could hear the sluggish *chug-chug* of a tractor.

'You said you wanted bringing to a camp,' Martha said, calling back over her shoulder at Owen and Irena. 'Well, folks, here it is.'

They rounded a bend. A single pole crossed the road and there were wooden huts on both sides. A couple of men in familiar-looking battledress raised the barrier and waved them through.

'Here she is, Ron,' one of them said. 'Where the dickens you been?'

'Round and about,' Martha said. 'You boys miss me?'

'Not half,' said the other with a cheeky grin.

'My God,' said Owen, with a sense of relief, 'they're English!'

Martha looked back at Owen and smiled.

* * *

They arrived at some barracks, an area of quadrangles, each consisting of clusters of four-storey buildings that spanned out in every direction as far as he could see.

It had been an old Panzer training school, Martha explained as they pulled up outside a main building.

They clambered out of the jeep, all slightly dazed. Janek wandered, stumbling backwards over his own feet as his head tipped back to see the buildings all around them: solid, concrete, functionary blocks, with rows of regimental windows. One or two faces hung behind the glass like ghouls; a couple of figures leant out through open windows, their thin arms hanging like broken sticks.

In the quad, medical tents had been erected, people in various military and medical uniforms pottering about, oil drums, a charcoal burner, and a couple of women in striped peignoirs sitting on a pile of straw mattresses drawing circles in the dirt.

Irena stood holding the baby tight to her, her gaze skittering about.

''Sall right,' Martha told her. 'Don't worry. You'll be quite safe here.'

Janek stood, his hand to his nose and his eyes screwed up to the stench of sewage and the warm dust that filled the air.

Martha handed him two boxes from the back of the jeep. 'Yep. It's pretty vile but you'll get used to it,' she told him. Owen took the third. 'And this is nothing compared to the camps.'

'This isn't the camp?' said Owen.

'Hell, no. We've ten thousand in here and this is just the camp hospital.'

* * *

The entrance hall of the admin block was full of military personnel, nurses and doctors hurrying through doors, talking in the foyer or passing each other on the curling staircase. *All hands to the pump*, his father would have said. Through partially open doors Owen could see small offices where uniformed men sat behind desks, talking on the telephone or scribbling notes. He felt a strange tangling of relief and confusion, as if he had fallen into another world but taken half of what he knew with him and now, thrown together, neither of them made sense. He had no idea where they were and yet everyone seemed to be English.

'They're all sorts, actually,' Martha said. 'But, yeah, English on the whole. I'm their token American. I reckon they got me down as a loose cannon.'

'And are you?'

'Oh, you have to be here,' she said as her gaze scoured the hallway. 'Otherwise, in my experience, nothing gets done. Oh, look! There he is. That's Hamilton. He's with the military government.'

Hamilton was tall and neat, with a slightly hooked nose and a cap pulled over his eyes. He wore grey British battle-dress, and had a notebook in one hand and a pen in the other that he was clicking furiously. He had the long face of a Dobermann, Owen thought.

'Ah,' Hamilton said, seeing Martha as he passed them and swinging around. 'Jolly good. You're back.'

'Yes. And with your penicillin, I might add.'

'Well done.'

He looked the four of them up and down.

'This lot with you?'

Janek and Irena fidgeted nervously, Irena holding the baby tight to her as if at any moment someone hurrying past might try to whisk him out of her arms.

'Yep,' Martha said. 'Picked them up on the way over. A present from my uncle.'

She made some quick introductions, but Hamilton seemed more concerned about whether they'd been dusted.

'Dusted?' said Irena. She looked terrified.

'DDT,' he said. 'It's regulation.'

'Typhus,' explained Martha. 'Gotta dust you down. It won't take a minute.' She turned to Hamilton. 'Owen here's English.'

'Oh?' said Hamilton. 'Right. God, you're not with Barker's lot, are you?'

'No,' said Owen. 'I fell out of a plane.'

'Oh, well, that's one way of getting here, I suppose,' he said, barely batting an eyelid. 'Certainly beats trying to use the ruddy roads.' He laughed, then leant in close. 'I say, you're not SOE are you?'

Owen had no idea. 'I don't think so, sir.'

'Good. Don't want any of that lot.' He took a closer look at the baby. 'Hello, hello, you don't look very happy.'

'He's sick,' Martha said. 'I'm going to whisk him over to one of the blocks as soon as we're done here. Get Haynes to take a look.'

'Ah, right. Well, what were you thinking

anyway, bringing in a child?'

'I was hardly going to leave the thing outside the gate now, was I? Anyhow,' she said, 'do you want the goddamned penicillin or not? You wouldn't believe the red tape I've had to duck and dodge to get my hands on this.'

She took the first box from Janek and pushed it firmly into the man's hands, then piled the other two on top. 'You owe me a drink. So I'll see you in the mess later — right? You can have mine ready.' She started to usher them out of the hallway, leading Janek by the arm. 'Double Scotch,' she called back to Hamilton standing in the busy hallway, holding the boxes of penicillin, his notebook slipping out from under his arm. 'I want to know what I've missed!'

⋆ ⋆ ⋆

For someone who had been resident in the camp no more than a fortnight, Martha had got herself rather well established. Everybody knew her. The benefit, she claimed, of being practically the only American on site. She had even managed to requisition a small office from a Red Cross liaison officer who had been persuaded to share a desk with a Jewish army chaplain who, Martha claimed, was hardly ever there anyway.

Now she sat at a table made steady with wedges of paper and nothing on it but some forms and a telephone. Owen and Irena sat opposite. Janek had been driven off with a member of the 32nd Casualty Clearing Station to his Czech dormitory in what Martha called

Camp 3, where internees considered healthy again were housed ready for deportation. Owen had said he'd track him down later but Janek still played on his mind. He felt strangely responsible for him and, now that he was out of sight, also a growing anxiety that something wasn't right. Janek would find comfort in being with the other Czechs, he assured himself; the same relief that he was finding among fellow Brits. It was as if he had finally found his voice, and with that his freedom. Another piece of him claimed back. He was almost complete.

'Oh, he'll be fine. You'll be fine,' Martha had said to the boy, but Janek hadn't looked at all sure. They had already started deporting those fit enough to travel, Martha had told them. Five thousand Poles had been despatched to Celle only a few days ago from where they had then caught trains back home.

'I'll try to make sure you're in the next batch of Czechs,' she told Janek, although she couldn't make any promises.

Janek's only concern though was his brother, and he'd stood in the middle of the parade ground shouting out his brother's name to no avail, quite convinced, it seemed, that Petr was there.

Owen, being a British officer of rank, would be bedded in a shared room with an ambulance driver called Wilkins, whom Martha hadn't yet come across but Hamilton vouched was a good sort. As for Irena, she would be placed in a shared room with other Polish women.

'Perhaps a couple of minutes in the office first,

though?' Martha had asked. All DPs needed to be registered, and she took down their details while Little Man was taken to a hospital block to be inoculated and given the once-over.

He half listened while Martha asked Irena questions: name, date and place of birth, last known address . . . She checked Irena's identification papers and handed them back. The girl seemed hesitant in answering anything about herself.

His eyes drifted around the room, which was barely bigger than a cupboard. There was a single shelf on one wall with nothing on it but a box file on its side and a French/German dictionary swollen with damp. A window looked down upon the quad and across to the hospital blocks; the pane was cracked and juddered in its frame every time a truck rumbled past.

'Some of them don't remember,' Martha had told him. 'They know practically nothing about themselves.' You had to find one thing with which to unlock them. A childhood nickname. A memory of some sort. Maybe even an object. 'And then, it's glorious. The door opens,' she said. 'They sit there and they start talking.'

Not Irena though. He saw the slop of bath water and Irena's wet hand on his stomach, her fingers moving down like liquid. Then the thought was gone. He tuned back in. He had missed something and now the half-completed form had been pushed aside.

'What about this incident then,' Martha was saying, 'with this man? You know.'

Irena looked at the floor, pretending not to

understand, then lifted her head again with some purpose, determined now to stare Martha out.

'Look, I'm sorry about what happened,' Martha said. 'I want you to know that. But, well . . . ' She took a breath. 'It wasn't one of our boys now, was it? It wasn't an American soldier who raped you.'

Irena held her stare, then blinked several times. Owen could feel his own chest tightening. He tried to catch Martha's eye. What the hell was she playing at?

'Oh, don't worry,' she went on. 'I don't blame you for lying. We get these kinds of stories all the time.'

He wondered what she meant by that, and how many other Poles like Irena she had questioned before.

'Anyway,' she went on, 'you said yourself that the child is a couple of months old now, yes? Well, you see, the way I look at it, that would mean that even if he was a month premature, whoever did this when you were in Aachen, if you were in Aachen like you said you were — that is right, isn't it?'

She waited for a nod that didn't come.

'Look,' she said, drawing breath, 'what I'm saying to you is that our troops hadn't got as far as Aachen by then. They didn't get there 'til September and the town fell in October. So, like I say, it's a bit unlikely — don't you think? — that it was a US soldier out on patrol like you said it was, given that the baby's a good couple of months old and it's now — what? — only just May.'

She waited for Irena to say something. Owen could feel his heart trying to squeeze its way into his throat. He couldn't believe that she had lied to him, and twice. Why had she made up such stories? What good was it supposed to do? He wondered now if that was why he had hesitated in telling the colonel. If deep within his subconscious he had been questioning her already, even though he had wanted to believe her, to think she'd tell him only the truth?

'Listen, I'm not mad at you,' said Martha softly. 'We're hearing these stories all the time. So, what really happened? Hm? Irena, why don't you just tell me the truth? We can't help you otherwise.'

She leant back in her chair and waited. Owen could hear a heated discussion echoing in the concrete passage below, men's voices babbling like water, then movement in the stairwell, people hurrying. A truck pulled up. More voices. The sun shone through the cracked window, four squares of light splashing across the table and the back of Martha's arm.

Irena moistened her lips. It was as if she were trying to pull out from somewhere within her a voice with which to speak.

'His name is Krzysztof Krakowski,' she eventually managed.

'Krzysztof Krakowski,' Martha said. 'Right.' She wrote the name down; not on the form, Owen noticed, but on a separate scrap of paper. 'That sounds Polish.'

Irena nodded. Her eyes were beginning to fill.

'So you were raped by another Pole. Is that

what you're saying now?'

Irena nodded again.

'Not an American soldier then, like you said.'

Irena started to sob.

* * *

It seemed highly unlikely, in Owen's mind, that of all the Poles swilling around Germany, the one whom Irena was looking for should wash up in this camp. Yet, Martha said, there had been thousands of Poles there. Along with the Russians, they were the biggest contingent in a camp of sixty thousand.

'You don't think she's been here herself?' Owen asked when it was just the two of them.

'No,' said Martha. 'But she's been in a camp somewhere, even if she won't say.'

'How do you know?' he said.

'You don't cut your hair like that out of choice.'

'I don't understand why she didn't just tell me the truth though? What difference would it make?'

'She's desperate. They all are,' Martha said. 'They'll say anything to get what they need — food, clothes, a ticket home, a new life in America perhaps. They think we'll just take 'em in. If they can persuade us that we owe them something, that America, Britain, whoever has somehow wronged them, well . . . And anyway, maybe now and again the story is true. We don't truly know what they've been through. We don't know what's happened. At the end of the day, the woman's been raped. In my mind it doesn't matter who did it. It's wrong, and I want to help her if we can. I know what she's going through.'

* * *

'You can't just give the baby up. It's a life. He's as much part of you as he is of this man,' Owen said to Irena as they had stood in the main entrance waiting for someone to lead her to her billet.

'You do not understand,' she said. 'It is not about love. I cannot love it. I cannot love something that I did not want — not now, not then, not any time, not ever, do you understand? And you cannot make me.'

'But don't you think you might be able to?' he said. 'If you gave the child a name — '

'No,' she said. 'I find Krzysztof Krakowski. I give him his child. He raped me. He must have wanted it. 'Well then,' I say to him, 'here, here it is.''

* * *

Martha said she could arrange for one of the lads to take him into Camp 1 and give him a tour of what was really happening out there if Owen had the stomach for it, but he hadn't. He slumped on a pile of crates not knowing what to do with himself. Why in God's name hadn't he taken the colonel's offer? So many times over the last two weeks he had closed his eyes and woken somewhere else. He squeezed his eyes shut again but when he opened them nothing around him had shifted. He looked out across the former parade ground at the tents, the dusty parked military vehicles, and the dishevelled nurses and soldiers milling busily around. Someone had a wireless playing big band swing music that a woman in a headscarf and shawl was spiralling around to and laughing as if she were drunk, her skirt fluttering up as she turned, as if it were trying to propel her off the ground. A line of white figures walked through, dressed from head to foot in overalls, hoods and visors pulled over their heads like strange aliens. As they passed he saw how filthy they were, blood spattered up the legs and the stench of shit wafting from their boots.

He kept thinking of the fencing he'd seen along the road, them driving past so fast that the barren wastelands beyond it, and the shape of barracks and twig figures, had come to him through the quickly shifting sunlight and leaves like strange blurring images he used to see through his grandfather's zoopraxiscope.

His memories had been like that, turning and turning and yet still not real. They were all trying to forget something and now he wondered whether in his own mind things were better off left as they were. *You haven't lost your memories, you've hidden them*, Irena had said. And perhaps she was right.

Now, though, Connie kept slipping into his mind. He couldn't keep her out. That treacherous kiss, the churn of desire, the realization of what he was doing — it all dropped through him like a bomb.

No, he had said, or maybe: *We can't*, or *We shouldn't*, or *Jesus, what the hell are we doing?* He remembered a girl sniggering from further down the landing of the hotel and, with that, Connie had suddenly slipped from within his arms and run. He hadn't known what to do with himself as he saw her go, slamming his fist against the wall, and then thinking he might be sick. He recalled nothing else of that night except being at the top of the staircase and wanting to call out to her. He had pulled the mask from his head but she was already lost to him. In that wave of drunken panic as he tried to hunt her out in the crowd, the countless heads below him had been a shoal of debris swilling in a sea.

He rubbed at his eyes now, trying to wipe the memory away. In the yard, two trucks had pulled up and bodies were being laid out, joining those already in long rows along the edge of one of the buildings. Three women were searching through them, peeling back the blankets that covered each of them in turn. He watched them for a while, two with Stars of David still stitched to their coats. When the third turned he realized that it was Irena. She was looking for a dead man: Krzysztof Krakowski.

* * *

The ambulance driver, Wilkins, whom Owen was supposed to be sharing a room with, never did show. The war, it seemed, was full of such little mysteries. He sat on Wilkins' bed and walked his fingertips across the window. *Come back*,

Connie had said, or *I need you*, or maybe nothing at all. And then, as if in the haze of a hot summer's day, she too had melted away.

He would fix the boy's watch, he told himself, and then he would find him and give it to him as a token of thanks. Sitting in that attic the previous night with the boy so inconsolable, and Owen's hand on his knee, he had felt them knotting tighter together. Two brothers looking for brothers, Janek had said. And now, without him, Owen felt lost.

He took the watch from his pocket and opened the casing, emptying all its tiny parts out on to the bed sheet. He had fixed things — taps, radios, carburettors. He would fix this. If he thought about it logically, every piece had its place, its function and connection, so that bit by bit the wheels and cogs turned, time would move again and events unfold, each one tipping into another — a downed plane, a POW camp, a long walk through the snow. And then what? He couldn't think. Only that at some stage the boy had pulled him into a field and then for some reason had left him for dead.

Slowly and methodically he pieced the watch back together, dropping each tiny element back into place with a bent bit of wire fashioned into tweezers, everything there for a reason and everything in its place. He found some comfort in returning to his old logical ways. He replaced the cover, fastening it with a *click* and then held the mended timepiece to his ear, and, with a satisfied smile, he heard the metallic ticking of its tiny beating heart.

* * *

It took Owen some time to find the Czech block and when he did there didn't seem to be anyone about apart from an elderly man on the concrete doorstep clasping a tin of food tightly in his hand.

'What boy?' he said in strained English when Owen asked if he'd seen Janek.

'He's tall and thin,' explained Owen.

The man humphed at that — they were all tall and thin.

'We arrived today. He's new here. Fifteen, maybe sixteen, I don't know.'

The man shrugged. 'People come and go. They are digging up a turnip field. Maybe he is one of them. Or in the forest. They do that now. Go to the forest.'

Owen wanted to know what for.

The man shrugged. 'I don't know. See what they can find.'

He asked Owen if he had any cigarettes and Owen said no. Then the man took one out of his own pocket anyway and took a while to light it.

'The boys, they come back,' he said, eventually taking a drag and coughing. 'Do not worry.'

Then Owen remembered and drew Janek's symbol in the dirt with his finger. 'What about this?' he said. 'Have you seen this?'

'Oh,' said the man. '*That* boy. You English brother.'

'Yes,' said Owen, wondering what Janek had been saying.

'He's upstairs,' the man said, pointing,

'planning revolution. I am too old for fight. And what is left for Resistance to resist?' The man shrugged again, befuddled by it all. He pulled another drag. 'Nothing,' he said.

Owen climbed four flights looking in every dorm for Janek: six beds in each, three on either side. Some rooms were partitioned into cubicles with narrow wardrobes and stacked luggage making precarious dividing walls or army blankets strung across on ropes. In one room a couple of men were playing draughts on a board scored into the floor with chalk and different coloured pebbles. In another women sat around a dusty wireless listening to a crackling news broadcast, sewing or threading laces through old, battered shoes. There was no sign of Janek. When Owen reached the last room, certain that Janek would be there, there was just his threadbare jacket on a mattress and the bird in the box scratched into the wall.

* * *

Martha wiped the last hunk of bread around her plate, soaking up the gravy juice before popping it into her mouth. With the mental and physical grind of what they were doing there, Martha said that the least the British government could do was ensure they were well fed. That said, the food was all provided by the Germans.

'You demand what you want,' she told him. 'Food, clothes, their homes — and they give. What choice do they have? It's like they're finally waking up after some crazy dream.'

She had made some inquiries and had asked a few of the Red Cross nurses and a couple of British doctors she knew, as well as some of the medical students who had been brought over from London. But none had come across a Pole called Krzysztof Krakowski.

'Is there no way the child can be taken into care?' Owen asked.

'Who are you kidding?' She pushed her plate aside. 'We can't really do anything until we got some procedures going.'

Nor was there any sign of Petr.

'There are new lists coming out of the camp every day, and other camps too,' Martha said. 'We put them up on the notice-boards. I'll keep my eyes peeled.'

On a brighter note, she'd not only got Janek's name on a list of Czech deportees who would be able to leave the day after next, but she'd also got the lieutenant on the case about getting Owen on to a flight.

He thanked her.

'Well, glad to finally be doing something right,' she said.

'And if Janek doesn't want to go?' he asked. 'He's quite determined to find his brother, and he's downright stubborn when he wants to be.'

'Well, there are countless other camps he could try. That's what many of them are starting to do. But you'd be better off persuading him to stay here, mind, so we can send him home. That way,' she said, 'if we find his brother at least we know where to send him.'

After dinner there was a daily medical

progress review that didn't finish until eleven and then they were joined in the mess by Hamilton and two other Brits — Haynes, a doctor who had spent several years as a surgeon at the Royal Marsden before joining the Royal Army Medical Corps, and Guppy, a sapper from Brighton whose real name was Fisher. A large consumption of alcohol was the only way to survive the horrors of the job, it seemed.

'It stops you going mad,' said Haynes. 'You do what you can to block it out. I don't want to spend my nights thinking about the things I've been seeing all day.'

'So we drink ourselves into oblivion,' Guppy said.

Before long Owen was indeed perilously drunk. Haynes seemed intent on providing an endless supply of Scotch and then vermouth and then flaming brandy that made everyone cheer. All Owen could think was that he was in a fucking circus. And he wished he could get out.

'And now look,' Haynes was slurring at Hamilton, 'we're treating them no better.'

'Codswallop,' said Hamilton.

'It's true,' said Haynes. 'Camp 1 — how long before we started to get them out? Before we got them any medical attention? Hm? Two fucking weeks. I had to wade through their shit. Pits,' he said, turning to Owen. 'Pits knee-high in bodies. And what help do we get? What did we get today?' He stood up now, unsteadily, and swung his empty glass around.

'All right, Haynes,' said Hamilton. 'We all know.'

'Yeah, c'mon, Roy,' said Martha. 'Sit down.'

'What do we get?' he shouted. 'Jam yesterday. And today? *Today*? Crates of fucking lipstick.'

* * *

'I'm sorry,' Owen said, or something like it. As Martha had escorted him to his digs he had hardly been able to keep hold of the wall.

' 'Sall right,' she said. 'We're on the Scotch every night. We got ourselves immune.'

'Haynes isn't.'

'Well, no, not Haynes,' she conceded. 'But then he's a doctor.'

He shuffled forward on the edge of the bed and sat with his head between his knees, feeling that he might at any moment tip right over or be sick. He felt her hand hot on the back of his shoulder. The other was holding a glass of water for him.

'I couldn't find him,' he said, meaning Janek. They had been here for half a day and already everything had changed. 'Will she be all right?' he said. 'Will they be all right?'

'Who?' she said. 'Irena and the baby?'

'I don't know,' he said. 'Everyone.' He felt completely desolate. 'I shouldn't have got drunk,' he said. 'I forgot about them.'

'They're not your problem any more,' she told him. 'We'll look after them. We'll send them home. They'll want to be with people from their own country anyway.'

'But they're all strangers,' he said. 'I know them.'

Martha sighed. 'Let's have another drink,' she said. She had a bottle of bourbon back in her room that she'd been waiting to open for weeks.

* * *

'In my experience,' she said, swilling the whiskey around in the glass and then watching it spin, 'there are three types of women here. The young ones who are here because they want an adventure of some sort, wanna travel and don't see why the hell you men should be gallivanting around having all the fun. Then there are the goody-two-shoes type who are here under moral obligation and see it as their ticket to heaven, you know, the sort who love being in the middle of a crisis and proving their worth. And then — well — then there are those, the third type, who are just here to escape from something, because it sure as hell beats the crap out of being at home.'

'And which one are you?' he said.

'My God, what do you think?' she said. 'I'm not a damn crusader.'

UNRRA had been recruiting men and women from all across Europe, she told him, not just America. She'd taken a boat to England and then a plane to Paris, and then a long bumpy ride to Granville in Normandy, where UNRRA had its training centre.

'And there we sat,' she said. 'We were supposed to be sent out into the field in teams to help with the refugee problem. But it was a goddamn fiasco. When they do finally send you out, you're completely under-resourced. My team, we had two old reconditioned army trucks with blankets, camp beds, water bottles, that sort of stuff. And that was it. We lost one of the trucks two days after we left. Tipped right over. Then Francine — she was the welfare officer from Montpellier — she got ill. And Stefan and Riordan were at each other's throats all the time anyway. So the team got disbanded.'

'And you ended up here?'

'You all get washed up somewhere. I couldn't abide all the damn paperwork that was part of UNRRA anyway. I tagged along with the American Field Service volunteers. There are still a few of them knocking around. I just wanted to get on with it. You know, get stuck in.'

He agreed that she didn't seem to be the type that much cared for rules.

'Listen, when you have five hundred, eight hundred, I don't know, a thousand people dying here every single day, you don't have time to cross the 't's and dot the 'i's. The war might as well still be raging for all the good the peace is doing us.'

Sitting on her bed, he leant back against the bedroom wall. He could feel himself succumbing. Beside him Martha shuffled, her neat legs crossed at the ankles, her skirt just over the hillocks of her knees. As she pressed her hand into the mattress, the springs groaned and the mattress dipped, their shoulders pressed together. He thought about Irena and Janek having sex, and then about having sex with Martha on the narrow strip of floor, or against the wall or on this bed, and how she might lie beneath him, gripping the sheets.

'I shouldn't be here.'

'No. But you could stay,' she said.

He hauled himself off the bed and stumbled up. The floor didn't feel as solid as it should.

'I'm going,' he said. He lurched for the door.

But before he reached it she had his wrist, and what happened next he wasn't quite sure, only that he pushed her hard against the wall, just like he had with Connie, and she gasped like Connie had too. He wanted to kiss her in the same way, to kiss her so damn hard and take her off her feet. Just like that night at the Stowe House Hotel when their faces were so close that he could feel her breath; when he could smell her skin against his.

But it wasn't her.

He pushed himself away. 'My God,' he said, 'I'm sorry.' Then he was out the door and in the corridor, crashing against the wall and clattering down the steps. Outside he doubled up to catch his breath in the empty yard, then he threw his head back, his mouth open, gasping as if he were trying to drown himself in the cold night air.

* * *

In the tearooms of the Connaught hotel, on the corner of Carlos Place, near Grosvenor Square — a place so out of his price range that he thought it most unlikely that anyone he knew would ever be there — he had sat in his RAF uniform and waited. He had listened to the polite clink of china, teas being stirred, spoons on saucers, and the endless murmuring chatter as he stared at the two teacups and felt himself slowly dissolving into the plush upholstery of the chair.

I came last week, he said under his breath when she finally arrived and had been shown to her seat.

Yes. I know, she said as quietly as him, her stare not lifting from the tablecloth either.

I sat here for an hour.

I know.

I sat here for an hour, in this very seat, in fact, and I watched your tea go cold.

Please. Owen. Don't.

He didn't know why he was being like this; so angry with her and him and the mess of them that he could have thrown himself across the table and kissed it from her face.

I checked my diary three times, he said. *I thought we had agreed.*

Yes, we had, she said, *and I'm sorry but . . .*

What?

She paused. *This has to stop*, she whispered. *Can't you see?*

Why?

For God's sake, Owen. I'm getting married.

Then don't.

What?

Marry me.

I love Max.

And so do I, he retorted.

I'm being serious, she said. *This . . .* She took a breath and tried again. *This is just a phase we're both going through. A silly infatuation.*

Then why the hell are you here?

The hubbub of the room fell away. Heat prickled on his face. At the corner of his vision a gloved waiter edged nearer and then thought better of it.

I'm getting married to your brother, she said under her breath. *I'm truly sorry but . . .* She pinched her lips together to stop herself from saying any more.

And not another word was said. He stared at their empty teacups and the doily and the sharply starched creases in the perfect white tablecloth. And then, when he couldn't bear it any longer, he abruptly pushed his chair back and, without allowing himself another glance, he walked out of the tearoom as fast as his legs could take him, through the reception and the revolving door and away from her down the crowded London street.

IRENA

Two gunshots and then a third, and he woke. Before that, just the sense of him being dragged through his sleep, hands at the back of his collar, someone hauling him through the dark.

He lay for a while, smelling his hands and his fingers and the cup of his palm, and then pressing his wrist and then his arm to his nose, trying desperately to find some scent of her, a spot where he could still smell her on his skin.

* * *

'Politically the war might be over but in here we're still fighting it,' Haynes was saying as he led Owen through the hospital ward, between the rows of army beds with straw mattresses, each occupied by a patient, many of whom were no more than collections of bone in thin sacks of skin. Owen had never seen anything like it.

They passed through another room, twelve beds on either side. Each had a woman in it, most with shaven heads like Irena and flat-chested from malnourishment. Haynes pulled a spare pair of surgical gloves from his pocket and handed them over.

'I'd put these on if you're going to help,' he said. 'And don't touch anything without them. We've dysentery, typhus, tuberculosis, the whole bloody Merck Manual.'

As they passed the beds, those with enough energy tried to grab at Haynes, begging for his assistance in rasping voices, '*Herr Doktor*'. Their lips were thin and colourless, cheeks sunken, and all the architecture of the skull visible, just a thin leathery skin pulled over a framework of bone.

'When they first arrived, do you know what our boys had in terms of medical supplies?' Haynes said. 'Aspirin and opium tablets. I mean, what good is aspirin going to do for them? I tell you, it's like trying to put out a forest fire with a bloody mouthful of spit.

'We've had ninety-six medical students volunteer from London,' he carried on as he hauled a window open and coaxed the air in with his hand, 'but they're up to their necks in shit and fighting a losing battle trying to stop those still in the camps from starving to death. We're taking in five hundred new patients here from the main camp — that's the equivalent of three of these blocks — every bloody day, and we're barely scratching the surface. Just a handful of half-trained volunteers, the Red Cross and whatnot. For the rest of the time we've to make do with internee doctors and nurses, but most of them are recovering from typhus themselves and those that aren't have been out of service so ruddy long they don't know a syringe from a fucking scalpel. It's farcical. Absolutely . . . *urgh*.' He threw his arms up in despair.

They carried on up the stairwell to another floor and another makeshift ward where the line of beds was even more tightly packed.

'Come on,' he said to Owen. 'I'm sure Nurse

Joubert has a list of things an arm long you can help her with. I hope you're of a strong stomach, mind.'

'How's the baby, by the way?' Owen asked as they went.

'Oh, he's going to be fine,' said Haynes. 'Perking up nicely, actually. We'll keep him under observation for another day perhaps. Just in case.'

'Well, that's good news.'

'Yes. Makes a change. And with his mother too. One of them is usually dead by now.'

* * *

Nurse Joubert was French and perfectly charming, and not much more than a sprite of a girl; small-framed with a cut lip and short cropped hair. She had been born and raised in Marseille, she explained, and then detained on a false accusation of aiding British servicemen on the 'home run'. It was God, she told Owen, who had saved her from the gas.

It wasn't long before she had Owen emptying bedpans and administering a liquid that smelt like Radio Malt. As he moved from bed to bed, he tried not to look at the faces cowered beneath the sheets, many of them asleep or barely conscious, others staring at him from dim and sunken eyes. His hand reached out to give them the liquid, while inside he could feel himself wanting to pull away. What had become of this world, he thought? Was it any wonder that lone soldiers walked out into fields and put bullets through their own heads?

Midway through the morning another nurse appeared on the ward. She stood in the doorway with a small card in her hand, calling out a name. When no one answered, she disappeared again and minutes later she could be heard upstairs trying again.

'What was that about?'

'They have opened an office in the hospital,' Nurse Joubert said, 'where they write the details of the deportees and all the people that are missing. They are swapping lists with the other camps. With the thousands here you could have a husband and wife in the same camp and they would never know.'

'And that's happened?'

'Not yet,' she said, 'but we live for miracles.'

* * *

Exactly a week after their last meeting, the very same day and time, he had stood outside the Connaught hotel with a ridiculous notion that, despite there having been no communication, she might come again. And she did, faltering a little as she came down Carlos Place and saw that he was indeed standing there outside the stone railings. He fell in line as she walked past.

I didn't think you'd come.

I didn't think you'd be here.

Well, it was never an arrangement.

No.

But there they were.

They crossed the road and walked through the

iron arch into Mount Street Gardens, the path swinging right and taking them past the Jesuit Church of the Immaculate Conception. They turned left down Audley Street and left again, hearts pounding, until they found themselves in Shepherd Market, and there down one of the passages was a narrow slither of a hotel called The Swallow, so discreetly tucked between other buildings as to barely be there at all.

They checked in, using a name that he had spotted on a painting in the foyer, and signed the date — 13 March 1943 — the boy at reception asking no questions and so getting no more lies; and then they went up the cramped staircase, four flights up to the room. She opened a window; he shut the door; and there beside the bed, with the breeze running its fingers through the thin pink curtains and the sounds of the market wafting in, he kissed her like he had kissed no other woman before.

* * *

He sat outside on the kerb. He had spent over half an hour cleaning a floor only then to have a patient squat down and defecate on it, the diarrhoea pooling around the man's feet. The stench had turned Owen's stomach and after mopping it up he had then needed to step out for air. With the situation so bad in Camp 1, many had been reconditioned.

'They can't help themselves,' Nurse Joubert had said. 'We have to bring them back from feeling like they are nothing more than animals.'

Now he was crouched over and spitting out the sourness, his eyes watery and the dreadful smell still seeping from his fingers. As he turned and wiped his mouth, he saw a group of boys all striding out from behind one of the blocks, and then turning towards the gates — twenty, maybe thirty of them, several with homemade Czech flags tied around their shoulders.

He stood up and shouted, 'Janek!'

From within the group a head turned. The boy stopped and stared, the rest of the group feeding around him with bags slung over shoulders, holding sticks.

'Janek,' he called. 'Where are you going?'

But Janek just looked at him, then without any acknowledgement he turned and carried on. As the group marched away, a call and answer chant started, while in among them two or three were kicking an empty can around as they went, laughing. On the makeshift flags tied around their necks an all too familiar symbol had been daubed in tar.

'Ah. I was going to have a word with you about him.'

He turned around. Hamilton was behind him.

'Seems your little friend has been rather busy since you got here.'

'That's his doing?' said Owen.

'The group? Well, we didn't have this trouble before, let's put it like that. Now look,' said Hamilton, 'I'm as anti-Nazi as the rest of you and we can't stop people coming and going from the camps. They've been liberated; can't go running this place like a prison. But we do have to have some rules. It seems your little friend and his comrades have been causing a spot of bother with the locals. Pillaging, arson, that sort of thing. Now, I know tensions are high but we're trying to retain a peace here, get some sort of stability and order in place, and, well, this sort of nonsense really isn't helping. I'd like you to have a word. You might get through to him.'

'I very much doubt it,' said Owen. 'But, well, I can try.'

'Jolly good,' said Hamilton. He smiled rather awkwardly. 'Seems this boy of yours is quite the little tearaway.'

'Yes,' said Owen, although he was hardly listening. Across the yard he had spotted the same nurse who had appeared at the ward door calling out a name. She was directing two large men, who between them were carrying a stretcher with a thin figure lying on it.

'Yes, well, anyway, he'll be off tomorrow,' said Hamilton. 'You know we're packing a whole load of his lot off, don't you? Your boy too, which will probably do us all a favour. You know someone was asking specifically for him, wanted him on the release list?'

'Yes,' said Owen. 'That was Martha.'

'No, I mean at their end,' said Hamilton. 'Asked for him specifically, I believe.'

'Oh?'

'Oh, I don't know who. You'll have to ask Martha. He's coming in person though, God help us.'

Owen watched the nurse and the two men with the stretcher as they squeezed it through the ground door into the hospital block, then turned to say something but Hamilton was already gone, heading towards the administration block, a hand slipping loosely into his pocket and the other clicking his pen.

Owen wondered if he shouldn't run after Janek now but Nurse Joubert's head poked out of one of the windows and she waved furiously at him.

'*Monsieur! Monsieur!*' she shouted, beaming. 'Come. We have our miracle!'

He walked hastily back across the yard, and then started to run. Krzysztof Krakowski, he thought. He now didn't want Irena giving the child they had carried all this way to him — no matter what he was like. Perhaps somehow, with Martha's help, he might persuade Irena to keep him. There must be some sort of assistance they could get for her in Poland. Martha or Hamilton or Haynes or someone must know the channels they'd need to go through. They couldn't just hand Little Man over to a man who had raped her when between them they had cared for him for so long. Then Owen thought — or hoped — *He'll be too ill*, because they were all ill. Perhaps he was dying or dead already.

He ducked through the main door and ran up the stairs. In the ward they were already squeezing in another bed.

'Oh,' said Haynes. 'Good stuff. Here — take this.' He thrust a clipboard into Owen's hand, a form attached to it, while he pulled on a pair of gloves and rummaged around in his pocket for a pen. 'Got someone here that might be of interest to your little friend.'

'Yes,' said Owen. 'I know.'

'We've just fished her out of Camp 1.'

'Her?' said Owen.

'That's right.'

Nurse Joubert was already at the bed and close to tears. She leant a little into Owen.

'God,' she said quietly to him, 'is with us today. This is just the beginning. All our wounds will be mended.'

Owen looked down at the two women, one he recognized from around on the ward. The other was much thinner, her cheeks drawn and hollow, and her skin grey around her eyes. Her head was bald but for the tiny wisps that lifted in the breeze coming in from a window. They lay side by side, not looking at each other but hands tightly clasped.

'They are sisters,' whispered Nurse Joubert.

'Yes,' said Haynes. He scanned through the notes. 'Both brought here from Buchenwald by all accounts. Must have got separated.'

'They'll be all right though?' asked Owen.

'Let's hope so,' said Haynes. 'They're together now. And that's the main thing.'

The two sisters lay quite still in their beds, their teary eyes staring up at the ceiling and the line of naked light bulbs that hung like translucent heads. It was hard to tell their age, but Owen thought they must have been much younger than they looked, with the beauty of their youth shaven from their heads and sculpted from their faces.

'You said she might be of interest to

someone?' Owen said.

Had Haynes meant Janek? He'd been half expecting to see a Krzysztof Krakowski.

'Ah, speak of the devil,' said Haynes.

Martha bustled through the door, Irena behind her. She looked terrified as she entered the ward and Martha briskly led her through the beds.

'Are you all right?' said Owen, but Irena didn't reply.

Martha brought her to the bed where they had already gathered, the two sisters staring blankly up at them all, their hands still clasped across the narrow divide.

Irena's hand fumbled for his and he held it. It was as if she already knew what to expect. She glanced out of the corner of her eyes at the line of beds on either side and the disease-ridden faces.

'I'm very pleased to see you together again,' Martha said to the two sisters. The newest of the arrivals was staring wide-eyed at Irena and suddenly looked scared. She murmured something in Polish.

'I don't think this will take long, do you?' Martha said, turning to Irena.

Irena's grip on his hand tightened. She stood quite solid, but Owen could hear her breath coming heavy through her nostrils. She was trying to hold herself together. Every reunion in times like this, he thought, must come as a shock.

'I'm afraid she's very sick,' Martha told her. 'But her sister has been good enough to give us all the details. I believe you know each other.' She looked at Irena. 'Is that right?'

Irena nodded.

'Perhaps you'd like to confirm her name then. We just need confirmation that what her sister has said is true.'

Irena stared at the sick woman, their eyes locked on each other.

'Can you tell us what her name is?' said Martha.

Irena nodded, her gaze slipping to the floor, and took a breath. 'Her name,' Irena said hesitantly, 'is Irena Borkowski.'

⋆ ⋆ ⋆

There was so little time. For twelve-hour shifts Connie fitted sparking plugs while he was out in Hertfordshire. It was a hell of a journey to meet her, even when he managed a few hours' leave. They would meet outside the Connaught, him falling in line as she passed, and only when they reached Grosvenor Square or the Brown Hart Gardens on Duke Street did they dare to speak. Mostly, though, they lived those hours in Shepherd Market; they walked its passages, ate pancakes in the café or made love in The Swallow hotel.

Every time he saw her with Max he burned; and with every snatched kiss, in the shadowy corners of his parents' house, he felt a tiny bit of him break off and go to hell.

It had to stop.

We need to stop this.

I know, she said.
But they didn't.

* * *

Irena — or the girl he had thought of as Irena — stood at the small window of Martha's office staring out at the empty sky, her gaze somewhere over the barrack rooftops, and her bony hand resting lightly on the sill. She had said that she would not talk to Martha, only Owen, and yet they had been there for fifteen minutes now and she had not said a word.

He sat looking at her, waiting. Her eyes kept filling but she would not cry.

When the real Irena Borkowski had given Martha her details, and then the information had been confirmed, Martha had realized the deception.

Owen felt angry, cheated by this girl yet again. *All these lies*, he had told her. *I don't know who you are*.

It made no sense. The strangeness he had woken to all those days before never seemed to clear, it just tangled tighter around him. He was so tired of it. Take him to a field now and he would lie there and shut his eyes. He would let the grass grow over him and slowly pull him under the earth.

Eventually she spoke, not turning to look at him but keeping her eyes locked on the sky outside, wisps of cloud seeming to judder within the pane of glass as below them another truck thundered through the dirt.

'When this is all over,' she said, 'for years after this, everyone will say how awful we were. That is what they will remember. That is what they will say. But I am ruined too. I am as ruined as they are. I have no home. I have no family either. I have lost all of that too. But I do not have the — how do you say? — the luxury of being the victim, of being the ones that everyone now will give to, or feel sorry for, or pity, or love. I see this now. I see it here. In this place. In all this. And all I have is the shame of my people. That is all I am left with.' She turned and looked at him. 'Do you understand? Right now, it is better to be anything but German.'

'You shaved your head so you could be like them.'

'I did what I had to do. People will feed you then,' she said. 'They will give you clothes, water. It's true.'

'So this Irena Borkowski — the real one — who is she?'

'She was a domestic servant,' she said. 'A cook. Krzysztof Krakowski — he was my mother's gardener. They had both been brought by my father from Poland to work for my family in Hoyerswerda. When the war started we were only allowed to keep them because my father was well respected in the Wehrmacht. They made concessions for him. He fought in Russia, you know. And then when that didn't work any more and my father had disappeared, my mother would pay the SS off, so that we could keep them and keep them safe.'

'And this Krzysztof chap, he raped you?'

She nodded. 'I have not lied about everything. And what he did, it was not revenge for anything, if that is what you think. Before the war we were friendly. He was young, I was young, but feelings like that soon became impossible. My mother was suspicious. The war was getting bigger. The Jewish Poles in Germany were being taken and my mother couldn't keep paying the SS off. It was only time before something would happen, I suppose: a different SS officer, one that could not be bribed; or we would run out of money; or someone would do something stupid. He wanted me to help him and I would not. I could not help him like he wanted me to. He kept saying that he wanted me to marry him, that I could protect him, but how could I? Everyone knew that sort of thing was not allowed, but he never saw sense. We fought about it. Then one night he got drunk, very drunk and angry with me about it and . . . well . . . '

'That's when it happened?'

'That's when it happened.'

'And after?'

'I don't know whether my mother heard or if it was only by chance, but the next day he was taken. Irena too. I knew — or thought — I would not see them again. I stole her identity papers just before the van came.'

'Why?'

'I don't know. I saw them on the table, that was all, and I was angry with them — with them both. I was seventeen. Still a child. I didn't know what I was thinking.'

'So you took them. And then?'

'Nothing,' she said, 'for a while. Then my mother was taken as well. She had been listening to your British broadcasts. She thought our news people were not telling the truth about what was happening on the eastern front. She was worried about my father so she would listen to your BBC, hoping to get something of the truth. Then a neighbour told the SS. She'd had the volume up too loud or perhaps someone had told them about the bribes. I don't know. Anyway, they came and they took her, just like they took all the rest. And that was that.'

'And you?'

'I was pregnant. They left me alone in the house to fend for myself. Then when it was clear that the war would be over soon and Germany was ruined, there was talk of Russians advancing, that everyone was going to be raped and murdered, so I left too. Germans were being taken from the road and beaten to death. It was like hell.'

'And is that when you took Irena's name?'

She nodded. 'I told you. My mother was a language teacher. We spent some years in Poland. Before the war my father was a site manager at a German shoe factory near Posen. My mother taught German to the Poles in the offices, and Polish to the Germans living there, like us. It was useful. She was useful. It was her that got my father the job in the first place. She knew Herr Blumenthal. Anyway, I realized I could pass for a Jew if I had to. I still had Irena's papers. She was older than me but she has a young face. With my head shaved no one would know any different.'

'You didn't think someone might question it?'

'You have seen it,' she said. 'The chaos. You understand. I thought I would never see her again. I was certain she was dead.'

'And what's your name?' said Owen. 'Your real name.'

'Anneliese,' she said. 'It is Anneliese Dreher.'

'Does Janek know?'

She shook her head.

He stood up and came out from behind the desk. There wasn't anything left to say. The girl turned back from the window. She was starting to sob now.

'Please. You have to help me.' Her hand was on his face. She was trying to stroke him, trying to kiss him. 'I'll do anything. You have to help me.'

He pushed her off. 'No. Come on, stop that.'

She backed away against the wall, shaking her head vehemently. 'Please,' she begged. 'You don't understand. You don't know what they will do.'

* * *

On a Sunday in early June 1943 — the last date he can fix in his mind with any certainty — she had driven him out to Wonersh in Max's Austin. It had been an audacious act that perhaps he would never forgive himself for but with only a few hours' leave left before he was transferred to Warboys — now his training was completed — they had done it anyway. The country lanes had been quiet and they had folded the roof down, Connie in her sunglasses and that familiar scarf rolled and knotted around her head.

They strolled out through the fields of rape, their arms held up as if together they were wading into the sea, and in the field beyond they sat in the grass smoking a couple of Woodbines as a heron flew by on lolloping wings, low and languid over the stream. For a while they watched a bumblebee busying itself among the cotton grass. She was playing with a grey scrap of material she'd found snagged like wool on a fence, turning it around and around in her hand and holding it to her cheek with her fingertips as if she were positioning a patch that she was going to pin to her face.

I've never understood how they manage to get off the ground, she said. *For such a bulbous body they have such frightfully fragile wings*.

That was why bees and birds were so much stronger than us, he told her, and that was how da Vinci had come up with the idea for his ornithopter, and that if mankind were ever to find a way off the ground, it would need to employ the use of mechanics. And thank God for that. Otherwise, without the war, he wouldn't have had a job. Da Vinci's ornithopter was, he said, the closest thing to strapping yourself within the ribcage of a bird.

Here was a girl who appreciated this, who had an inquisitiveness that was rare, he thought, in these days where planes were just expected to fly and no one questioned what it took to get 70,000 lbs of metal off the ground and moving.

It wasn't just power, he told her. It was a three-way love affair between aerodynamics, mechanics and art.

Sydney Camm had said it himself: Aircraft design is an art and not a science.

These are the things he remembered from that one afternoon in June, or perhaps many afternoons gathered before: the weight of her arm looped through his; the touch of her lips as she'd stretched to kiss him; how when he'd laid out on the grass, the side of his face pressed to it, she had danced and swung herself around, and all he could see was her feet and the swishing hemline of her skirt wafting by his face. Was that when he had sketched her, that very first time? Was that when she had said to him: *Aren't you going to give me a face?*

Long after they'd finished in fields and cafés and rented hotel bedrooms, their conversations would linger in his mind and bring with them secret smiles.

How do you feel, she quizzed him once as they sat in bed, *about me having a slight schoolgirl fancy on the late Amelia Earhart?*

I don't much mind, he joked, *as long as she's still dead*.

And this, he announced on another day, holding his sketch to the hotel window so the sun bleached through, *is the mechanics of a bee. Reconfigured — as you can see — in the style of the late da Vinci*.

They had laughed those days — in those few and fragile piecemeal hours when they could cocoon themselves away from the world, when there was him and her and no one else, and they could pretend that everything about them existed only in that room.

Then, on that June day at Wonersh, as he'd helped her across the stream, she'd slipped and, grabbing his jacket, had pulled a button clean away. It dropped with a splash and had tumbled through the current some way before they had scooped it out with his cap.

Oh no, she said, *it's your RAF jacket. If we don't sew that back on, my God you'll be in trouble*.

While he'd dozed in the grass, his cap drying on his knee, she sat with his jacket heaped in her lap and sewed the button back on. *Only you and I will ever know*, she said, and then she leant over him and he felt the warmth of her kiss.

* * *

They didn't know what to do with her. It had gone up through the ranks almost as far as the lieutenant colonel. She'd have to go, Hamilton speculated. They couldn't house a German as if she was a Polish Jew. It was a displacement camp for victims of the Nazi regime, not a bloody hotel.

'She *is* a victim,' said Martha.

'And you believe that?'

'She was raped!'

'That's not under debate,' argued Hamilton. 'It's whether we let a German stay or not, regardless of what's happened to her.'

'We had Germans imprisoned in the camp,'

Haynes pointed out. 'Victims of persecution.'

'Yes, people who had already been incarcerated here. And now we open the gates to everyone?'

'We can't shut people in or out,' said Martha.

'We'll have half the nearby villagers turning up,' said Hamilton, 'wanting to be fed. And all because, in their eyes, we've pillaged their gardens, emptied their cupboards and stolen half of their clothes to care for Germany's so-called victims, to compensate for the crimes carried out here that they're now all claiming they know nothing about!'

'They don't come in though,' said Haynes, 'and there's a very good reason for that. If they do they know what will happen. You only have to see what happened to the German nurses they sent. Their uniforms practically torn from their backs. They turned on them like bloody animals. I've never seen anything like it.

'When we first liberated the camp,' he told Owen, leaning in, 'there were Russian and Polish prisoners hurling SS guards out of top-floor windows. One man was strung up and skinned. I mean, *skinned*. They want revenge, and I tell you, sometimes I want to do it myself, just for the sheer bloody awfulness of the things I've had to deal with here.'

They had already needed to move her. Guppy the sapper had told Owen that they'd put her in a private room.

Can't have her lot with the Poles, he'd said. *They'll have her for sausages*.

'I mean, what does she want anyway?' said

Haynes. 'She's one in sixty thousand here so even the fact that we're wasting time talking about her is winding me up. I don't give a flying fig whether she comes or goes.'

'Well, you should do,' said Hamilton. 'We'll be setting up a precedent.'

'I don't think she knows what she wants,' said Owen. It was the first time he'd dared to speak. They'd been debating it for half an hour and didn't seem to be getting anywhere. 'I don't think she's capable of thinking straight at the moment.'

'Well, she's not alone there,' grumbled Haynes. 'I can't think straight here either. It's bloody impossible.'

'And we need to consider the kid,' said Martha.

'Well, that's easy,' said Hamilton. 'They'll just take it off her.'

'Why the hell would they do that?'

'We must have lists of orphanages,' Hamilton said. 'She's not fit, is she? She's not a fit mother.'

And so the conversation went. Owen felt that he had nothing to offer. He didn't know the systems or the procedures, or the paperwork that needed to be dealt with. The only thing that seemed to be evident was that no one particularly wanted the issue to take up much time. As Haynes had pointed out, she was only one in sixty thousand.

* * *

The Czechs were being prepared for the trucks arriving the following day. They would be driven to Celle where trains would be waiting for them to return them home. Each deportee had to be registered, carefully printed SHAEF cards filled in, one copy of each sent to the destination reception centre, the others held in Germany. Janek was processed along with the rest. This time tomorrow he would be on his way home, but still nothing had been unearthed of Petr.

Outside Janek's block there were now Czech flags hanging from several of the windows, one or two daubed with the familiar marks. Owen passed the old man on the step outside, politely greeting him, and then ran up the four flights of stairs. He didn't expect Janek to be there but he had the watch anyway. Perhaps he could slip it into the boy's bag for him to find later. It would make Janek smile.

As he ran up, voices echoed — boys of Janek's age and younger dispersing down the stairs, alive with their strange chatter. Their sense of excitement was hardly surprising, he thought, as he let them clatter past. They would soon be going home.

Janek was sitting cross-legged on his bed, struggling to fix a brooch, trying to bend the clasp back into position with his fingernails and then his teeth. Two other boys whom Owen recognized as the ones who had been kicking a can about amid their parade out of the camp that morning sat around on the floor among a litter of items: kitchen utensils, boxes of chocolates, empty rucksacks, photograph frames, various Nazi memorabilia, and what looked like a musical box. One had a pile of clothes on his lap. He lifted one up and shook it out — a ripped Nazi jacket. He poked his finger through a bullet hole and wiggled it like a worm, and the three of them laughed. It was only then that they saw Owen.

'May I come in?' he said.

The one with a pile of trinkets around his feet hurriedly gathered them up, shoving them into a bag. Janek and the other boy stared.

He walked nervously into the room, three sets of eyes following him.

In among the clutter, something that resembled a campaign headquarters had been set up. On the wall above Janek's bed he had stuck all the newspaper articles that Owen had found in his bag — pictures of Petr caught in the crush of a demonstration or a riot or a protest, sometimes with his fist in the air, but always he was there in the thick of it. Beside the clippings, the scraps of map that had once been Owen's had also been stuck up and pieced together. The name Sagan circled and clinging to the edge, and other names circled now too — dotted across the whole of Germany and elsewhere — that he couldn't quite make out.

'Looks like someone's been busy,' he said. He wondered what they were playing at.

As his eyes took in the rest of the room with a growing sense of unease, he noticed maps scattered across a desk, piles of sticks thick as wrists, more flags — some draped over the back of a chair, others hung from a line pinned across the room, drying where Janek's bird had been newly painted. There were empty bottles and scraps of cloth too and, to his horror, even a rifle kicked under a bed, gun cartridges scattered carelessly across the floor.

He motioned at the bed — 'May I?' — and then sat down at the foot of it anyway. Janek carried on what he was doing, his elbow sticking out at an awkward angle as he struggled to fix the clasp.

'Do you want me to have a look?' Owen said, offering his hand.

'No!' Janek held the piece of jewellery closer to him. He didn't want Owen touching it.

The two boys sitting on the floor watched him with suspicion. They were about the same age, Owen thought, but thinner even than Janek, and yet somehow they had survived and now they too were fit enough for sending home.

He took the watch from his pocket and dropped it on the bed.

'I mended it for you,' he said. 'I thought you might like it.' They had brought it all the way back from a pool in Czechoslovakia, after all. Everything would be mended, they had said, starting with a watch.

Janek held his arm up so that the sleeve fell back to reveal another newer and cleaner watch already on his wrist. He carried on working.

'Look, will you just take it?' Owen said. He'd damn well mended it for him. He tried to force it into Janek's hand. 'I want you to have it.' Grudgingly Janek took it and held it to his ear and then pushed it into his pocket, tossing the brooch on the floor.

'You said you will help. Look for Petr,' he said.

'*Můj bratr.*' He sounded resentful. 'You promise. Now you send me home.'

'I'm not sending you home,' Owen said. 'No one is going to force you, but you should go.'

'No,' he said. 'You are *lhář*.'

'I'm not lying. Listen,' said Owen. 'Your brother is going to find you. He will come home to you in his own time. You don't have to be the hero and find him yourself.'

'No,' he said. 'I look for Petr. I save you. Two lives. And now you don't care.'

'I do.'

'Now you with English.'

'That's not true,' Owen said.

'*Co jsem všechno pro vás udělál!* I do for you.' He was getting upset now. 'You English are all *stejní*. Same.' He held two fingers up together. 'Mm? You leave me like you leave our country. You sell us. To Hitler. It is not your country to sell. You betray us. Hm? You owe us.' He jabbed his chest. 'Me.'

'I know,' said Owen, 'and I'm sorry.'

'You know *Angličani*. People. You promise help. You don't remember.'

'I didn't promise anything,' he said. 'Anyway, help who?'

'Petr,' said Janek. 'He will lead. We find Petr. You and me bring him back. Then, *revoluce!*'

'What revolution?' said Owen.

'*Sokol zase bude létat*,' he said, flying his hands as if they were a bird.

He meant his symbol — the *sokol* — Owen thought.

Then Janek pulled out a black strip of material

from his bag and threw it into Owen's chest — the familiar-looking armband, Petr's symbol threaded on it, just like he'd seen another man wearing in the photographs now above the bed. He tried to force it into Owen's hand. He wanted Owen to wear it.

'No, I'm not getting involved.'

'*Pomůžete nám!*' Janek shouted.

'It has nothing to do with me.'

Janek scrambled off the bed. 'Yes! Yes!' he cried. He took one of the books from the desk, found a blank page and ripped it out, then held it out for Owen. 'You write, hm? You write. *Napište anglické vládě*. English government. They give help. You tell them. Help to us. Help to Petr. Help *revoluci*. Yes? You betray us. Now you help us. Yes?'

He kept on talking but Owen had heard it before. They would clear all the Germans out, all the Hungarians, all the Russians. Just Czech, Janek had told him. Nobody else. It was their country.

'And you help. Yes?'

Owen laughed. 'Write to the British government and do what? Ask them to help you? But I don't know anyone. Who am I supposed to write to? No, I'm sorry, but no.'

'*Musíte!*'

'Why?'

'You owe me. Two lives!'

'Yes. I know. You saved me. You saved my life two times. I know!'

'No, two lives you owe me. Not *your* two lives. *My* two lives. For me. Mine.' He pulled out his wallet and snatched out a photograph, then shoved it in Owen's hand. It was the portrait of the boy's parents.

'Two lives!' Janek shouted.

* * *

He walked out of the block, through the camp, out of the gates and some distance along the road through the field, the woods closing in around it until eventually he slumped on the verge and pressed the heels of his hands into his eyes. He felt quite sure that he would splinter and break.

He kept seeing the same images: the dark sky and trees lurching over him as the boy dragged him up the short bank from the river and into the field, the sound of his efforts as he heaved and struggled towards a house, and then could drag Owen no more. Cold wet hands undoing the buttons at the top of Owen's shirt, and then taking hold of his wrist. There was nothing else, no other clue, before he lost consciousness. Just the vague sound of two shots, and then a third; and in the darkness the boy had run.

* * *

In the mess his eyes followed Martha to the bar, watching as she poured them both a Scotch and then reached up to replace the decanter, her whole frame rising a little as her feet exalted her on to her toes and held her there for a moment. Nothing had been said about the night before.

All day she had kept her eyes anywhere but on him, while he had scrutinized her for clues that she was about to turn and say something. Now it hung between them, this rumbling aftermath.

Taking her seat across the table, she set his glass down and lifted her own to her mouth, slopping the Scotch around the ice cubes before she drank it in a mouthful and sighed as if she'd needed it.

'Isn't it a little early for this?' he said, staring at his glass. It was still afternoon.

'You know Hamilton is doing everything he can to dig out some information about you,' she said, ignoring the comment. 'He's sent a communication over to your Bomber Command that we have you safe and sound. They're going to get you on a plane home. If not tomorrow, then the day after. You'll be back in London by Tuesday, with a bit of luck.'

'That would be nice,' said Owen. He had prayed someone would tell him these words so many times over the last few days but now, hearing them for real, the relief did not come.

'What will you do?'

'I don't know,' he said. Strange that he hadn't thought that far. 'Find out what I was doing before all this nonsense and try to put my life back together, I suppose.'

'Do you know what your Bomber Command also told Hamilton?' she said.

'No.'

She held his eye and then leant forward a little across the table as if she were about to whisper him a secret. 'I don't think Anneliese Dreher is the only person we know who's been spinning little lies. Do you?'

'What do you mean?'

'You told me you were a pilot.'

'But I am.'

'You're not though,' she said with a vaguely triumphant smile. 'You're a goddamn liar. You're not an RAF pilot at all. Your brother was. You're just a flight engineer.'

* * *

Outside he sat against a pile of boxes that had been stacked beside the main entrance of the admin block and held his head in his hands. Why had he ever allowed himself to think he was a pilot? The truth was that there was no hero in him, no matter how deep he dug. There had been days when he had believed it — days when he saved an infant from the road or stopped an innocent farmer being clubbed to death — but now all of that belief had fallen away. With every new thing he had learnt, every new memory bolted on, he felt thinner, not fuller, as if the real Owen was only a splinter of the man that he rather hoped he had become.

Not a pilot then, but a flight engineer.

Always his brother's sidekick.

The role he knew was designed for men like him — monitoring and operating the plane's systems, the fuel management and engine oil and temperature coolants. While Max pushed the plane through the sky, hands at the yoke or edging forward the throttle, Owen had logged and noted and recalculated those fussy little details, his eyes fixed not on the sky ahead but on the dials in front of him. Was that why his natural instinct all those days ago had been to log everything that came to him? BOY = CZECH = BREAKFAST.

It had always been Owen, not Max, who had snuck away to read copies of *Flight* or spend his evenings hunched over *The Aircraft Engineer* supplement, trying to understand the articles on wiring lug design and airscrew performance, all the strange equations and terminology that had intrigued him with their mystery, while Max had been the one on his pushbike bombing it down the lane. It had never been the accolade of flying an aircraft that had fascinated him; it was the science, the physics and aerodynamics, the nuts and bolts and wiring and pistons that somehow got the crate up into the air. Beneath the gleaming skin of a Lancaster there were 55,000 identifiable parts all playing their intricate role.

In the end, he thought, leaning back and considering this with a strange relief, everything came down to mechanics: the workings of a plane or a watch or a frog; the joints that held a man together; the mechanics that propelled him forward and walked him through the snow and dust.

Max and he, of course, had therefore been on different training schedules, not even at the same station half the time. That must have made the thing with Connie easier, allowing him to duck and dive the days when Max might be around. For a month she had even given Owen a key; and on leave days he would take the number 2 tram from Victoria Embankment, following the rails through Kennington, Stockwell and Balham, along Tooting High Street to Colliers Wood and then Wimbledon. There at the station he'd hop off, changing on to the 604 trolleybus that took him along the Kingston Road until it dropped him on Caversham Rise. Sometimes before he went in he would sit on the front steps, collecting up the fallen geranium petals while he took a cigarette, satisfied by the warm weight of the key in his pocket.

Only once more did he ask her to leave Max.

You know I can't do that.

He poked his finger into one of the boxes he had been sitting on, where under the weight of the others one of the sides had split, and pulled out a lipstick. It must have been the delivery that Haynes had been complaining about. Still, no one had bothered to move them. He took the lid off and wound it up. He held it up, a slight wetness to the crimson colour in the sunlight. There must have been hundreds of them in the boxes. He would give it to Anneliese. She would look pretty with a bit of colour.

'Oh, hello.' A young man in army overalls had appeared out the door and was standing beside him. 'You busy?'

'Not especially,' said Owen. He slipped the lipstick into his pocket.

'Guvnor wants this lot shifting. I don't suppose you could gi's a hand. They just need running up to the stockroom. Jesus.' He scratched the back of his head as he looked at the boxes. 'I didn't realize there was so many.'

Owen said that would be fine.

'I can probably take three,' said the boy. 'Do you want to load me up?'

He handed the lad a box and piled another on top, then moved some of the boxes around, getting the one from the bottom that was split so he could put it on the top of the pile in the boy's arms. As he moved them away from the wall he stopped. He bent down. My God, he thought. There was the symbol — the swooping wings and the 'v' for a head, the box around it scratched into the side of the wall with something sharp, like a nail or a knife.

'You all right there?' said the boy.

Owen got down on his knees to take a closer look. He ran his finger over the scratches in the stonework. This wasn't the work of Janek. It was a wound that was old and weathered. The symbol, he realized, had been there in the wall for some time.

'What is it?' said the boy.

'Nothing.' He stood up again and passed the box.

Then it quickly dawned on him who must have left the marking.

'Actually, do you know what? I can't help after all. Sorry. I need to see someone. It's urgent. Sorry, but I just remembered.'

'Oh, all right,' said the lad. He seemed a bit disgruntled but Owen was already running.

* * *

Martha said it would take some time — time she did not have — but she would go through the cards that the nurses had started to complete and there were new noticeboards going up with names from other camps.

'You'll need to be patient, mind,' she tried to explain, but Janek would not.

He went from block to block, ward to ward, and bed to bed — a Czech man, he said, Petr Sokol, showing them the photograph and newspaper clippings, saying all manner of other things that might prompt someone to remember.

The two Czech boys — Otmar and Mikoláš — went with him. Owen too. They paced from ward to ward. *Does anyone know anything of a Petr Sokol?* But Owen kept on forgetting who they were looking for. His eyes kept being drawn to the women in the beds, seeing reminders of Connie in every face: the shape of her eyes, the line of her jaw, the indentation of her lip.

The same nurse from yesterday appeared at the doorway. She held a familiar-looking card in her hand. 'Petr Sokol?' she called.

But there wasn't any answer.

* * *

Strange how things came and went. In all the turmoil of the day he had quite forgotten about some things, but seeing the button on the ground stopped him. He bent down to pick it up where it had been trodden into the dirt. It was covered in mud, round and metallic, almost the size of a threepenny bit and with four eyelets, dusty broken threads tangled between them. It looked familiar.

He took the tin button out of his pocket and weighed them both in his palms, and then held them up to the sunlight. They were the same — the same size, colour, style and shape, and each with the same four eyelets and broken strands of thread still knotted and tangled around the holes. It was only when he laid them each in the palm of a hand and brought his hands together that his palms seemed to form a face; the two silver-coloured buttons stared back at him like eyes.

* * *

A single tin button lay in the shadows. It was only the sunlight streaming through the carriage window as the train clattered on that had made him notice. It soaked in through the glass and was sliced by the wooden slats of the seat opposite him where the girl sat, a dusty shaft cutting through the dark beneath the seat and falling on the button so that in that moment it had caught his eye. For a while he had looked at it, hidden there behind her ankles, the stark white of her socks and the red gleam of her sandals, her suitcase parked beside her. She held the teddy bear on her lap, the same styled button for an eye, the other fallen from it, and now he saw it lying beneath the seat. Behind him he was aware of the SS troops making their way through the carriage, getting closer, checking everybody's papers.

He bent down and said something in German like *Excuse me*, before he reached under her seat. *Ich glaube, es ist Ihnen etwas heruntergefallen*. I think you've dropped something. He pulled out the button. *Hat Dein Bär ein Auge verloren?* Has your bear lost an eye?

What made him pick the button up? What made him bend at that moment, just as the SS officer making his way through the carriage, going from passenger to passenger, had finally reached them? Owen looked up — *Has your bear lost an eye?* — the button still in his hand, and something in that moment had passed between them. Perhaps she had seen the help he needed, the ink on his hand, the now smudged and useless documents. Or something in his own eye that told her that he was not who she thought he was. For even though he had said it and she had quite clearly seen the button there in his hand, the bear still held tightly in her lap, when the officer had approached them and said 'Papers', she had still made a fuss.

Mein Bär! she said. My bear! *Oh, mein Bär!* she cried. She was up on her feet and then down on her knees looking under the seat, scrabbling around on the floor of the carriage and between people's legs, making them move, getting everyone up. *Sein Auge!* His eye! *Oh, nein!*

Papiere! He needed to see their papers.

But no one was taking any notice. All around them people were lifting their feet up or bending over to look beneath their seats, moving luggage, shaking out coats, and saying things like: *Oh, let's have a look*.

It must have rolled somewhere.
Are you sure you've lost it?
Yes, look, she said.
Papers! I need to see your papers!

She held the bear up with its missing eye and then started to cry, so that in that moment's distraction while a dozen people at the end of the carriage looked for a button that both she and Owen knew very well Owen was holding in his hand, she created for him an opportunity.

And there it was now — this button that in those crucial moments had distracted the officer from his papers long enough for the plane to come over, for the sound of it to fill the carriage just as it filled his head now, the train slowly rattling over the bridge, while all around him the good passengers hunted for a button to appease a distraught child travelling on her own. In that briefest of commotions, merely seconds, he had pushed past the officer to the outside door and, unnoticed, opened it and stepped out on to the end of the platform. The train had slowed to cross the bridge. Up above them the plane had passed overhead but when he looked up he saw that, slowly and deliberately, it was beginning to turn, curling back towards them as it started its descent.

* * *

That night the Czech contingent threw a farewell party. They lit fires around the parade ground and sang Czech songs, encouraging the other refugees to join them so that before long, the whole square was filled with a throng of people. There were trumpets and accordions and percussion played on anything that would hold still long enough: pots and pans and the bonnets of jeeps, discarded tins strung up on twine, the back of someone's head . . .

The two boys from Janek's room — Otmar and Mikoláš — had made firecrackers that popped and fizzed through the dirt, crackling as they scurried beneath people's feet, making them jump, or shoot off somewhere like miniature rockets. There was alcohol, of course, taken from nearby houses, and Owen was not surprised to hear rumours that earlier a nearby farm had been held up at gunpoint, a group of 'liberated prisoners', it was claimed, forcing their way in and stealing a wheelbarrow piled with bottles of homebrewed beer.

Many of the military team came out to join in. They had as much to celebrate as the Czechs, said Martha. Every refugee sent home was one less to worry about.

'You don't get many moments like this,' she said, 'when you get a chance to take stock and realize that actually, yeah, we're doing all right.'

Most of the medical staff and volunteers sat around on chairs outside the tents in the square, smoking and swigging beer. Guppy sucked on a foul-smelling cigar that a Hungarian had given him, and for a while there was some debate as to what was actually in it.

With a drink in his hand and puffing one of Martha's Luckies, Owen allowed himself to relax. He thought only of that night and his strange sense of belonging, and his gratitude that come tomorrow, Janek would be on his way, and then him too, and Martha had at least made promises about Anneliese and that she would do everything she could to ensure that Little Man would be all right. The only moment when the past crept up on him was when someone released a makeshift Chinese lantern from a top-floor window. For a while they watched it floating up into the sky, where it drifted over the rooftops.

'God. Looks like a bloody lung,' grumbled Haynes.

But Owen had seen it as a scarlet heart or a box kite sent up on a string held by him and his father.

* * *

In the bedroom of The Swallow hotel, booked under the name of Gainsborough, he had sketched her. Not the mechanics of her. No guidelines. Not the muscles or structure of bones or where the heart might sit or the liver or lungs or how the major arteries ran through her body like wires. He sketched her clothed in only her skin as she sat on the end of the bed, her head turned to the window.

My face, she had said with a smile.

He glanced up at her over the edge of the paper.

I want you to draw my face.

* * *

The man was called Myska. He was a small, timid creature with surprisingly large earlobes and a diminishing hairline that had retreated to such a degree that it now formed little more than a crown around his head.

At first Janek didn't seem to know him but the man was evidently pleased to see him, grabbing him out of the throng of people, talking fast and excitedly, all the time holding Janek's arm and gesturing at perhaps how well he looked or how tall, and then talking just as fast at Owen, not realizing that he was English and hadn't the slightest idea what the man was going on about.

'*Myska?*' Janek said eventually.

'*Ano! Ano!*' said the man.

Janek's face cracked into a smile and then a laugh. 'Myska!' He clutched the man by the arms and they gave each other an awkward hug, squeezing each other hard.

'Josef Myska,' Janek said. He held his head between his fists and circled about. He clearly couldn't believe it.

Owen wondered whether he should wander back to the tents and leave the two of them to it. Nearby a couple of French girls from the Mission Militaire de Liaison Administrative were trying to teach a group of Russians how to dance the jitterbug. Someone shrieked. Another firecracker whizzed through. Otmar and Mikoláš were shouting and laughing.

Janek dragged Owen over and slapped him on the back. 'Josef Myska.'

'Yes,' said Owen. 'So I gather. Nice to meet you.' He shook the man's hand.

'He is my friend. He is . . . er . . . ' He spun around on his foot with excitement and frustration. Then he pulled his wallet out and took out a newspaper clipping. He pointed out a man in a photograph, a man too short to be seen within the demonstration but for a hand held up in a clenched fist. Janek held Myska's own hand up and manipulated the fingers into that same fist. 'Myska,' he said. 'Look, look!'

'Ah, I see,' said Owen. 'Very good. So you're the one with the armband. I remember now.'

'Yes,' said Janek. 'Old friend.'

'Old friend,' said the man. He thumped his fist in the air and shouted. '*Československo Čechoslovákům!*'

'*Československo Čechoslovákům!*' Janek yelled. Both of them laughed, then they took each other in a headlock and circled around for some time, grappling playfully.

'*Kde je Petr?*' said Janek, releasing him and still laughing. '*Je tady Petr?*' He looked around as if expecting his brother to appear from a tent or walk out from among the people around them, drunkenly dancing and shouting.

'Myska and Petr,' he said to Owen. '*Jsme bratři.*' He squeezed the two fingers of one hand together. 'Yes? Comrades. *Československo Čechoslovákům!*' he bellowed again, punching the air. This was where his revolution would start — from here in the camp now that Myska was here with him and surely Petr too.

'*Kde je Petr?*' he said again anxiously.

Myska then said something: '*Není tady.*'

'*Co?*' Janek's tone changed. The enthusiasm

and fervour fell from his face. He asked the man the same question again. This time it sounded more like a demand but the man gave the same reply, then added, '*Opustil nás.*'

'Ne,' said Janek. He shook his head, but the man nodded.

'*Je v Americe*,' the man said. '*Už nevěří našemu poselství*.'

Janek's frown tightened. 'Ne,' he said. 'Ne.' He shook his head again and kept on shaking it, saying the same thing again and again, over the top of everything this man was trying to tell him. 'Ne. Ne,' he spat.

Then, without warning, the boy hurled himself at Myska, bringing the man heavily to the ground, and he had smashed two punches into the man's face, shouting, '*Lháři! Lháři!*' before Owen had a chance to pull the boy, still kicking and then sobbing, from him.

'*Můj bratr*,' he said to Owen. 'Gone.' Then, with a voice that bellowed out of him, he shouted it out: 'Traitor!'

* * *

Owen found him among the trees, some distance outside the camp, far from the muffled voices and singing and the heady sounds of music.

Josef Myska had gone, shouting abuse at Janek and Owen as he wiped the blood from his nose. There was no sight of Otmar and Mikoláš either — the first sign of trouble and the boys had disappeared. Now Owen sat beside Janek on an overturned oil barrel, the woods around them dressed in gloom, with only the slight gleam of moonlight catching on the leaves. The boy was huddled with his knees up, the torn flag wrapped around him like a blanket. Owen didn't know what to say. In the photograph that Janek had shown him, Petr had been a soldier, but through the newspaper clippings Owen had seen and the snatches of things he'd understood, the man had grown to become something else. A revolutionary, someone had said. Or a resistance fighter. A member of the Czech underground. Or just an idealist who had pulled other people in with him only to lose faith in it and wrangle himself a flight to America, abandoning the hopes and love and loyalty of all the people he once knew.

He saw how similar he and Janek were now, both caught up too much in the lives of brothers whom they could never keep up with, and chasing after shadows when all they had really needed was to stand up on their own. Janek seemed so young now, like a child again, wrapped in a flag that was made of nothing but ripped and sewn bits of material and painted with a blurred and faded symbol. He wondered when the boy had last seen his brother. On their journey together, Owen had always imagined Petr might simply appear from the trees one day, elusive to the end.

'Thank you,' he said under his breath. 'I wanted to thank you, for pulling me out. For saving my life.' He had been meaning to say it for some time.

The boy gave a faint smile, then brought his arm out from under the wraps of the flag and rested it lightly on Owen's shoulder. The moonlight caught in the glass of his watch — the watch that Owen had mended for him and was now fastened around his wrist.

* * *

Owen returned to the party and the warmth of the braziers. A collective drunkenness had infused the revellers, the whirl of dancing and cacophony of sounds merging into a wash that even in his own soberness made him feel sick. And between the swirl of bodies, he could just about see them — Anneliese holding the infant in its papoose and Janek leaning against the side of a building, his arms folded, a bottle of something held in his hand that occasionally he would uncross his arms to slug from, stone-faced, and then knit them back together. Owen could see that Anneliese was pouring out a desperate babble of words. She would turn herself inside out for the boy. Owen had said to her that she couldn't live with those lies.

'Believe me. I know.'

Now here she was cutting herself open in front of the boy. *This is who I am*. Janek gave her nothing. He let her talk and talk herself into crying, and then the baby too. She was pleading with him, this girl whom Owen thought maybe Janek had fallen for, but now everything was changed. Then he saw the boy drop his arms. He drew himself up and he spat into her face.

Owen pushed hurriedly through as Janek strode away. He grabbed hold of Anneliese by the arm and led her swiftly away from the crowd, the spit still there on her face. Her eyes were full of shock.

'He spat at me,' she said.

'He thinks you betrayed him. You slept with him. You let him fall for you. Don't you understand?'

'But I didn't mean to,' she said. 'I didn't want it to matter. Why does it matter what I am? I didn't do anything to hurt his people.'

He took her to a doorstep and sat her down, the baby still crying in her arms. It was dark and cold away from the fires and she held the infant close, her eyes staring, wet and glittering. How fragile she had become, he thought, now that she wasn't Irena; how vulnerable and broken. She sat there, gently rocking the infant, trying not to cry.

Owen didn't know what to say that would comfort her. In the morning the trucks would come to take Janek away, and a car to take away him. No decision had been made about Anneliese other than that it was impossible for her to stay at the camp.

'I'm glad the baby is well again,' he said. 'I tried to see him on the ward but he'd already been discharged.' He didn't tell her that he'd looked for her too but hadn't been able to find her. 'What will you do?' he said.

She was silent, and then she lifted the infant a little. He was quiet now, dozing in her arms.

'Will you take the child?' she asked.

'Of course.' He held his hands out.

'No,' she said. 'I mean will you take it with you? When you go.'

He paused.

'Please.'

He felt himself flush. 'I can't,' he said quietly. 'How can I?'

There was a silence.

He stared at her. 'Oh good Lord, Anneliese, you know I can't do that.'

'I could leave it again,' she said after a while. 'I could put it down somewhere and — '

'No. I thought you were going to find the father. You might still find Krysztof. Who knows? Maybe he will take him; maybe he will love him. People change. Wars change people.'

'No,' she said. 'His name was on one of the lists from the other camps. I saw it on a noticeboard.'

'That's good news then, isn't it?'

'Not that list,' she said.

'Oh.'

Krzysztof Krakowski was dead.

Another silence grew between them, long and large enough for the space to fill again with music and voices around them, and the crackle of a bonfire.

'I can't take the child,' he said again. 'You know that. I'm sorry.'

She nodded. 'Yes,' she said. 'I know.'

* * *

At 1745 at RAF Warboys — the Huntingdonshire airfield Owen had been stationed at since he'd completed his training — they were called into the briefing room where Group Captain

Collings gave them their operational instructions. After a first sortie to Hamburg three nights before, they would be going out again.

Max had been out of sorts all day, and in the crew briefing he took several verbal swipes at Owen that made even Budgie, their navigator, raise an eyebrow. Owen tried to think nothing of it. They were all tired. The squadron had already lost a Lancaster on the first sortie, taking six men with it. The strain was starting to show. It was a week since Owen had been reposted to the airfield — and since he had made his last deceitful trip to Caversham Rise, while Max had been journeying from where he'd been previously based at Wickenby.

Owen remembered when he'd first walked into the Warboys canteen.

I'm nabbing this FE, Max had shouted to anyone who cared to listen as he leapt over to the table to grapple Owen around the neck. *That's my brother. Best bloody FE you boys are going to see*.

Barely a week in, though, and something had abruptly changed.

By 2130 they were at their lockers, nervously checking their kit and pulling their flying suits on over their uniforms, then their flying boots and parachute harnesses, fixing their shoulder straps. They collected up all the paraphernalia of gloves, helmets, oxygen masks with their intercoms, and then their Mae Wests. This was the point when Owen always felt most sick. By the time the WAAFs drove them out to their craft, the adrenalin was usually kicking in. Tonight, though, he felt sicker than ever, glancing across as Max did up his laces with a yank and fastened his straps.

Dear Christ, Owen thought. He knows.

The rest of the crew filed out.

Blinkin' 'eck, I hope you ain't planning on flying at this speed, Skip, joked Tapper. *We'll never get off the bloody ground*.

Then they were gone and, as Owen turned to fix his harness, he realized that only the two of them were left.

Max took a couple of folded sheets of paper from his locker and shut it with a clang.

Max, for God's sake, what — ?

But Max had already slammed Owen hard against the lockers.

Owen gasped. *Jesus Christ*.

His brother's face was seething. *I want to show you something*, Max said.

What?

And I want you to be honest with me for once.

What on earth are you talking about?

Max thrust the papers hard against Owen so that he had no choice but to take them. *Go on*, he said. *Look*.

Owen held the crumpled sheets. His heart was in his mouth. Even though they were still folded he recognized the cream weave of the paper and the worming indents of his pencil markings showing through like narrow trenches of deceit.

I said look at them!

His hands shaking, Owen slowly unfolded the first and stared at the drawing. It looked so pathetically childish now: the bumblebee drawn to look like a flying machine with a cog for a heart and its wire-frame wings, the pulleys and pistons for hauling the wings up and down, and swag bags of pollen that he'd humorously labelled. He had held it up to the hotel window.

The mechanics of a bee. Reconfigured — as you can see — in the style of the late da Vinci. It had made her laugh.

Look, Max, this isn't what you think, he said.

He hardly needed to unfold the second sheet — he knew what it was — but he did.

I thought you couldn't draw faces. I'd say you tried pretty hard with this one.

Max was right. With the same intricacy and precision with which he had plotted every screw and rivet at Hawkers, so too had he reproduced Connie's face: the lines in her irises, the curve of her jaw, the blemishes of tiny freckles . . . This creation though, unlike the Hurricanes or the prototype Typhoon, had been crafted out of nothing but his love.

There was nothing in the picture to suggest that she had sat naked for him but for the bareness of her shoulders. She had said it herself: *I want you to draw my face*.

I bumped into her, he blustered. *In town. That's all. We had a quick tea in* . . . But he couldn't think and he didn't know what he was saying anyway.

Here. Max snatched the pieces of paper and rattled them in his face. *Right bloody here. You must think I'm a bloody fool*.

Owen stared at the stationery, at the small but treacherous footer:

The Swallow Hotel, Shepherd Market, London W1

It was somewhere near dawn when he woke, Anneliese playing heavy on his mind. The air in the room was cold, and colder still outside as he picked his way through the parade ground, the embers of the bonfire still burning, the shadows of tents and little pockets of litter seeming to loom up out of the ground.

He saw her up ahead hesitantly making her way with nothing but a bag, the baby and her grubby coat around her. He could hear her hushing the child, the hard soles of her shoes crunching over the stones. He knew where she was going but he did not try to catch up with her, nor did he call out to her, although he could have, the words there and ready: *Don't, Anneliese. Come back*.

She walked on oblivious, but then at the gates she stopped, hoisting the child further up on her shoulder and repositioning the strap of her bag around her neck. And then she quietly pulled the gate open and slipped delicately through. Only then did he glimpse the pale skin of her face. She turned and walked down the road, and he watched as she disappeared almost silently into the dark.

JANEK

Connie's arm was wrapped around him and hot against his chest. It was the lifting of it away from him though, the unpeeling of her from him, that woke him properly.

He opened his eyes.

Has your bear lost an eye? Six words, and a hand reaching beneath the bench to pull out the button that had been lost in the dark. And she had seen right into him, perhaps heard the slight English tone in his accent, seen the tension in his neck, or the nervous way he gripped the papers, fingers stained with sweat and ink that was lifting from the documents. She had given him a chance. In the chaos that then ensued — the upheaval in the carriage this small child was making for him — he had inadvertently slipped the button into his pocket as he had made his escape. Now he sat on the bed and held it in his hand.

He had ducked unnoticed from the carriage and was standing outside on the timbered platform holding on to the rail, looking up at the plane — sleek, silver and beautiful, turning above them as the train pulled across the bridge and the river rushed below. He had stared as the plane passed overhead, its engine guttering over the rattling clank of the train's wheels. From the swollen belly of the plane, a single pellet appeared. He watched it fall, slowly at first and then gathering speed as it plummeted through the sky, faster and faster, falling furiously towards them.

* * *

Out in the compound, dawn had broken and the morning was making a sluggish start. People wandered about, the odd truck kicked up stones as it rumbled through, and the medical students were trudging out in their ghost-white suits, skirting puddles where it had rained during the night. He had seen neither sight nor sound of Janek since last night's party. But here was Anneliese, returned, standing behind the wire fence staring in, the forest stretching on behind her and the grass growing around her ankles as if she had been there as long as the trees. Her mouth was open, her eyes wide and gazing blankly at him, not with fear but bafflement. It was only then that he realized how dirty she was. Her arms were locked rigid and plastered in mud right up to her elbows. She couldn't catch her breath.

He walked closer.

'Irena,' he said without thinking, and then corrected himself. 'Anneliese, I mean. What are you doing? Are you all right?'

She stared at him. She tried to speak, her mouth shaping a sound that would not come.

He stepped closer and took hold of the wire.

'What is it? What the hell's wrong? And what are you doing through there anyway? Where's the baby?'

Then the realization dropped.

'Oh my God,' he said slowly. He saw it in her eyes, in her soil-covered hands and arms, in her shaking. 'Jesus, no. Where's the baby? Where's the baby, Anneliese? *Anneliese*? Listen. Listen, look at me. Look at me, Anneliese. For God's sake look at me! Where's the baby?'

Her eyes were red, her chest heaving. Behind him the sounds of the camp faded. He tried to keep his voice calm as he clung to the wire.

'What have you done?' But she wouldn't answer. He shouted it again: 'What have you done?'

'He is gone,' she said, her voice no more than a whisper.

'What?'

'I had to bury him.'

'What? Oh, Jesus, no. No, Anneliese.'

'No one wanted him,' she said. 'But it is all right now.'

The girl was in a dream, sounding so distant even though she was right there. He flushed pale. He shook the fence so hard it rattled, and then shouted: 'Where is he?'

'It's all right,' she said. 'I buried him properly. I planted him like a seed.'

'Jesus Christ. Where?'

'In the field,' she said. 'You didn't want him. Nobody wanted him.'

But Owen wasn't listening. He was already running. He flew along the perimeter, yelling: 'Martha! Janek! Somebody! Help!'

There were people looking at him.

'Oh God! SOMEBODY HELP ME!'

He reached the gates and pushed through them, then ran out across the road, beneath the hang of trees with their dappled light and shadows, then swerving off over the grass to the field, all dug up in earthy furrows. He ran across it, tripping and scrambling. She wouldn't do it. She hadn't. She couldn't have done it.

He thought he was going to be sick. In the middle of the field he stopped, turning again and again, hunting for any sign, but everywhere he looked the field's surface looked the same. He saw Anneliese had reached the edge of the field.

'Where is he?' he shouted at her. 'Where is he?'

He fell to his knees. He started to dig, desperately clawing at the soil, doubled up and gasping, unable to breathe.

He was dimly aware of voices and figures approaching, slowly at first and then breaking into a run, and his own frantic cries of 'the baby, the baby', as if the words alone might push the infant up and lift him from the earth.

Anneliese was being dragged across the furrows, but she couldn't tell them where the child was. They couldn't even shake a voice from her.

He didn't know how many there were but they dug frantically with their hands, scrabbling at the earth, and all the time he kept thinking the field was falling away from him. It kept rising up and tilting so that clods of soil skittered away, the earth trying to tip him from it.

Then a voice. A sudden rush of people hurriedly gathering into a circle. Guppy was there, and Hamilton too, nurses he'd seen from the hospital, and inmates drawn by the cries for help. They collected around a single spot, two or three on their knees, furiously digging and brushing the dirt away. He didn't move. Nor Anneliese. She stood a short distance away, her arms limp at her sides and sobbing. They dug and dug until the murmurings of encouragement stopped and then something small and pale was slowly lifted, and a woman in a shawl had to quickly turn her head away.

* * *

At 11.00 on Tuesday 15 May 1945, they buried him. No one knew exactly how old the child was, not even Anneliese. The engraving on the cross simply stated: *An unnamed infant*.

There were mass graves in Camp 1 filled with the infected, but Little Man was buried among the trees at the spot where only hours before Owen had sat with Janek on an overturned oil drum. The small group huddled among the ferns, while the Jewish chaplain and then Hamilton spoke a few words. Throughout it all Anneliese's gaze was lost in the distance. Martha stood beside her with her arms folded, seemingly unsure whether her face should be showing sympathy or rage. There was no sign of Janek and no time to find him.

By 11.15 it was done. The Czech deportees were leaving at twelve; there were plenty of other things to be getting on with. One by one they dispersed, the chaplain back to his office, Guppy back to the estate car he was attempting to fix, Haynes and the handful of nurses back to their blocks and the tens of thousands of others who still needed their attention. Martha had last-minute paperwork to collect before the transport convoy arrived. She stepped towards Owen before she left and brushed his arm with her fingertips.

'You'll need to be back before twelve,' was all that she said.

He stood there alone, his eyes on the little cross that Guppy had hastily fashioned. He would dig another grave if he could. He would bury himself in it and let the earth gather itself around him. He would take comfort in its embrace.

Turning, he then saw Anneliese just as she had appeared that first night, stepping out from the undergrowth with no child in her arms. This time, though, he could not meet her gaze. He pushed through the ferns right past her, not knowing or caring any more.

She came crashing through the foliage after him as he headed towards the road. She was talking so fast. She kept grabbing at his arm, saying: 'I had to. Don't you see?' And then: 'Now I can come with you,' she kept saying, over and over. 'Take me. Take me with you. Take me with you. Please.'

He could knock seven bells out of her; knock her into the ground. 'For God's sake, no!'

'Why not?' She tugged at him. 'Please. Please,' she said, 'I beg you.'

He stumbled over the grass, walking blindly

out on to the road, his hands and arms as muddy as hers now. He could kill her with them. He could slap her right down.

'Don't leave me,' she said. 'You don't have anyone either.' She clung to him. 'Just take me with you.' He kept trying to pull her off but her hands were all over him, pulling at his neck and his face, trying to force him to look at her.

He tried to wrench her away — 'Get off!' — but she wouldn't let go. 'I said get off!' He took her by the shoulders and shook her as hard as he could so that she sobbed even harder, shouting: 'What the hell have you done?'

He shoved her away, and walked on, his blood roaring in his ears. He left her in the middle of the road, muddy and weeping.

In the distance behind him, trucks were coming through the field.

They barely slowed as he stood on the verge, a jeep and four trucks with open backs, their dark canvas sides buffeting in the wind. They rattled past, wheels rumbling and spitting up stones, before turning through the gates.

He paced after them with such a filthy, brutal rage storming in his head. He should have taken the child from her. He should have taken him from her and not given him back. He could put her in the ground beside him. He could push her into the soil.

The trucks disappeared around one of the blocks into the parade ground. People stood and stared at him, at his muddy hands and his face that could so easily crumple into tears.

* * *

The four trucks were parked in a line, each with their back to the square. A handful of Czech soldiers milled around, smart in their uniforms, a couple of them smoking cigarettes before the drive to Celle. From there, Martha had said, the refugees would be put on a train to Prague, other Czechs joining them from the countless other DP camps scattered across Germany; each changed for ever, broken and rebuilt again, survivors who had somehow clawed on to life and — against the odds — had finally regained some of their dignity. He saw it around him now as they waited, clutching their few possessions, a man playing a harmonica, a child holding a naked doll, its hair cropped as short as the child's.

There was no sign of Janek. Nor Martha. Hamilton wandered about among them with a clipboard and list, trying, Owen thought, to evoke an air of orderliness, while Haynes was ushering the Czechs together, his arms open wide as if he were a goatherd readying himself in case one of them suddenly bolted from the group.

Around the square others had appeared too: the French, the Poles, some Yugoslavs, all eager to wave the Czechs off, knowing that in the days and weeks that followed, it would be them piled into jeeps and trucks as the whole camp cleared out. Some of the women were hurriedly decorating the trucks with ivy vines and thin blossoming branches and sprigs of wilting wild flowers, festooning the vehicles with garlands like festival floats.

'You've not seen your Czech boy then?' It was Hamilton with his list.

'No,' said Owen. 'Have you asked those two?' He pointed out Otmar and Mikoláš.

'They say they haven't seen him.'

How fast friendships were formed and forgotten, Owen thought. The two boys did not seem at all bothered that Janek wasn't there. They sat in the dirt playing cards and slapping at each other's hands. They would soon be up on their feet and pushing, as the tailgates of the trucks were lowered and there was a rush for seats.

'Where's Martha anyway?'

'With this major,' Hamilton said. 'Some bloody high-ranker. It's usually a bunch of lackeys. Half the time we have to organize the transportation ourselves, but this time they've actually sent somebody.'

'Yes, Martha said,' said Owen. The major had been asking for someone but Owen couldn't now remember what it had been about.

'Look, are you all right? You look as white as a sheet.'

'Dicky stomach,' he said. It was true. He felt incredibly faint, as if Anneliese had taken the life from him too and only the shell of him was left.

Over Haynes' shoulder he saw Janek appear from behind one of the blocks, his bag hauled over his shoulder, moving with a nonchalant air as if it made no odds whether he went home or not.

'Oh, here he is,' he said with relief.

'Well, thank Christ for that,' said Haynes.

He slipped through the crowd to intercept him and Owen would have gone too but Hamilton was blocking his path and saying something.

'And I hear you're being ferried up to Hamburg. Someone's landed you a cushy flight.'

'Yes, something like that,' remarked Owen. He could see Haynes and Janek talking. The boy was paler than ever. He nodded at something that Haynes said. With a hand at the boy's back, Haynes then guided him over to join the other Czechs as a nervous anticipation started to fill the square.

'If the major has Martha giving him a guided tour, we could be standing here for bloody hours,' Hamilton grumbled. 'And that's not going to go down well. They want to be off and out, and you can't blame them. We'll have a bloody riot on our hands.'

Haynes raised a hand to one of the Czech drivers and the soldiers dispersed to their trucks. As soon as the first tailgate was dropped the refugees were swarming, clinging on to friends and family, elbowing their way forward and fighting for seats. Bags got caught in the crush, and then the shouting began. Before long, as the trucks filled and the scramble for seats became more ferocious, the inevitable happened. There was a commotion as families, lovers and friends were split, hysteria starting to set in as if they didn't believe the trucks were all going the same way.

Hamilton tried to calm the situation before somebody got hurt. 'There's room for everyone!'

he shouted, but no one took any notice.

The Czech soldiers pushed people back with their rifles as the first truck became full, and soon the tailgate was hoisted and bolts pulled across, a dozen or more pale but excitable faces cramped inside, and those who could extending an arm or hand to wave. At last they were going home.

Janek stood motionless in the parade ground, the crowd feeding forwards around him as he stared dumbly at the trucks. Owen pushed through and took his arm.

'What the hell are you playing at?' he said. 'Go on. Get in!'

Janek shook his head. 'No.'

'Petr's gone,' said Owen. 'Listen.' He took the boy by his shoulders and forced Janek to look at him. 'Look, listen to me, Janek. He's gone. Left you. Do you understand? You have to go home.'

The boy's eyes were wide — hazel, he saw, in the sun — cheeks so pale and flecked with sparse stubble. He was so clearly still a boy.

'You must have someone left,' he said. 'Some family.'

The boy shook his head. 'Only Petr.'

Owen let out a heavy breath and looked up instead at the windows around them, some of them open where patients well enough to get out of their beds were leaning out. The tailgate of another truck was lifted, bolts pulled in place, and then the third. The last stragglers crushed around the final truck.

'Listen,' he said to Janek. 'You can't stay here. You have to go.'

'I find Petr.'

'Petr's gone!'

'Ne!'

'Yes! For fuck's sake, Janek, will you get in the bloody truck.'

'He can ride with me,' came a deep voice.

Martha had emerged, bringing a large man with cropped silver hair with her. He was in a smart olive uniform, a single gold star on each shoulder, one arm held firmly behind his back. There was something familiar about him that Owen could not place.

'The major was just telling me how a certain young Czech saved him,' Martha said.

'Plucked from the rubble of a collapsed building,' the major said. 'A bomb blast,' he then added. 'And with barely a scratch.'

He took Owen in with a flash of recognition. 'That is why I must absolutely insist that the boy travels in the jeep with me.'

Martha said, 'Shall we go then? I'm sure Major Nemecek is keen to be on his way.'

The realization struck. Owen felt a cloud of heat quickly fill his head and prickling at his face.

Nemecek took a step closer to the boy. 'It would be an honour,' he said. His smile widened. 'I've been looking for you, Janek Sokol.' He turned to the crowd. 'And what a relief I must say to have finally found him.'

He pulled out his arm from behind his back and held it out. '*Nepodáš mi ruku?*' he said to Janek.

Owen, his pulse quickening, glanced at

Hamilton and Haynes and then at Martha. The major seemed to want Janek to shake his hand, but there was no hand to shake, just the arm and the end of the jacket sleeve, and within the dark hole the nub of something like the snout of a creature lurking in its burrow. He held it out, waiting for Janek. Martha gave a nervous laugh.

'Go on. *Nepodáš mi ruku?*' he slowly repeated.

'It's all right,' Martha said to Janek. 'He's joking with you.'

But when Nemecek spoke again, it was without the smile. '*Podej mi ruku*,' he told Janek. He pulled his sleeve back a little to show the wound, angry and pink, the threads of stitches still in place where the hand had only recently been removed at the wrist.

Dropping into a bucket, Owen thought. Taken off like dead wood, and falling in such a way that it hooked its fingers on to the rim as if it was trying to crawl its way out. *Well, don't just stand there*. It was the voice of his father. *Shake it!*

There was no more laughter, just a thick and awkward unease.

'*Podej mi ruku*,' Nemecek said again. Not an invitation but an order.

Janek stared at the offered stump. Martha glanced at Haynes and Hamilton. Owen felt all eyes turn, the camp revolving on its axis, all the faces in the trucks on them, and then Nemecek suddenly laughed.

'I am teasing,' he said. 'It is just an old war wound.' He withdrew his arm and pulled the sleeve back down. 'You must forgive me,' he said, addressing the crowd. 'The war has done strange things to my humour.' He looked at them for acknowledgement, smiling. 'I must insist that he rides with me, though.' He placed his remaining hand on Janek's shoulder. Owen saw him grip it, Janek's face flushing.

The boy, Owen realized, had become strangely docile since Nemecek had arrived, as if he had been deflated by the realization that Petr was really gone. He watched Janek let the major steer him by the shoulder around to the side of the jeep, and then the major opened the door and motioned him in.

'Don't worry,' he said, directing the comment squarely at Owen. 'He is in good hands.' He laughed.

He got in beside Janek and slammed the door, laying his arm over the back of the seat behind the boy as his driver took his place in front. Around them the trucks had started their engines, the onlookers pulling back to give them space to reverse out and then edge forward through the gates. There was calling and waving as they threw flowers over the trucks, then a sudden swell of noise as people started playing accordions and trumpets.

Across the yard, Owen spied Anneliese watching from the other side of the fence, her fingers at the wire. He felt his stomach turn. From inside the jeep Janek's eyes were locked on Owen's. He looked terrified.

'I don't think he should go,' said Owen.

'Don't be insane,' said Martha. 'He'll be fine. He's going home.'

'Yes, he'll be fine,' said Hamilton.

'No, you don't understand. We need to stop them. Hey!' he shouted, but his voice was lost in the surge of noise as the trucks pulled out through the gate, the crowd making way to let them through and then starting to close again, shouting and waving and singing.

Owen tried to push through as Nemecek's driver edged the jeep forward, hooting his horn to clear the path.

'No, wait!' Owen shouted. 'Wait. Martha! Haynes! For God's sake, stop them!' His voice was lost in the cacophony of cheers and excitable flurry of flag-waving.

The jeep pulled out and Owen squeezed through, freeing himself from the crowds at the gate, and started to run after it. His eyes locked on the jeep as it accelerated away down the road, and on the two figures seated in the back, the distance rapidly expanding between them.

The line of trucks grew smaller, the jeep kicking up clouds of dust from behind, and the sound of them became fainter and fainter. Owen slowed to a halt. He watched them go, disappearing, and then his heart stopped as Nemecek's jeep abruptly turned, swinging left away from the line of trucks, heading out instead across the field and towards the woods beyond.

Owen stared, bewildered. 'Oh Christ.'

Before he knew it he was running.

* * *

The jeep had followed a narrow track until the trees had grown too dense around it and it could go no further. Owen followed Nemecek's voice. He was irate and shouting at Janek; he sounded half crazed. Crouching low, Owen pulled the pistol from his pocket; it was too late now to get help. He picked his way through the ferns that were lush and still wet from rain, the sodden leaves quietly squelching under his feet and his shirt fast becoming damp on his back.

In the smallest of clearings, Nemecek was standing over the boy, who was kneeling at his feet, the mouth of Nemecek's gun pressed at the back of Janek's head.

Owen stepped forward.

'I wouldn't come any closer,' the major said, not taking his eyes from Janek. 'And put that thing away. We both know that I can put a bullet through his head before you've even managed to cock it. There is only one person who has ever taken a shot at me and lived, and now I have him on his knees.' He laughed. 'We have an old score to settle. *Máme nějaké staré účty k vyřízení*,' he said to Janek. 'Mm?'

'Is that what all this is about?' said Owen.

'You have no idea.'

'The war is over.'

'Your war, perhaps. Not ours. When the Germans leave the Czech republic, who will control it then? Hm? The Soviets? The Poles? The Hungarians? You can't leave it to the Czechs. They let you sell them to the Germans. No, not even sell them.' He laughed. 'Give them away. A gift to Hitler from your Mr Chamberlain. And what do they do? Nothing. They give themselves to the Führer. They welcome him in.

They let him terrorize them. They sleep with the devil.'

Janek shouted: '*To není pravda!*'

Nemecek struck him hard with the butt of his pistol. '*Co ty o tom víš?*' he said. He gave Owen a sideways glance. 'His loyalty is touching — don't you think? But completely misinformed.'

Janek clutched the side of his head. Owen could see the blood beginning to seep between his fingers. The boy muttered something.

'Petr?' the major said, smiling. 'Always Petr. *Petr uletěl, jako pták.*' He made a whistling sound. 'Flew away, hm? Like the coward he is. The great Petr Sokol,' he scoffed. 'He was a big fish in a small bowl. All talk. The new Czech republic, he said. Czech for the Czechs. And what happened when the Germans came? Hm?'

The boy said something and Nemecek laughed.

'They did not take him prisoner,' he told Owen. 'I don't know where this boy gets his crazy ideas from. He wasn't a threat to the Germans. He wasn't anything. Nothing. He ran away. Like I keep telling you. He abandoned you. All of you. You,' he said, poking Janek in the back of the head with his gun, 'just don't listen.'

'Stop it,' said Owen. 'Just let him go.'

'Let him go?' He laughed. 'I'll do no such thing.' He turned his attention to Owen, the gun still held against Janek's head. 'Let me tell you something: I used to work with this boy's father. I was loyal. I was hardworking. I was the voice between him and us Sudeten employees, his go-between, his lapdog. His factory would have been nothing without us. We made his father rich. And when the economic crash happened, what did he do? He let us all go. He kept only the Czechs. Only them.

'I lost my job. We all lost our jobs. He told us we all had to get another job. There were no other jobs. But he turfed us out anyway to save his own neck, feed his own family, but without a care for us or our families. He made me hate him. I didn't want to.

'And then his son, this Petr.' He spat the name into the back of Janek's head. 'The great Petr Sokol,' he mocked. 'He made us believe he was on our side. He organized a demonstration outside the factory gates. He was going to demand his father give us our jobs back; stand with the workers, he said. But his father would never listen to him. It was just Petr trying to placate us, disowning his father for his own ambitions. The demonstration got violent. He wanted them to riot. His father called the police. There was fighting, and a boy got shot. My boy. A boy his father had employed and then, like us all, he had thrown him out on the street.'

Owen remembered the clippings. The rioting crowd. Petr's fist in the air. The headlines that he had not been able to make out but the odd word as he'd scanned the page — *sabotáž* — and two names: Petr Sokol and Antonín Nemecek. A boy aged fifteen — perhaps the same age as Janek.

'This boy's family,' Nemecek went on, 'has taken my job, my livelihood, my son, and now this,' he said, holding his handless arm up. 'They have caused me nothing but pain. But I am Sudeten. I fight for me. I play one side against the other but this is my war, not theirs or yours or anyone else's, and I say it is not over!'

'This boy,' Owen said, 'has lost his family too, you know. His parents.'

'Do you think I don't know that? You can't trust anyone these days, not even family.' He nudged Janek with the tip of his gun once more. 'Hm? His sister let slip where they were,' he told Owen. 'She was dating a Sudeten German. She had walked out on them for him, this man. She told me where they were.'

'What do you mean?' said Owen.

'I mean the war was in pieces. The *Protektorát*, the so-called government. Martial law. I went to find them. Someone else would have done it if it was not me.'

Owen relived the sensation of a figure hauling him up into the field. And then, like a distant echo in the far recesses of his head, two shots and then a third before the figure crouching over him in the dark had turned and run.

A house. Two graves. The boy standing over them. He had seen them from a bedroom window. Then, in his mind, he was stepping once again through the debris of a room, the chair with a penny-sized hole puffed into it, the sunlight coming through another hole in the wall. He remembered the crackle of smashed china beneath his feet and the snap of broken photo frames, the photographs already taken.

There, in the woods, his legs gave a little. He stepped out from under the trees, straightening his arm, feeling the tightening of anger within him. He pointed the gun at Nemecek, ready to fire it.

'Let him go,' he said.

'No.'

'Haven't you done enough? I said let him go.'

There was the sharp click of a safety catch. The major's driver stepped out from the trees, his gun fixed on Owen, while Owen pointed his at Nemecek who still had Janek kneeling before him, his own pistol pressed into the back of the boy's head.

'Do you think I drove all this way, orchestrated all of this, just to pat him on the back and wave him off? No. He has made me a joke. This,' he said, holding up his handless arm, 'is a joke. You're right. I want to ruin him, not kill him. I want him never to forget. So, do I take his hand? Hm?' He glanced at Owen. 'When he took mine? What is the most important thing to him right now, do you think? Not his parents.' He laughed. 'Not his traitorous sister or his cowardly brother. Not his two little siblings, gone. What's the most important thing to him now?' He signalled for his comrade to keep his gun trained on Janek, and then he took a step closer to Owen, pointing the gun at Owen instead.

'What is the most important thing to him now?'

'I don't know,' said Owen.

'I think you do,' he said.

Two shots simultaneously, and in the split second that followed Owen was aware of a third, and of Nemecek twisting and turning with the impact.

On the rattling train Owen found himself looking up at the sky. He could see the bullet-shaped pellet falling from the plane, closer and closer as the train edged across the bridge. The river roared below. And just as Nemecek's bullet hit him, bolting through his skin, the bomb struck the end of the bridge. The bullet tore into his body, tearing through the flesh below the ribs as the bomb blasted through the railway tracks, blowing a hole right through and exploding against the gorge beneath. His insides crumbled. From the train he clambered on to the side of the rails at the end of the carriage as the brakes shrieked and passengers screamed. And then he jumped. The bridge was collapsing and the front of the train started to tilt. He felt his whole body lurch, and all of this came to him in a second — the moment of a bullet's impact.

He fell.

He was falling, the ground rushing towards him. He could hear voices, see Nemecek's body slip to the ground, Janek still there with his hands to his head as Owen's legs gave way, and he fell from the bridge, the river rushing towards him fast and furious. He hit the woodland floor as his body crashed through the water. The sudden roar of the river as it tore him away, the rumbling of underwater explosions, bits of bridge and rock starting to hit. His head burst to the surface. He was only aware for the briefest moment of the huge wrenching sound from above him as the engine toppled, peeling the carriages with it one after another. The tremendous eruption of water as the train and half the bridge smashed into the river around him.

Then, in that same moment — as Owen's bulleted body hit the woodland floor and in his mind the thunderous roar of water crashed down upon him — everything cut to black.

⋆ ⋆ ⋆

He is at a bus stop in the quivering heat, the hill rising up in the distance. Inside his uniform he has the heart secretly stitched into the pocket. There is a canvas RAF bag on the pavement beside him. He is going to meet Max. They've been called to the station to deliver 14,0001bs of fire-makers. He looks at a familiar wristwatch. The number in the tiny date window reads 18. Eighteenth of July, he thinks. Nineteen forty-three. The bus is already five minutes late.

The street is deserted. Just him and — in the far distance there on the brink of the hill — her. She is standing on the pavement outside the gate where the steps lead up to the flat. He can see her quite clearly, still standing where she had said goodbye when she had put her hand to his face, and he had kissed those lips, that cheek, that skin. It is all coming back to him: when she smiled at him, a breeze lifting her hair. She pats his breast pocket and takes his hand. She kisses the knuckles and then plants a kiss in his palm, closing his fingers around it as if to keep it safe.

Come back, she says. *Come back to me*. She puts his hand to her belly. *I need you to come back*.

She straightens his jacket and pulls it tight, and then kisses him one last time; and that, in his mind, is when the first drip falls. It lies on the ground like a petal, and then another and another. She opens the jacket, and there where the bullet was that Nemecek had fired, that pain that Owen has carried with him all this time like a premonition of the pain to come, he can see that he is bleeding.

* * *

In time he would call it a miracle, for it was Martha who saved him, clawed him back from the dead, and would not give up on either him or the heart that for those few seconds stopped. Or perhaps it was the cotton heart stitched next to his own that had pulsed first with the love of someone lost and for some time forgotten that eventually reignited it, not the pumping hands or the cries for help. But for those few seconds he was adrift in a timelessness, with all the time in the world to find himself, to walk through the rooms of a frozen ice house, or run through the wheat fields with a brother, or spot a button, or catch a bus, the tears streaming down his face. Or kiss someone goodbye.

* * *

He wakes in a field. He is not at all hurt or injured. He is in his office suit. He has been sleeping, that is all. And when he wakes and sits up he knows exactly where he is. He has done this all before. He freewheels through the images. The line in the grass where Janek had dragged him from the river. The zip of a bird. The deep blue sky. The button is exactly where it should be. No gun yet but he knows where to find it. First he needs to stand up. He needs to look around. He looks for Max but he isn't there. There is just the field, the gentle tilt of it. He is quite sure of where he is going. He has walked this walk before.

'There you are!'

It was Martha. He at least knew that.

'I thought we were going to lose you, but you've pulled through,' she said.

His jaw felt loose. He wanted to ask where Janek was, where Irena was, and the baby. He knew that some of this was wrong, but he couldn't think what. His fingers curled around the bed sheets, the soft feel of cotton.

'He's gone,' she said. 'Before you ask. Janek, I mean. Went yesterday. Haynes drove him down to Celle. There was a train we managed to get him on.'

Owen tried to speak. She leant in close and he tried again.

'You've been here three days,' she said. 'He sat with you for two of them. I'm sorry. I know I'm not much of a substitute.' She pulled something from her pocket and pushed it into his hand. 'He wrote you this, by the way,' she said. 'Haynes helped him with the English, so you'll have to blame him for the spelling.'

The folded sheet of paper had been tied with string around a watch. He held it tight in his hand.

'Oh, and that goddamned major of yours is dead,' she said. 'Haynes took him down. I think you shot as well, but God knows where that went. Lucky, I suppose. You might have been court martialled.'

She went on talking but he was already falling. The darkness pooled over him so that when he came to, he was no longer in the hospital block, in one of a thousand beds.

He is clambering instead over the wrecked remains of a train. The iron is hot in the sun, the heat blasting off the metal. A cloudless blue sky reflected in the broken windows. He picks his way across the overturned carriages, the smashed wood and timbers caught among the broken rails. Standing on the side of a carriage that now has become its roof, he wrenches open a door and peers down through it. The carriage is full of dirty water, bodies floating about. One of them is a small girl, wearing white socks and bright red sandals. She is floating face down. Beside her there's a scattering of his forged identity papers floating like waterlilies, the ink draining from them, and there, nudging against the wall of the carriage, a stuffed toy bear. When he lies on his stomach and reaches down to pull it out, he sees that one of its eyes is missing and the other is a single rusted tin button.

He drops the door shut and sits for a while, then climbs on to the fender and slides down to the boiler. He wades into the water and pulls out a canvas RAF bag that has got caught by a branch. He knows what is in it. It has his camp identification number — 4993 — scratched into the canvas. He unhooks the buckles, opens it and finds the rye bread. He takes the letters out and reads each of them one last time, committing every word that she has written to memory, the letters he had carried with him all that time, before, just like then, he lets them slip into the water, and the river washes the ink from them and, like scattered waterlilies, sweeps them away.

* * *

The field ambulance took him from the camp, with Haynes at the wheel. Martha and Hamilton waved from the gate, along with a French girl with cropped hair whom they all called Nurse Joubert. The remaining Czechs had gone; the Dutch and Serbs too. Before long the camp would be empty, all signs of what had happened there vanished entirely.

As for Owen, he was on the road to recovery and Haynes would drive him to Hamburg, where he would spend the night before his flight home.

He didn't see the girl standing at the edge of the field as the ambulance bore him through the camp gates and out along the road. He didn't see her waiting, hoping to see him one last time if even for a second through a grubby passing window. She stood with her arms as if in the crook of them she still carried a baby, and as the truck passed, she turned and watched it go, knowing perhaps that it was Owen and she would not see him again.

OWEN

From the line of tables outside the café along the Alsterarkaden you could see both bridges across the Alsterfleet and the view across to City Hall, which had hardly any war damage at all, he noted. The sun etched its way around it, drafting its outline against the blue, sparking on the clock face that topped the central tower. While below, in the main square, British tanks were lined up, the taking of the city and victory over Germany now complete.

He nursed a barely warm coffee. The sun shone over the water through the arches, the shadows of the railings tangling around his feet. He closed his eyes for a moment, the pain beneath his ribs real now and throbbing beneath the bandaging. The clock chimed the quarter hour. She was late; he knew she would be.

Along the neat row of tables people sat, basking in the sun and making small talk. Mostly they were German but occasionally a British voice would rouse him. Two women were quibbling over whether they should leave a tip. Through the arcade, a deliveryman hauled a cart of bottles over the cobbles. It rattled through Owen's chest and out through the hole where a bullet had once been. Life, it seemed, went on.

He saw it all around him. He had walked though the city's flattened streets, picking his way around the rubble of the train station and gazing around him at the forlorn carcasses of buildings, the endless flurries of dust blowing out and swilling around his feet, and all he could think was: we did this. Max and I. Deliverymen delivering bombs. They couldn't be held responsible, but he felt responsibility all the same. He was filled with an almost unbearable shame just seeing the faces of the children sitting about on kerbs, or the single mother struggling to push a pram through the debris.

Here though, on the arcade, the rubble had been swept up, the pavements washed down, wooden boards laid over holes and streetlamps righted. Across the way, a woman was banging the soot from a rug over a balcony, while two floors up another was helping a girl to water a window box. People walked with shopping bags. He'd seen them queuing for bread. He had even stopped to watch two boys playing with a broken tennis racquet — one tossing ball-sized chunks of rubble that the other would strike, blasting it against a half-tumbled wall and leaving pellet-shaped marks among those already there.

He saw her crossing the bridge and knew instantly that it was her. She was dressed efficiently in a grey skirt suit, a collection of files held in her arm. He watched her turn off the bridge and swing a right and then come flurrying through the arcade, threading through the passers-by.

'Flight Sergeant Thomas?' she said, a little breathless. Her words were clipped and well spoken. How refreshingly English, he thought. 'Cathy Bridport. RAF Liaison Officer. So sorry.

Have you been waiting long?' She pulled up a chair and sat down, dumping the pile of folders she had been carrying next to the ashtray. 'I've only been here a week myself. I'm still getting lost.' She lit a cigarette and offered him one, which Owen politely declined. 'Not helped, I suppose, by the fact that you never know which roads are going to be blocked. You think a building's safe and then down it comes. *Bosh*. It's a wonder anyone sleeps at night. I know I don't.' She took a puff and blew it out. 'God, that's better. I'll just grab a coffee. Then we can get down to business.' She glanced at her watch. 'Oh look! I'm sorry, you've been here an age.'

She signalled for the waitress and a thin girl with floury fingerprints on her apron stepped out from the café. Cathy ordered a coffee. 'And one of those nice pastries, please. *Eine kleine Konditorei*.'

The waitress nodded.

'And you?'

'Coffee and cake,' said Owen. 'Yes. That would be lovely. Thank you.'

'Well, least I can do for keeping you waiting,' she said.

* * *

In the July 1943 bombings, forty-five thousand of Hamburg's inhabitants had been killed, she told him. Half the city destroyed.

'We've taken over the Gestapo headquarters,' she said. 'The British Army Field Security, I mean. The boys are in their element there. Can you believe it — the place was still fitted out with all their old telephone-tapping devices? They've been having high old jinks.'

'Forty-five thousand?' His head seemed stuck on the number.

'Well, it wasn't just us,' she said. 'The Americans too. It simply had to be done, didn't it?'

'Why?'

She gave him an odd look over the rim of her coffee, then leant across and stubbed her cigarette out in the cracked ashtray.

'Perhaps we would be better off looking at your files,' she said. 'Fill in a few gaps.' She opened the folder and leafed through. 'Last dated sortie: twenty-seventh of July 1943. Declared missing: twenty-eighth of July. Last radio contact: somewhere over Hamburg. You've rather come full circle,' she said, scanning down the page. 'Captured on landing.'

'Yes. If my memory serves me . . . '

'Well, we'll come back to that, shall we?' She turned the page and read on. 'From what we've gathered, you would have been taken to Dulag Luft, west Germany, then a camp over in the east. One of their Luftwaffe places, right?'

'I think so,' he said. 'Then it gets murky.'

She rifled through more papers. 'From our intelligence, there's a record you were all moved to Nuremberg.'

'Nuremberg?'

'Yes. In the west. You arrived in early February.'

'Yes, like you said, we were moved.' He

remembered the long walk, the snow and then, at some point, a train ride with other men crowded in with him. 'How long was I there?'

She scanned the page. 'Not sure. The camp in Nuremberg was evacuated about a month ago as well, in mid-April, just as we were closing in.' She gave him a weak smile. 'God, it all seems so long ago, doesn't it?'

'And then what?'

'And then transferred again, to Moosburg. Southern Bavaria. They were getting desperate by that point, I shouldn't wonder; moving you all into the furthest reaches they had.'

'And I was there as well?'

'You see, that's what I was hoping you could tell me,' she said. 'We rather think not. It's our belief that you never actually arrived in Moosburg. There's been no mention of you on any records or from the men we pulled out from there. We think you disappeared in the transfer at Nuremberg. It was rather chaotic by all accounts. I like to think you might have slipped away, managed to get on a different train — hm? — going somewhere else. How does that sound? Feasible?'

He didn't know.

'But I was heading east,' he said. 'I remember the train now but I don't understand why I would be heading east.'

'I'm not sure I can help with that,' she said.

He remembered now: the crowd at Nuremberg station. The guards had become lax, drunk and careless half the time; the war as good as over, their cause as good as lost. In the throng of people amassing on the platform there had been a scuffle and in the confusion he had slipped away, ducking into a lavatory. The room was empty but for a small gentleman at the sink. Owen had stood there in his battered RAF uniform and had known then that if he was to head back into Germany, he needed to change his appearance. He took the man quite by surprise — a sharp crack as his head hit the sink — and then Owen dragged him into the cubicle. The shirt was too small, the trousers too short and the shoes were falling apart, but they were less conspicuous than what he was wearing. He couldn't get the man's jacket on though — the arms were too tight — so, in a moment's decision, he ripped the insignia from his cuffs and shoulders and then, instantly regretting that, stuffed the jacket instead into his bag, hoping that at some point he might be able to find another.

He saw in the mirror how ridiculous he looked, but there wasn't time to change back. He could hear the shouts coming down the platform. He needed to run. He wasn't going to Moosburg. He wasn't even going home. He had been intent on nothing else at that point but heading back to Sagan.

'Max.'

Cathy looked up from her folder.

All this time there had been a terrible fear that he had left his brother somewhere: in a camp, a field, on a path in the snow. *We have to go back*, he'd said, but Janek had been adamant.

'I need to know if you have any information,'

he said, 'on Flight Lieutenant Maxwell Thomas.'

'Ah.' She turned the page on the file. 'Perhaps we ought to get another coffee.'

* * *

At 0120 hours on the twenty-eighth of July 1943, it was reported that a Lancaster Avro Mark III, flying a sortie over Hamburg, was shot down. Of the seven crew members of 156 Bomber Squadron, two were known to be found dead, two were eventually reported by the German Luftwaffe as 'captured', and the three remaining were eventually classified as 'missing in action'. These were the facts as reported in the documents held in her file, and communicated to Owen over a second cup of coffee and a third cigarette. This was his plane. She wondered what he remembered.

Not his plane, Owen thought. Theirs. 'Suzie Sue' — a bomber so beautiful that they had named her twice.

It had been a calm night: clear and star-filled as they flew out from Warboys and left the English coast at Mablethorpe with the rest of Groups 1 and 5, heading north-east across the North Sea, before dipping in a south-easterly direction north of Heligoland. Owen remembered the battle roar of the engines as he had sat at the flight deck next to Max, their Lancaster flanked on either side by other bombers, Halifaxes and Blenheims too — over seven hundred aircraft in total. The night's sky swarmed with them, their engines throbbing.

He was always edgy on the outbound journey, but that night an anxiety had gripped him harder than he could bear. Since the incident at the lockers, Max had hardly said a word — none of his usual banter and bravado — and now, glowering beside him like a thickening cloud, he was making Owen nervous. He could sense the awkward glances passing behind him in the cramped fuselage: Budgie, their navigator directly behind them, plotting their course, and Tapper at his radio desk, listening to the airwaves. How could the plane be so cold and yet so hot, he thought. He could feel his guilt leaking out from every burning pore.

Beside him Max gripped the yoke with his gloved hands, his face like stone. His brother's eyes seemed so intensely fixed on the sky that Owen thought he might explode. Owen looked out himself: nothing but the night sprawling endlessly around them, dark and empty but for the deeper shadows of other bombers migrating through the sky.

He needed to carry out his system checks and log the readings but his mind kept falling through a thousand moments, a thousand kisses, looks and touches when he should have stopped himself. And now it was over, and everything was going to hell.

He could hear the growl of the Merlin engines through the floor, and something rattling beneath him, the vibrations seeming to roll around in his head. Then through the earpiece he heard Tapper quietly sending out code, and a cough came from somewhere through the tunnel of the plane, probably Smithy, their new bomb aimer. With the air pressure and freezing temperatures, they were all in perpetual possession of a cold.

At the back, Peri, and Barnes, who was their tail-end Charlie, were getting into their gunner positions. Speaking to each other through the radio had become second nature but now their voices testing the intercoms sounded strange, as if they were communicating through little more than thought. He could feel his own words bunching at the front of his mouth, all the things that he had not said but meant to, like: *I'm sorry* and *I love her* and *I tried not to, Max, I promise*.

Navigator to pilot, said Budgie through the intercom. *ETA — twelve minutes*.

Owen stared out at the black bulks of planes flocking around them.

Max did not respond.

Owen looked across. He could barely see any human sign of his brother at all beneath the paraphernalia of oxygen mask, jacket and helmet. There was just the cold stare of his eyes, the bridge of his nose and top of his cheeks. The sound of his brother's breath came amplified through the microphone.

Max, he said. But it was too late.

Peri's voice cut in. *Mid-upper to pilot. Sporadic flak bursts coming*.

Barnes' voice broke in too over the heavy burr of the engines. *Rear gunner to pilot. Confirm. We got Krauts*.

Owen pulled out his log. He was supposed to note it. *0058. Sporadic flak bursts*. They'd had encounters before but now his hands were shaking so violently that he couldn't control the pen.

Three Bf 109s swept into view as if they'd been pulled in on wires, and now he could see their silhouettes alongside them and the sharp bursts of light.

Messerschmitts on the starboard, he said into his intercom.

Coming close at the back too, added Barnes. He could hear the tension in Barnes' voice.

Through the side window the flak bursts were visibly heavier, but Max still wasn't responding. Goddamn it, he needed to do something.

Max. Come on, he said.

Barnes' voice broke through. *Yes, come on, skipper. Get us out*.

Owen could hear Max breathing heavily now, coming loud through his earpiece. Was he doing it on purpose? He saw his brother's hands tightening, squeezing at the control yoke.

Skip, we need to manoeuvre.

More flak, said Peri.

They're coming in.

For Christ's sake! someone shouted. *Manoeuvre!*

Flak burst around them, flashes of light around the sky. Owen's hand was at the parachute storage, the other clinging to the overhead struts, bracing himself.

What's going on? Communicate! This was Smithy from the back. *Why aren't we doing anything?*

Owen pulled his intercom away and leant in so

he could shout. *Max! Max!* He grabbed at Max's arm, trying to shake him from his trance. It was as if he'd fallen so deep within himself that he couldn't be pulled out.

Max, look, for the love of God, I'm sorry. But you need to snap out of this.

There were tracers going into the wing and he was aware of a barrage of voices through the radio. Peri and Barnes were firing. The cabin was filled with noise as the darkness around them lit up with staccato blasts.

Corkscrew port! came a voice. *Max! Corkscrew port, goddamn it!*

What the hell's going on?

Budgie was standing behind them, head cowering against the arc of the fuselage and one hand holding an overhead strut. *Max*, he shouted. *For God's sake!*

Then, without a word, Max suddenly turned the yoke and dipped the plane. Owen rammed the throttle levers out to the stops. Max banked her violently down and to one side, then turned her towards the oncoming fighters so that Peri could get his aim. But it was too late. The cannon shells popped, scattering through the side of the plane, in a rapid fire of blasts.

Christ!

An inner light exploded.

Owen saw the starboard outer engine backfiring and lighting up the darkness.

We're hit!

The flaming engine spluttered and stalled.

Engine down. We're hit!

Max jammed the throttle and swung the

Lancaster into a dive. They lurched forward, the dials on the instruments twitching around as they lost altitude, the plane accelerating, twisting and turning, the air rushing hard against it.

Through the intercom all Owen could hear was shouting. Smoke issued into the cockpit as the self-sealing tanks blazed. He could no longer see any of the controls, or Max, or even his own hands. They were in a gushing, blasting, raging fog. The plane filled with the foul-smelling smog as it screamed and turned, hurtling down, Smithy shouting: *For the love of God!* and Max yelling: *Get out!*

Such a noise, such a deafening noise, as the windscreen cracked, flames scoring around the sides, starting to fill the cabin and coming through the electrics. Owen fumbled at his chest parachute, clipping it on. Max or someone — he couldn't tell — prised back the escape hatch and clambered up as it opened. There was a sucking roar that took the smoke and flames with it, the figure also disappearing. Owen hauled himself up and, with a hard kick, he too was away. He fell fast, the air whistling painfully in his ears, the pressure of it against his body so forceful that it scorched.

Below him his beloved blazing bird fell like a beauty, the dust and smoke and flecks of debris whipping up around him, and he saw nothing but the thick smog-filled sky that he was falling, blasting, tumbling through. When he thought he must be at about 1,500 feet, he pulled the ripcord and felt the jerk of the parachute opening. Some distance away the plane hit and exploded, still full-bellied with its bombs. Above him his white canopy billowed. Shreds of the Lancaster, metal and cloth, still fluttered past like smouldering ash, the flittering silver strips of window.

A thousand feet up and slowly drifting, everything cold and quiet. He looked around him. The sky was empty. No dark silhouette of anyone else parachuting down.

And only then did he realize that he was crying. The wrecking of the plane was burning in the distance.

Max! he screamed. *Max!*

* * *

'I say, are you all right?' It was the woman opposite him, her name momentarily gone. 'You seemed to blank out there for a moment.'

Perhaps he had. The images now came too fast. The heat of the smoke burning his eyes. Its foul stench. The billowing dust.

He had drifted for some time over black fields and the occasional nub of a house. The air buffeted at the canvas. He felt the cold bite of it at his legs. As he came in over a pasture and then crossed an empty lane, he could see people with flash-lights hurrying, the lights swinging over the crop at him and then a voice. All the torches shone up at him coming down like a black angel. They started to run — he could hear their voices — as they followed his descent over the field.

He was going to collide with the wood beyond but he could do nothing to stop himself. The wind threw him over the treetops, the branches scratching and scraping, lacerating his legs, and then he fell through, caught within the branches. He hung breathlessly, helpless. The torchlight shone up through the limbs of the tree towards him, strung up like a marionette.

'Any news then of the others?' Owen said now. 'Any survivors, I mean?'

'I'm sorry,' she said. 'I don't know. Look, I know it's all terribly muddy for you but if there's anything you could tell us that might help join the dots . . . '

There wasn't, he told her. He just needed her to go.

* * *

In a darkened cinema he stared at the screen. There was a newsreel playing images, a commentary running over the top of it. Some man from the BBC. Two seats down from him a woman was crying into her handkerchief, and further across a couple of soldiers both sat with their fingertips pressed to their lips. No one spoke — there was just the commentary.

The images flickered, but he barely saw them. It seemed impossible that it had been the same camp that he had just come from. By the time he had got there, most of it had been cleared up and he had seen hardly anything through the wire. But now the full horror of it was played out before him, the bulldozers sweeping up the hundreds of naked bodies, no more than bones dressed in skin, their matchstick limbs turning and tumbling over each other, bodies splitting as the bulldozer pushed them over the dirt and shovelled them into a pit. In the distance a wooden building was being torched. There were images of huddled people, their faces hollowed out, their eyes bulbous and watery. The commentary droned on.

When it ended, the rest of the people in the auditorium slowly got up and left, the woman taking her snivelling out into the foyer. But Owen didn't. He sat there in the darkness staring until eventually, with the last whirr of the projector and a click, the screen went blank.

The tram from Victoria Embankment took him over the Thames, moving with slow persistence past the lines of traffic. London felt surreal. The streets were recognizable but the war had cast a shadow over them; the blackened buildings seemed to loom despite the mid-May sun. His greatest fears lay scattered around him. Even buildings here had been taken out, bombs and fires ravaging the city in much the same way as he had seen in Hamburg. It seemed to Owen to be a city damned beyond repair.

After he had come out of the Ministry, he had walked along the river and cut across Victoria Embankment Gardens, where in a bandstand a group of returned soldiers were singing hymns and women from the Red Cross rattled collection boxes. All the men were parcelled up in bandages, one or two even missing an arm or leg. He wondered if any of them had been at St Mary's and dealt with by his father; whether his father, in fact, was still working there. He stood for a few minutes on the neatly trimmed grass and listened to the tune he'd carried all this way in his head — 'Guide Me, O Thou Great Redeemer' — being sung out, proud and strong.

At Wimbledon station he changed on to the trolleybus. Gazing through the window now as it took him down Kingston Road, the tune still lingered. He held the button tight in his palm and watched the windscreens of passing motorcars blinking in the heat.

The streets became more familiar still, remembered images turned real again, like: the buildings of Hawker Aircraft, and the window propped open by someone's shoe, and inside a figure that might once have been him, leaning over a drawing board and drafting out a future in nothing more than pencil lines.

Then they were curving right at a junction and heading towards Caversham Rise, where outside a gate almost two years before she had patted his breast pocket and, taking his hand, had kissed his knuckles and palm, closing his fingers around it. *Come back*, she had said. She had then put his other hand to her belly. *We need to tell Max*.

On the trolleybus that had taken him away from her that last time, his RAF bag on the seat and her silhouette on the pavement at the top of the hill watching him go, he had looked out the window — just as he did now — and outside the street and people had blurred, washing down the glass as they turned to liquid in his tears.

Now here he was again. The trolley whirred to a stop and he stepped off and waited as the wire sparked and the bus surged forward once more. Nothing much had changed: on either side just a line of terrace houses on an ordinary street. He set off up the hill feeling rather anxious as a boy on a pushbike came freewheeling past him. He had no idea, he realized, what to expect from her, what she looked like now, what she might say. She probably didn't even know that he was still alive. The official report had stated 'presumed dead'.

He slipped his hand in his pocket, expecting to find not a button or a map or a scrap of paper but, perhaps, a forgotten key; and with it he would go through the gate and up the steps, past the pots of geraniums, and he would unlock the door and step inside and she would be there to meet him and he would see her face again. What if Max was there? What would he say? He tried to think of all the things that should have been said. He could feel his heart racing.

As he drew nearer to the house, though, and its single gate and wooden steps leading up to the door — the door and steps he had so often imagined, the round-bellied bowls of the ceramic pots and geraniums scattering their petals — it wasn't there. He couldn't see it. He picked up his pace. It wasn't there. No, he thought. No! But there was just a gap. He reached the spot and stopped sharply, his heart beating so damned hard now that he thought he might pass out. He stared, horrified, across the empty space: nothing but the piled remains and juts of wood; nothing but bricks and rubble.

Oh God, no. He looked at where the house had always been, then scrambled over the debris.

'Connie!' he shouted. 'No, Connie! No!'

He clambered over the piles helplessly looking for her.

This was their retribution. This, he thought, was for Hamburg. With a single bomb and pinpoint accuracy, they had blown out his heart.

'Connie!' he yelled.

After all these miles, all these days . . .

She had been nothing when he had woken in

that field, not even as much as a thought, but he had searched and searched until he had found her, and now he was here; miles and days and infinite lifetimes later, he had come all this way for her, because she had said it — *Come back* — and he had. He was here now. He was here.

He felt that bomb drop again through him, breaking every bone within him as it fell and blasted, and he crumbled until he was on his knees in the bricks and timber, in all the dust and shards of glass. He strained out a voiceless cry, retched, and then shouted. He couldn't help it. He tugged at his stomach and wept so hard — for there among the shattered pieces of blasted terracotta were pale and washed-out petals. They looked like shreds of skin.

The car provided by the Ministry bore him along the lane as he stared blindly through the window at the stark yellow oilseed rape, the field burning so bright.

When they finally arrived, his mother was standing in the doorway, already crying just seeing the car pull into the drive. She bustled him through. She was kissing his cheeks again and again; she couldn't stop touching his arm. Everything was strangely familiar: the wooden boards that Cedar used to skitter across; the kitchen floor his mother fell on; the stairs his father had come down that day; and the light shining through the stained glass window, the way it fell across the floor, leaving pools of different coloured light that he and Max had lain beside, passing their hands through it to see the colours chase across their skin.

She led him through the dining room and out the double doors to the garden.

'Your father is doing the usual. He hasn't changed. Oh, darling, I can't believe that you're back. I prayed for you every night.'

And there he was standing at a flowerbed with a large floppy hat. He nimbly snipped the dead head from a rose, pocketing it in his summer jacket, while Cedar scrambled up from his sleep and came padding across the lawn.

'Oh, jolly good, there you are,' his father said

matter-of-factly, as if Owen had been gone for no more than an hour.

'And what of Max?' Owen later asked.

His mother tried to smile but couldn't manage it. 'It's short, you know, but lovely handwriting. They must have taken some care.'

* * *

He had died on the second of May. Pneumonia, as reported by a German doctor in a town called Sagan — somewhere in the east of Germany, his mother had explained. He had been transferred to a camp for aircraft pilots that, it had been written in the letter, had been evacuated, but he was found to be too ill to make the walk.

That was indeed why Owen had been going back, he realized — the sense that he had left Max there, the pull coming from a memory that he had felt all along but still couldn't unearth; going back for the love of a brother or as a final act of atonement for the guilt of an affair. Either way he had sat on a train, watching a girl in red sandals and white socks being settled into a seat opposite by a kindly aunt before she'd kissed the child goodbye and handed her a teddy bear.

Sometimes now — in his memory or his imagination or a dream — he saw his brother stumbling out of a truck, newly arrived from somewhere or other, or in a hospital bed in a camp about to be emptied, as the snow battered the windows and men gathered outside in the dark, stamping the cold from their feet.

At that bed he had slipped a promise into

Max's ear, and sometimes, in his dreams, an apology too. He would feel Max press a watch into his hand, and then closing Owen's fingers around it as if, like her kiss, that might somehow keep it safe.

Now this watch that had once been stolen — unfastened from him in a field in the dark, six hundred miles away — had been returned to Owen and was on his wrist once more, fixed and no different from how it had always been but for a small engraving on the back — two tiny 'v's that were only visible when you turned it and they sparkled in the light.

So much was lost and yet every day something would come back to him — a snatch of dialogue or a name or a face, blowing through his head like leaves, that he would see for a moment but couldn't quite catch. Other things returned and lingered, as if he had opened curtains to a view that now could not be closed. He thought about Max and their final minutes together, and the long trudge away from him through the forests, the biting cold and driving snow. Sheltering that first night in a brick factory in Muskau with thousands of other men, he had cried. In the flickering light of a gas lamp, seated among the shivering bodies, and with his jacket in his lap, he had chewed through the threads and unpicked the heart that she had sewn there, trying to unpick everything that had happened, everything that he had done. Then, without thinking, he'd slipped the threads into his pocket, where they were now and had always been, and only when the square of material was left in place had he realized what he had done.

* * *

'I'll take you down the garden,' his mother said.

She led him across the lawn to where his father was still among the flowers, secateurs in hand. It was as if nothing had changed. Owen felt the warm sun against him, the first scents of summer already pervading the air.

'Ah, here he is,' said his father. He called into the nearby potato plants. 'Leo. Come on, out you come.' A small face appeared between the stalks. 'Come and say hello.'

They walk out across the Hampshire fields, heading away from The Ridings and the *clip* of his father's secateurs. The day is warm and sunny, with the scent of pollen in the air, bumblebees and dragonflies, and vapour trails pulling like fraying threads across the sky.

Sometimes the child wants to walk, so progress is slow and meandering as he grasps Owen's finger in his hot hand and totters slowly forward, but mostly the child is content to sit and ride in Owen's arms. They watch Cedar lolloping ahead, disappearing in and out of the long grass so that every time he is found again, the child points and laughs.

Eventually, in a field overlooking the Downs with a slope just like he has been looking for, they stop to sit and rest. Cedar nuzzles scents out of the soil and the boy stumbles around, still finding his feet. He finds wonder in the smallest things, like ladybirds opening up their mechanical shells and folding out their wings.

Owen lies back in the grass and the child eventually clambers on him and, before long, is asleep. He holds him close, enjoying his weight, his smell, his warmth and, above all else, the sense that he is his. Sometimes, in his head, he can hear Irena telling him that he is good with him — not Little Man but this Little Miracle, this little infant found alive in the rubble when all else around him was lost. He listens to the child's breathing now as he had done on that first afternoon, sitting on the bench at the bottom of his parents' garden and holding the child tight to him as he cried at all the confusion of his desolation and his thanks.

All the clues he needs to remember Connie by she has left for him in this face — her eyes, her nose, the shape of her chin, the soft pinkness of her cheeks. And there she is vivid once more, more vivid than she has ever been, so that when he shuts his eyes — as he does now — she is with him. She is kissing him at a party down a darkened corridor, or potting geraniums on a step, or sitting beside him on the remains of a train engine writing him letters, every word of which he now knows. Or she is at the top of a street waiting for him, or turning to glance at him from the back of an open-topped Austin that is disappearing down a lane. Either way, she is not lost any more. She is in his head and heart and everywhere that he looks. He just has to close his eyes.

Author's Note

Devastation Road is a work of fiction. The only historical figure to feature in the story is Sir Sydney Camm, Chief Designer at Hawker Aircraft. All the other characters have been imagined, as have the events of Owen's journey. That said, much of the background detail is true.

Although not named, the camp that acts as the main location in the final third of the novel is Belsen, south-west of the town of Bergen, near Celle in northern Germany. As the war entered its final phases and the Reich found itself being squeezed from every side, the death camps were evacuated and the inmates moved. Many of these ended up at Belsen — among them its most famous inmate, Anne Frank. In February 1945 the population of the camp had grown to 22,000, but by 1 April this had exploded to 43,000. To make matters worse, in February a typhus epidemic had broken out as well, then the food supply failed and the water was cut off. The camp was reduced to chaos and the situation was so dire that there were even reports of cannibalism.

When the British 11th Armoured Division finally liberated the camp on 15 April 1945 the sights that met them must have truly horrified them. By this point the camp's population had reached a staggering 60,000, disease and starvation were rife, and the bare dusty grounds were littered with a further 13,000 bodies lying unburied where they had fallen. One of the first to enter the camp over the following days was a young BBC reporter, Richard Dimbleby. His report and film footage shocked the world.

Slow responses and some ill-advised decisions meant that despite their best efforts a further 14,000 inmates died *after* they had been liberated, including an estimated 2,000 dying from being given the wrong food. The main concentration camp was called Camp 1 — or the 'Horror Camp' — while the barracks of the nearby Panzer training school became the location of Camp 2. This was where the hospital was established. As Haynes says to Owen, they took 500 patients out of Camp 1 into the hospital every day, the equivalent of three blocks. Even with the help of various relief and aid agencies, including the International Red Cross, they were woefully under-resourced. Those deemed healthy enough were then housed in the smaller facility at Camp 3 awaiting deportation home, the first group to leave Belsen being a group of French and Dutch on 24 April. The 'Horror Camp' was fully evacuated and the last of its barracks burnt down on 21 May. It had taken over a month just to clear out all those who were sick.

While none of the characters portrayed really existed and some of the geography and environment of the camp has been altered, some of the smaller events did occur. German nurses brought in to assist were indeed ravaged by hospital inmates; ninety-six London medical students volunteered to assist in the evacuation of Camp 1; former inmates such as Nurse Joubert, many of whom were themselves recuperating from typhus, were drafted in to help in the hospital barracks; and a delivery of lipstick indeed took place, causing consternation among those desperate for medical supplies. In fact, the lipstick proved to be a considerable turning point in the recuperation of many of the patients, returning to the women a sense of worth and humanity — which their Nazi incarcerators had been hell-bent on eradicating.

For more information on Belsen I highly recommend Ben Shephard's *After Daybreak: The Liberation of Belsen, 1945*.

The second camp featured in the novel is at Żagań, western Poland (formerly Sagan in eastern Germany before the borders were realigned). Anyone with much knowledge of World War II or Hollywood war movies will recognize it as Stalag Luft III, the location of the Great Escape. Although the camp was evacuated at the end of January 1945, in reality it was taken over by the Russians when they arrived the following month and, in a stroke of irony, used to house German POWs. That said, many other camps were left abandoned by the Germans and so the sight that Owen finds himself facing was not at all unusual.

Stalag Luft III was one of many POW camps run by the Luftwaffe and used to hold captured aircrews. Camps run by the Luftwaffe were rather more relaxed than their Wehrmacht counterparts. At Stalag Luft III there was a theatre, library, and the opportunity to play sports, and from spring 1943 captured airmen were allowed to keep their uniforms. If you want to find out more about Stalag Luft III there are countless books available on the Great Escape, and I would recommend *Stalag Luft III: The Secret Story* by Arthur A. Durand.

Leipzig suffered aerial attacks by the Allies in July 1944, with the United States First Army capturing the city on 19 April 1945, just over a fortnight before Owen's arrival. In autumn 1944, the United States, Britain and the Soviet Union had agreed to divide Germany into occupation zones for administrative purposes come the end of the war; however, when peace was at last declared, the US Army had pushed far beyond the boundaries that had been agreed. In July 1945, the US Army was forced to withdraw from the city and the Russians moved in.

A word or two should be said about Hawkers. The company had originally been named Sopwith Aviation Company (founded in 1912) with its premises, even back then, in Kingston-upon-Thames, on Canbury Park Road. The firm became H. G. Hawker Engineering Co. Ltd. in 1920 and Hawker Aircraft Ltd. in 1933. Sydney Camm joined the company in 1921 as a draughtsman. However, by the time Owen was there, Camm would have been Chief Designer. It was during this period that Camm designed some of the most innovative aircraft of the twentieth century, including his most famous fighter plane, the Hawker Hurricane. Owen would have been in the Experimental Drawing Office during the development of the Hurricane, which went on to defend England during the Blitz. Indeed, on 18 February 1941, an article in the *News Chronicle* went so far as to claim that Sydney Camm was the man who had saved Britain. The company closed its doors in 1992. It is sad that its significance in British history and the defence of England is almost forgotten; if you would like to know more about the history of Hawker Aircraft I thoroughly recommend you visit the Kingston Aviation website: www.kingstonaviation.org

Janek says to Owen of the British people: 'You give Czech land away.' There is an element of truth in this. Since the formation of the first Czechoslovak republic in 1918 there had been tension over the border regions where a significant German population lived, and whether the areas should be part of the Czechoslovak republic or affiliated to Germany. One of these border regions was known by the Germans as the Sudetenland. The situation there was exacerbated in the 1930s by the rise of the Sudeten German Party, and in a congress of the Nazi Party in September 1938 Hitler accused the Czech government of suppressing national rights and promised to ensure the liberation of the Sudeten Germans and the annexation of the Czech border regions to the German Reich.

What happened in Munich on 29 September 1938 will be well known to most readers — the four-power conference instigated by Neville Chamberlain and the French prime minister Édouard Daladier, along with Italian dictator Benito Mussolini and the German Führer. Wrongly thinking that the Munich Agreement would appease Hitler and that all he wanted was the reclamation of what he considered to be German lands already populated by Germans, Chamberlain and Daladier signed an agreement on the ceding of Czech border territories. Chamberlain famously stated to the British people that the agreement meant 'peace for our time'. How wrong he was. Representatives of the one government this most concerned — the Czechs — were not invited to the talks, and, as a result, they felt they had no choice but to capitulate. On 1 October 1938, the Czech army evacuated the border areas and the German units moved in. Then, on 15 March 1939, Hitler finished what he had started: the German Army moved into the rest of the country and the next day an order was issued on the formation of the Protectorate of Bohemia and Moravia.

Underground resistance groups quickly formed, leading ultimately to the assassination of the acting Protector, Reinhard Heydrich, in May 1942, and the resulting reprisals, including the terrible destruction of the village of Lidice. After that the resistance groups fell quiet but the spirit was never lost. Acts of sabotage and revolt still occurred, while the Czech government-in-exile continued to do what it could from London and Czech pilots joined the British RAF. If you are interested in reading more about the plight of the Czech people, I highly recommend *Prague Winter: A Personal Story of Remembrance and War, 1937 — 1948* by Madeleine Albright, or *Border Crossing: Coming of Age in the Czech Resistance* by Charles Novacek.

Unbeknown to Janek, the day after he meets Owen an uprising occurred in Prague, while elsewhere in Bohemia, US forces moved in. The Soviet Union told the US that they would begin their Prague operations the following day and asked the US to halt their advance, which Eisenhower agreed to. On 9 May, as Owen, Irena and Janek join the hordes of refugees on the road to Leipzig, the first Soviet tanks entered Prague. Three years later, in 1948, the Communist party took control of the country in a coup supported by the Soviet government. Czechoslovakia would remain under Communist control for forty years, until the Communist government was finally overthrown in the Velvet Revolution of 1989.

There are many excellent books available about the immediate aftermath of the war. Two that I found invaluable are *Endgame 1945: Victory, Retribution, Liberation* by David Stafford and *The Long Road Home: The Aftermath of the Second World War* by Ben Shephard.

By 1944, there were reportedly 11.5 million people displaced in Europe, 7.7 million of those in Germany. *Devastation Road* is about just a handful of them.

Acknowledgements

I would like to thank Jessica Leeke for her early encouragement and invaluable feedback on the first draft of this book. I am also hugely indebted to my subsequent editor Rowan Cope for her hours of work, advice, support and scrutiny, and, most of all, for her patience. Huge thanks to the rest of the team at Scribner, including Jo Dickinson, Dawn Burnett, Elizabeth Preston, Jamie Groves, the production and sales teams, and everyone else who has been involved, including Natalie Braine and Nancy Webber, my eagle-eyed copyeditor and proofreader, and Matthew Johnson for the wonderful jacket design. Thanks also to Will Francis for his endless enthusiasm and tireless work on my behalf, as well as everyone else at Janklow & Nesbit.

If you've come this far you will no doubt have noticed that not all of the novel is written in English, so I would like to thank Sophie Hardach, Justina Hernik and Jeanne Corcos-Conisbee for assisting with the German, Polish and French; as well as special thanks to Terezie Holmerova for not only translating the Czech but also teaching me the basics of a language that I have grown to love.

I am greatly indebted to Bill Downey, who provided a wealth of information on Hawker Aircraft and showed me around the site on Canbury Park Road in Kingston. Thanks to

David Hassard for providing some of the finer detail on the history of Hawkers and putting me in touch with the right people; and to Dave Betteridge, who welcomed me into his home and gave me a fascinating insight into what life was like as a draughtsman in the Experimental Drawing Office under Sir Sydney Camm.

Thanks to Jeremy Bright for providing hours of documentary footage on the RAF Avro Lancaster, and to the staff at the British Library, the Imperial War Museum, the London Transport Museum, the Museum of Allied Prisoners of War in Żagań and the Bergen-Belsen Memorial; as well as Ewan Eason, and his family, who allowed me to read the diary of his grandfather — a real-life survivor of Stalag-Luft III who made the infamous Death March. Also to my early readers: Sam, Karen, Jenny, Becky, Anthea and Pam, and to Kathryn Race, who has lived every bump and jolt of this journey with me, and has been the endless provider of cups of tea and moral encouragement.

Finally, and most importantly, my most heartfelt thanks go to my family and friends, who have supported me more than I could ever have hoped for; in particular, my parents, whose belief in me seems to show no end, my adorable nephews William and Henry, sister-in-law Helen, and brother Jonathan — this one is for you.

Other titles published by Ulverscroft:

HAG-SEED

Margaret Atwood

Felix is at the top of his game as Artistic Director of the Makeshiweg Theatre Festival. His productions have amazed and confounded. Now he's staging a *Tempest* like no other: not only will it boost his reputation, but it will heal emotional wounds as well. Or that was the plan. Instead, after an act of unforeseen treachery, Felix is living in exile in a backwoods hovel, haunted by memories of his beloved lost daughter, Miranda — and also brewing revenge. After twelve years, his chance finally arrives in the shape of a theatre course at a nearby prison. Here, Felix and his inmate actors will put on his *Tempest* and snare the traitors who destroyed him. It's magic! But will it remake Felix as his enemies fall?